Norway
1716

Baby
Nikko

D1174207

Behind Every Myth Lies the Reality

KRIS

The Legend Begins

Part of the *Santa is real*-series based on the original story by J.J. Ruscella

KRIS

The Legend Begins

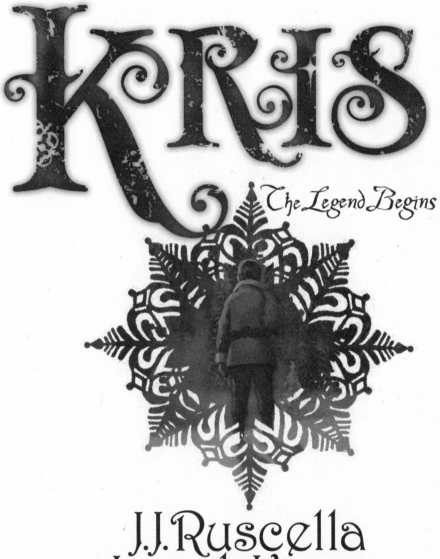

J.J. Ruscella
with Joseph Kenny

HIGHERLIFE
DEVELOPMENT SERVICES, INC
Oviedo, Florida

Kris—The Legend Begins
by J.J. Ruscella with Joseph Kenny

Published by HigherLife Development Services, Inc.
400 Fontana Circle
Building 1 – Suite 105
Oviedo, Florida 32765
(407) 563-4806
www.ahigherlife.com

This book or parts thereof may not be reproduced in any form, stored in a retrieval system, or transmitted in any form by any means—electronic, mechanical, photocopy, recording, or otherwise—without prior written permission of the publisher, except as provided by United States of America copyright law.

Copyright © 2010 by J.J. Ruscella

All rights reserved

ISBN 13: 978-1-935245-41-4
ISBN 10: 1-935245-41-4

Cover Design: r2c Design—Rachel Lopez

12 13 — 9 8 7 6 5 4 3 2

Printed in the United States of America

To the man who fills our heads with dancing sugar

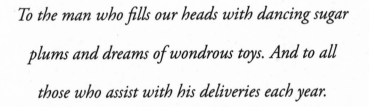

plums and dreams of wondrous toys. And to all

those who assist with his deliveries each year.

Table of Contents

The Prologue

There are some among you who may say, and may believe, the story I am about to tell is but a myth. A fanciful legend. A tall tale full of wishful imaginings. That no soul so steeped in pain or so lost and inconsequential as a snowflake on a mountain drift could ever have chanced to rekindle hope in a life that seemed so endlessly beyond control.

Yet I am here to comfort you. To tell you this tale with great earnestness and confidence. And to assure you it is true. For this is more than a story of pain and suffering, of helplessness and fear, of confusion and endless wanderings, of separation and loss. This is a story of hope. A story of transformation. A story of great passion and forgiveness. Of mystery and magic. Of beauty and wonder. And of the Majesty of the world.

Yes, my children, you can believe me when I tell you this story is true, for it is a story long known and long told. It is a story from my heart. And I know that it is true. For it is my story. I am Kris and this is my gift to you.

Chapter

Delivering

lickering flames of orange and red reflected in the eyes of my brothers and sisters as we looked on the burning remnants of our childhood home. I snapped the reins, and Gerda responded intently. Through the snow we slipped, gliding furiously over the trails and across the crests of hills. When at last we stopped to look back and measure our distance, black clouds of smoke rose in pillars to the skies. The mountains of Norway were all I had ever known, but our once sacred, now savaged, mountain enclave faded into distant smoky memories of all we had lost and left behind.

Aged Gerda, her strength not what it once was, tired quickly. As we went ahead, we slowed to a more measured pace, giving us time to think and focus on the moment, if not the future. Which way should I go? Which way to safety?

Inside the sleigh, Garin, my weary brother of nine, waited. He denied the world his sadness as he played with a toy wooden bear, the only familiar element he was allowed to carry on our desperate journey.

The snowy-blond twins, Tamas and Talia, were only seven. They sat in awkward silence and clutched each other's hands. I hoped their bond would not be broken somewhere along our path. If nothing else, they might have each other as a reminder that they had once belonged to a family.

My freckled sister of five, Kendra, held our sleeping younger sister of three, Jess, in her arms. Kendra stroked Jess's curly red hair. They seemed to glow with a gentle radiance in the illumination of my torch.

Shivering next to my mother was my beautiful, violet-eyed two-year-old brother, Owen, who began to cry.

My mother smoothed her palm down Owen's cheek. "Hush."

We paused momentarily atop the ridge that was the boundary to our mountain home. Near the end of the trail stood an ancient, sprawling tree that was burdened and twisted like the weakened body of a dying elder, a tree I had climbed countless times but no more. From the tops of those branches I had look out across the lowlands and dreamed of a different life. One I was now destined to discover.

The children huddled around my once beautiful mother, now as twisted and as tormented as the tree looked to me. They seemed to be waiting for something, some clue, some comfort, and so I began a song that was familiar to them—a favorite we sang each winter as Christmas was approaching.

Crystal snowflakes, crystal night,
keep my brothers in your sight.
Watch my sisters, safe and dear,
through this Yule and through this year.
Falling snowflakes from above,
each unique and filled with love!
Keep them safe until I call
my Christmas wish as snowflakes fall.

How I loved my brothers and sisters. How I lamented every mean word and accidental bruise born of childish arguments. How I wanted us to be safe, to remain together. My mother would not allow me to care for them in her absence. Back in the village, I had argued with her, insisting I could find a home for us all and watch over them.

"I am thirteen!" I exclaimed. "I have had my coming of age."

She only scoffed at me, mocking my earnest desires.

"You are just a boy. A crumb. Not yet a man," she said, while struggling to catch a painful breath. "You cannot care for these children or protect them."

She cut me cruelly with her words. Furious and frustrated, I struggled to fight back welling tears.

"You must leave them," she continued harshly. "Tie them to the pillars at the crossroads. Leave them in the road for travelers to find. Together you are doomed to be discovered for what you are. There is little chance they will live, unless some stranger should discover them and take pity. They are in God's hands now."

How could I leave my brothers and sisters tied helplessly along the roadside in the bitter cold? God would find them? God would give them shelter? Who would give them shelter, except to place them in a shallow grave or leave them buried under mounds of snow and ice?

I hated her.

I realize now that I did not want to face her undeniable truth. I knew I would have to separate them as my mother commanded, and I hated her for what she asked me to do, even if she was right.

For who would take in so many desperate souls? Who would willingly provide us all with sustenance and shelter? Though none of us showed signs of the illness, who would endanger themselves with the plague God had brought upon my innocent village?

Each time I asked myself those awful questions, I knew with certainty I would have to unlink our fingers, if not our hearts, and find new families and new homes for them to start their lives again. While I hoped our love would never fade, I had to face the grim reality: they would not survive another day in this cold if I did not find them sanctuary.

We swept across the wasteland seeking salvation, some modest place of shelter from the perils of winter's hostile breath, until before us a windblown roadhouse appeared like a gift from heaven.

Who will be first? I thought to myself.

Then I saw my mother struggle to free herself from Owen's desperate grasp, and I knew she had already made the choice. I hid the sleigh among the trees and looked to my mother.

Gently, she stroked Owen's face and spoke to him almost teasingly. "As happy as I am to be getting an uninterrupted sleep, I will miss you at night, crawling in bed with me. When I see your smiling face, all is right with the world. No more night scares now. Sing them away, like your father would."

Owen couldn't fully form words yet, but he had a language all his own that he spoke just to us. At night when our father would sing as my mother slowly rocked him, Owen would sing along in his little sleepy voice.

"You are the most wondrous thing," she said to him. "I knew all too well these days would end. And though I am not ready, it is time you were off without me. I love you more than words can say."

I took Owen's hand and cautioned the others to be silent as I started off toward the isolated roadhouse. Watery eyes revealed their understanding.

It was a long march across the snowy meadow. Owen did his best to keep up with me, nearly waist-deep in the snow, until I swept him up into my arms and carried him the rest of the way.

Gently I sat him on the stairs and began to make a small snowman, forming the mounds and molding the face. Slowly he joined in.

I left him playing on the steps, quietly backing away to rejoin the others. Owen gurgled and laughed the way children do.

Just then the roadhouse door swung open and slammed against the wall. Owen began to cry. The roadhouse man, a grizzled, ham-handed giant, filled the doorway. He gazed out past Owen shrieking on his steps. Then he saw me, skulking off into the distance, and yelled,

"Hold!"

I was driven by fear that he would pursue me. I did not hold. I ran faster than I had ever run before, spurred by my stumbling anguish. Don't catch me. Don't follow me. Don't look at me. Don't see me for what I am, for what I've done.

I had left my little brother behind in the hands of a strange giant, a man who could squash him in his mighty grasp. Sobbing, I ran, fearful that I had made the greatest mistake of my young life in leaving him there alone. The distant cries of my brother proclaimed my betrayal.

Please forgive me. God forgive me. Let this be a home. God give him a home. Please, if you are up there, don't abandon him the way I have. Give him love.

But I had little faith in a world where love was scarce. Whatever hope I had was dashed when I looked into my mother's swollen eyes.

"Get on with it," she commanded.

The morning sun glanced off the crystalline snow and sprayed a glaring light upon our ragged and weary group.

In such a harsh light as this, we now found ourselves illuminated, our desperation exposed as our sleigh moved forward across the powdery snow.

The devil time now became our enemy, waiting for us to falter, watching with glee as we drifted onward in hope of finding yet another way station or sheltered hostel in which to deposit one more piece of our hearts.

As we moved ahead, I noticed feral shadows peppering the snow, interrupting its glaring whiteness in slinking, threatening movements. Wolves, I thought. Or was I so tired that my mind now birthed twisted imaginings?

Vicious wolves, I imagined, marking time, waiting for us to hesitate or pause, so they might strike. This was their land, their hunting ground, their home, not ours.

Wolves know the value of time and how quickly it passes and changes us. They know the value of patience and of waiting for opportunity.

They surround their prey and paralyze it with fear while they stalk and distract and close their ranks in anticipation of the moment when they might spring.

The whole world can feel full of these savage predators, always advancing, always stalking, always ripping away at our youth. But sometimes the world offers salvation, and sometimes the wolves are imagined.

Another modest cottage. Another chance to dispense a desperate and hungry child and save him from the wild and release him to the vagaries of fate.

Bread. The sweet scent of bread. Hot loaves placed upon a windowsill to cool by the mistress of the house. Hot loaves of bread calling to me, making my mouth water, coating my wind-parched lips.

We all smelled it. Our forgotten hunger now pulled at our rumbling bellies. And again our mother chose, another boy, a twin, my brother Tamas.

"I am torn," my mother said to him, "by wanting to know what kind of man you will be when you are grown up and wanting to keep you, my child. I cannot imagine a time when you will not be my little man. You were so excited to be six and with the toy whistles and bells your father hid about the house. So very frustrated with your sister for taking forever to find the gifts and then to play with each one before she moved on to the next treasure hunt. You are stubborn and bullheaded, and I love that about you. I hope you keep those qualities as you get older. I look at you and I see such possibilities. How excited I am for you and your new life."

As my mother kissed and held him, he reached for our sister Talia. I pulled my brother Tamas toward the house and the scent of freshly baked bread. He began to fight me, screaming. I placed my hand across his mouth to silence him and held him fast, though he kicked and lashed out at me in his desperate anger. I was so afraid I might hurt him as he fought. But what could hurt him more than tearing him from his family? He would hate me for leaving him here alone.

He struggled. I walked.

I told myself over and over this must be done. "This must be done!" I said aloud.

I ignored his tears. I ignored his pleas and his struggles. Then, suddenly, he stopped fighting. The tension released from every muscle in his body. Talia's fingers intertwined with his. She stood there holding his hand, their look sharing what only twins could possibly understand.

For a moment they glanced up at me with tears in their eyes, then turned and walked to the cottage.

How brave they were, how trusting. How beautiful they were, like lost angels filled with grace walking hand in hand as they approached the cottage door.

Who ever could have dreamed when they were born that such a day as today would arrive? My mother's glorious twins, her pride, now pushed aside and sent out into the world alone.

I rushed to the windowsill and snatched one loaf of bread for the others, then ran back to the sleigh, nearly breathless in my desire to flee. The twins knocked upon the cottage door.

Of all the pain I had ever felt, none was so savage as the misery of separation. When my father died, I felt a wound that would never heal. He did not mean to leave us, I now know. But as he died, I was filled with rage.

"How can you leave us?" I demanded to know as he lay there dying. "How can you go and not think to take us with you?" I shouted when he was gone.

I wanted to walk with him no matter where he went, in worlds dark or distant. I wanted him to be strong and take my hand or caution me away from dangerous dispositions. He was my heart.

It was not so much the pain of loss but its permanence that echoed again and again for me—loss that could not be reclaimed in this world, or maybe even in the next. Everything I counted on was gone. Every memory. Every hope. Every small achievement measured by this man whose death left me abandoned one winter day. I was not ready to take on this world alone.

This is how my brothers and sisters must have felt. They had trusted that our parents would be there. That I would be there as an older brother should be. But that too was denied by my mother. I blamed her. However wrongly, I did blame her.

I knew I could not end our reckless journey until each of my brothers and sisters was given some chance, some place of shelter. So on we went, our sleigh glancing across the rugged terrain.

After we traveled for so long that it felt we might soon come to the world's end, the music of mighty axes and the singing of lumberjacks floated out from a distant stand of trees. I reined in Gerda and slowed our pace, listening to the rhythm of the axes as I planned our next engagement.

THWACK, THWACK, THWACK, THWACK,

A lumberjack's life is a worrisome one, though some call it free from care.

THWACK, THWACK, THWACK, THWACK,

It's the ringing of the axe from morning till night in the middle of the forest fair.

THWACK, THWACK, THWACK, THWACK,

While life as a jack can be bleak and cold while the wintery winds do blow,

THWACK, THWACK, THWACK, THWACK,

As soon as the morning star does appear, to the wild woods we must go.

Then came a mighty and thunderous CRACK, and a giant tree surrendered its majestic form to the earth.

Garin did not wait for my next thought. He never seemed to need the rest of us. That is not to say he wasn't part of us. He loved us, and we him. Sometimes he would play with the rest of us, and sometimes he was a kind of loner. It amazed me how independent he was at nine years old.

He leaned his tired frame across the bench and kissed my mother on the cheek. The kiss held for just the slightest moment, and as he leaned back my mother spoke words to him that rang in my ears for years to come, "Don't ever let them know where you are from."

Before I stopped the sleigh, Garin leapt out onto the snowy ground and began his trek toward the lumberjacks. I loved that he struck out on his own without looking back. He got that from our father.

He was strong and embraced his new calling with resolute purpose, like some tragic champion of old. My deep sadness and regret was that he might someday forget us all in his effort to cut away the painful past, forgetting all the happiness that once lived there.

The sleigh came to a stop, and I watched as he walked across the snowy expanse. He didn't look back.

THWACK, THWACK, THWACK, THWACK,
  Some would leave their friends and homes and others they love dear,

THWACK, THWACK, THWACK, THWACK,
  And into the lonesome pine woods their pathway they do steer.

THWACK, THWACK, THWACK, THWACK,
  Into the lonesome pine woods all winter to remain

THWACK, THWACK, THWACK, THWACK,
  A-waiting for the springtime to return again.

A snap of the reins and Gerda was off again, leading us forward into evening and tomorrow. Garin's old wooden bear, left behind, collapsed onto its side as if felled by one stroke of an imaginary axe. And it rolled to the rear of the sleigh, where it came to a halt as abruptly as Garin's childhood.

My mother coughed behind me. It was clear her time was coming to an end. I struggled with confusion. She was stern in the demands she placed on us and especially on me, but she always had watched over us and protected us in whatever ways she could. Now she was determined to see us scattered to the wind with only the smallest hope we might again take root. At the time, she seemed to me without feeling or compassion for our young lives as her own began to drift away.

I did not know what else to do, except to carry out this task as she demanded. I was helpless to change the path we were now upon, so I executed her dying wish because I could think of none to surpass it.

I became determined to take what little control I could in my effort to find real shelter for my brothers and sisters. It would be their only opportunity for survival. That my mother wanted me to leave them by the roadside or wandering alone in hopes some stranger would discover them only added to my frustration, deepened my anger, and left me feeling weak and pitiful. It would be years before I uncovered the simple truth that facing your own death was almost inconsequential compared to losing a child.

In the evening light I spied a modest country inn and set it as the next destination on our quest for gentle refuge.

My mother stroked Jess's hair. "You're beautiful. So, so pretty and red is your hair and your long, long lashes. Our neighbors would stop us to tell me how beautiful you are. I wish I could say it was embarrassing, but I never tired of it, because not only are you beautiful on the outside, you are even more so on the inside."

Jess had a sweetness, a kind of rosy glow around her wherever she went. She also had her own world that she lived in all the time. She loved to dance and sing and would make us call her by her name of choice for the day and would not respond to any other. Penelope was her best friend, though none of us could see Penelope. Jess was a joy.

With Jess in hand, I walked to the inn and sent her inside. I found a slightly open window through which I could see and feel the raging fire radiating from the hearth within.

A buxom bar matron busily served patrons and travelers, men and women that had gathered inside for warmth who ate and drank in great measure. They shouted raucous songs and engaged in playful banter in the spirit of holiday revelers and were so occupied with their merriment they failed to notice Jess as she entered through a swinging tavern door. I watched from outside and could see Jess make her way curiously through the room until she stumbled and fell in a carpet of scraps and sawdust. All eyes turned to Jess, but no one came to her rescue.

"Whose child is this?" the bar matron finally demanded. There was no response. Bewildered, the matron swooped Jess up and took her to a chair where she sat, placing Jess upon her lap. She combed Jess's curly red hair with her fingers and made an occasional playful tweak at Jess's nose and laughed with her as the singing and drinking carried on around them.

I raced back to the sleigh, feeling emptiness at losing Jess and great hope for her chances of survival.

As we pushed onward, night wrapped its gossamer cloak around our sleigh, concealing our secrets and the illness inside. Empty as the world around us, I prayed for some newfound fuel to carry us into tomorrow.

The church ahead, visible in the silvery moonlight, woke me from my delirium like a beacon of salvation created for us. In that moment, I believed in miracles, but simple momentary miracles are often forgotten in a moment.

Kendra was sleeping now, too exhausted to remain alert. Quietly, my mother spoke to her as she slumbered.

"I will miss our days together. I will miss eating fresh snow peas and watching the ducks and even laying on the bed talking. You are going to be a powerful woman. You are tough, but with the kindness you embody you will never be mean, just tough. It is a rare woman that can carry it off, but I believe it will come to you with ease. There is sometimes an old soul quality about you. You are my little wise one. I couldn't love you any more."

I don't think my mother was done talking when I lifted Kendra from the bench of the sleigh and carried her into the vestibule of the church. I didn't care. Kendra was cold and needed to go inside, I told myself.

Her beautiful, freckled, five-year-old face was radiant in the candlelight. She did not stir. She did not waken as I lay her upon a large wicker mat on a table in the vestibule and left her there for God and his messengers to watch over. On the table beside the mat was a small, rough nativity, crudely carved from some dark obsidian rock. For a moment I bowed my head; then in a burst of anger, I swept the figurines to the ground, bouncing and scattering across the stone floor.

As the sleigh pulled away from the church, I felt someone watching, perhaps the eyes of heaven upon me. I didn't care. The only forgiveness I wanted was from the family I had left behind.

Snowflakes.

Lazy, floating snowflakes.

I ran through the experiences of the day as we rode through the slow, soft snowfall. My mother's task accomplished, I was done. Something good had taken place today. Something unexpected. Something impossible. But over and over again I lived each delivery. I critiqued each moment. And all I wanted was to turn around and gather us back together.

Sometime past the dark early hours of morning, my mother's shawl broke free, unraveled from about her head, and sailed into the night. I watched, mesmerized. It floated, turning gracefully in the sky like the snowflakes. Defying nature, it danced upon the air rising higher and higher.

I stopped the sleigh and retrieved the shawl from where it had finally come to rest on the snow. The peace of the quiet snowfall was calming. Still fascinated by the descending snow, I watched one oddly large snowflake fall as I walked around to give my mother her errant shawl. The flake landed on her face and didn't melt. I gently placed the shawl around her head, almost afraid to wake her from her endless sleep. A small, wooden snowflake pendant rested upon her neck. She had worn it my entire life. A gift, I believe, from my father. Carefully I untied the necklace and wrapped it in my hand. Then I wrapped my arms around her. "What about me, Mama? What words for me? How am I special, Mama? How do you see me?"

The blankets covering her body began to stir, and a cry broke the tranquility of the silent night. I recoiled.

"My God."

I had forgotten. I had forgotten the precious life my mother held to her breast. I had forgotten I even had a days-old infant brother. Frantically I tore at her clothes and pulled my naked brother from the ebbing warmth of her grasp. The wind whistled through the barren winter land surrounding us. Nikko cried as I held him away from my body.

What was I to do with this squealing infant who had no protection from the world? I trudged across the snowy field toward a gathering of trees.

How would I find him comfort in this forsaken land now that my mother had died? Surely, he would not survive until morning. Who would feed him?

Would it not be better for him? It would happen so soon. He would have no recollection of loneliness and suffering, only eternal life.

So I walked, the snowflake pendant dangling from my fingers, the tearful shivering infant in my outstretched arms.

I walked to one tree. And then the next. What I was horrified to consider I could not find the will to do. I walked through the stand of trees knee-deep into the fresh powdery snow. Slowly, I pulled him into my protective body, and I walked through the rolling snowy hills.

I walked until I could not walk another step. Until weariness over-took me. Until my legs became so heavy that I stumbled and fell. Until I had no other choice but to accept our fate and surrender to exhaustion.

I removed my old cloak and laid it over the snow then gently placed Nikko upon it, laying my own unprotected body in the snow beside him.

"Don't worry, little one. The cold will not last long."

As we lay there, gazing into a glittering and translucent sky, I held the wooden snowflake pendant and thought about the way snowflakes formed and fell to earth. Each like a crystal jewel. Each unique, with unrivaled form. Each drifting from heaven like a silent prayer or a gentle kiss from God. Each finding its own special place, yet joining so many others, as the world embraced and absorbed them.

And then I thought of Nikko and all my brothers and sisters, who were as delicate as any of these snowflakes. Each unique, each now sent drifting in search of a special place and hoping for the world's embrace.

"Nikko, do you think it is Christmas yet?" I asked.

A star flared in the night and raced across the sky, then was followed by sparks and cinders that floated upon the wind. A fire, I thought. We must be near a fire.

I wrapped Nikko in the cloak and headed off to follow the trail of burning, pulsating embers.

From beneath the crest of a hill poked a smoking chimney. Attached to that chimney, among the hills of nowhere, was a cottage. When I found that cottage, with its chimney spewing sparks into the sky, I set about devising a way to deliver Nikko to his new home.

I laid him in the snow outside a window that had not been sealed and peered inside to see who might be within the small house. An old couple sat at the table near the fireplace, eating stew. I ran to their door and knocked on it boldly.

Surprised, the old cottager arose, picked up a walking staff, and headed to the door. His curious wife followed close behind. As they opened the door to see what sort of wandering stranger had beckoned them, I crawled through the window with Nikko in my arms.

"Who goes there?" the cottager called out to the empty night.

Quickly and quietly I set Nikko near the hearth, on an old blanket that lay folded there. I placed the wooden snowflake on his breast. Nikko's tiny little hand held onto my thumb. I peeled his hand off my finger, and in the blink of an eye I was gone out the window. For the first time in hours Nikko began to cry.

The cottager's wife must have turned to discover Nikko lying near the hearth, for I heard a muffled shriek from inside. Minutes later the old cottager started up again.

"Who goes there? Hello?"

But I was a far distance by then, now truly alone as I walked away into the night.

It is difficult to look back and remember the pain of that long day's delivery because there were so many good times to follow. Though weary beyond belief, I did eventually make my way back to the sleigh and Gerda, who somehow braved and survived that chilling journey. As I think about it now, I realize that I wasn't fully alone. I had her. She was with me through all of it, just as she would see me grow into a man over the coming years.

I wasn't there yet. It was the early 1700s, and though I wasn't a boy, I was not yet a man. You see, tragedy doesn't make a man. It may end a childhood, but only learning to embrace responsibility of your own free will makes a man. So far I had only been on the ride. Now I had to learn to do something with my pain and my experience. It helps to have an example, if not a teacher, for a young person to truly come of age. God was good enough to give me both in the years to come.

You might think of my story as tragic. I want you to know that I am grateful for the experience. It made me who I am, who I was to become. Heroes must pass through a trial of fire. In time I would pass through mine to become someone I loved and respected, someone, I hope, who brings joy to others. But once again, I wasn't there yet.

You may be curious about my mother and what became of her. I could tell you a story of a child frantically trying to dig into the frozen earth with hands and sticks. Or I could tell you about days of looking for rocks to pile, or of hands too frozen to light the smallest of fires.

In the end I laid my mother's body near the roadside, propping her head up gently with a mound of snow until it seemed she was at last peaceful in her eternal sleep. I remembered Garin's toy bear and retrieved it from the sleigh, placing it in my mother's arms as a reminder of the children she had planted along the road. I prayed that in time her body would be discovered and given a more fitting burial, which I could not do alone.

Eventually I realized that we had to move on and that I had decided to live.

Chapter

2

Rebuilding

Galloping horses broke the peaceful solitude of the fresh winter's morning. A wagon filled with wooden furniture and other wares passed me, bucking and bouncing on the rough trail. Its boisterous passengers, a group of three boys, kept the older driver from noticing me as they moved past. Thankfully Gerda and the sleigh were well hidden in the trees beyond the roadside.

Behind the old, rugged driver, in the overloaded wagon bed, the three young men about my age were cavorting, poking and smacking at each other as the wagon rumbled past.

A storm was beginning to build in the distance, its dark clouds and steadily growing winds heralding the approaching blizzard. I decided I would secretly follow this group to wherever it was destined, in hopes of stealing some form of shelter.

In a short time the wagon approached a modest cottage on a ridge above the road and skittered to a halt. I left Gerda behind the last bend in the trail and moved closer so I could watch and listen without making myself known.

The old man, Josef, a salt-of-the-earth grandfather whom the boys called by name, jumped from the driver's seat of the wagon and walked toward the cottage.

"Jonas!" he yelled. "Paddock them horses. Markus, you and Noel grab them chairs. We need to beat this weather."

He paused there for a moment and turned back to the boys. Unaware, the boys started to roughhouse. Josef barked at them again, "No horsing, hear? That's a blizzard brewing."

Then the door opened, and he entered the cottage, leaving the boys to their work.

Jonas, perhaps thirteen and the smallest of the group, seemed somewhat shy and timid in his manners. He nearly fell as he awkwardly dismounted the wagon and hit the ground. Regaining his balance, Jonas gathered several large pieces of wood that he wrestled over to the wagon wheels where he wedged them to hold the wagon in place. As he stood, a mound of snow hit him on the back of the head with a THWACK. He yelped.

Markus, a fresh-faced and powerfully athletic boy, along with Noel, a thin and sneering lad, both about fourteen, jeered at Jonas and continued their snowy assault from the protection of the wagon bed. Jonas couldn't find cover. Every time he blocked one assault, another would find the opening it left. Sputtering and jerking, he moved in first one direction and then the other, until finally he dove with desperate courage at his attackers, crawling beneath the wagon in an effort to avoid being pelted.

Markus turned his attention to one of the tarps covering the chairs in the wagon bed. He grabbed it firmly by one side and yanked on it, flipping it off the chairs and onto Noel, who screamed in entangled self-defense, "Hey! Get this off."

Markus laughed as Noel stood in the wagon, squirming beneath the tarp. In his struggle to escape, Noel tripped over the side and landed with a great thud in the snow beside the wagon. Markus, a laugh now half-caught in his throat, flopped onto his belly and looked down at Noel with concern.

"Noel, you hurt?" Markus asked in a worried voice.

Noel frantically popped his head out. "I did that just to make you laugh," he said with false bravado as he struggled to catch his breath.

Markus threw another tarp over him.

While Noel continued to thrash about once again, Markus grabbed two chairs from among several in the wagon and placed them on the ground. Jumping down from the wagon, Markus stacked the two chairs in the snow. As he turned to lift out another chair, a snowball exploded against the side of his face. Markus looked about in newly fueled anger.

For a moment, Noel stood champion atop the wagon, sneering; then his smile froze. Markus vaulted onto the sleigh. Desperately, Noel staggered through the wagon and tumbled over the side, running. Markus chased him relentlessly, a predator on the tail of his prey, and when Noel finally stumbled, Markus leapt upon him. They tumbled end over end, head over foot, to the ground fighting.

Jonas crawled out to watch Markus pummeling Noel and rubbing his face in the snow. I followed, initially caught up in the fiasco. Beside me in the back of their wagon sat a chunk of salt-cured meat. I devoured it before I even remember picking it up.

Josef's voice boomed through the open door of the cottage, "Markus! Noel! If you are playing the fools, you will feel the lash! Hear?"

I turned to dash back to the trees in the hope I would not be discovered and ran directly into Markus. I spun and tried to move in another direction, but Noel blocked my escape and pushed me back toward Markus once again. As I struggled to get my balance and escape in yet another direction, Markus grabbed me and tossed me into the chairs that were sitting in the snow. They snapped and splintered as I hit them, sending pieces of wood in all directions.

Josef yelled again, "If we're caught by the storm, I'll be looking for new apprentices, and your parents will have to find something else to do with you."

As I lay on the ground, Noel grabbed one of the satchels from the wagon and threw it at me. I caught it as it hit me on the chest. "Thief! We captured a thief!" Noel began to scream loudly in an effort to muster Josef's attention.

I tried to stand.

Markus ruthlessly pushed me to the ground and yelled, "Josef!"

"You've got it coming now," Noel taunted.

This was what I wanted. I wanted this more than anything in the world. A reason to injure. A justification to hurt. A deserving enemy to destroy. A fight.

I lurched up at Markus, who was looking toward the cottage. He never had a chance. My body, launched from the earth, drove my momentum. My arm swung back for maximum damage. And I screamed at him from the depths of my pain as I swung my fist forward.

A powerfully strong hand grabbed me by the back of the collar and spun me around, suddenly ending my attack.

Josef looked down on me with drilling, intense eyes.

"He broke the chairs," Markus yelled angrily in accusation.

"He was pinching our food," Noel added in an echoing chorus.

Josef looked at each of the boys, as if to warn them not to lie.

"Jonas?" Josef asked after a moment in his deep, commanding voice. "What have you to say? Is this what happened?"

Jonas stood nearly frozen with worry and did not dare to speak.

Josef closely scrutinized him, waiting for an answer, and Jonas nodded his head timidly.

Josef then grabbed the satchel, which was resting in the snow, and pointed to the broken chairs. "Your people will pay for those," he said to me gruffly.

I wiped my dripping nose with the sleeve of my threadbare coat and looked away from Josef in embarrassment. "I have no people," was all that I could say.

"Then you'll work it off," Josef barked at me. "All of you! There will be no more fighting. Now, get these chairs up to the house. Grab the tarp and tie everything down. Quickly now."

I moved to help the others with the chairs.

"Not you!" Josef said to me forcefully.

The apprentices went about their duties unloading the wagon and carrying the chairs up the slope.

Josef approached me and set his hand roughly upon my cheek, lowering my bottom eyelid as he searched. I knew what he was looking for. But the signs of the plague are not always left on the body. He saw nothing but the story of my misery in the tears that never spilled from my eyes.

"I have a horse."

"Then you'll work his keep off too."

We didn't beat the blizzard. Gerda didn't have a sprint left in her. Slowing his pace to ours, I would have thought Josef was endangering everyone on his wagon if he didn't give off the impression of unquestionable control. The last few stretches of land were the most difficult as the road all but disappeared. Despite the last span of days, Gerda seemed to know that a true rest was just ahead and, though not fast, she kept a modest pace.

The world was nearly an impenetrable blur of white by the time we deposited each of the apprentices at their homes. Jonas's family was so relieved when they greeted him at the door. Hugs and kisses.

"Please come in! It's safer to stay!" they hollered over the deafening wind. Josef waved them off with a polite refusal. Marcus's father met him at the door with a pat on the shoulder and a simple nod at Josef. No one welcomed Noel home.

The carpentry shop and Josef's home were connected, though I couldn't tell how large they were from the outside. I couldn't even tell how he located the building until it was right in front of me. We put the horses up before we went to the main house.

The barn had been mucked out and was just roomy enough for all three horses. We lit the corner stove, though it didn't quite warm the whole space. I cried when we liberated Gerda from her harness. As we removed each piece, the terrible toll on her body was revealed as was the horrible injustice done by me. There were minor cuts and abrasions from the sheer toil of our hard journey. But the worst, almost too difficult to look at, were the gashes created by the tackle and straps. The breaching, the girth, and the tug had all cut deep wounds through her skin and into the muscle beneath. When we removed the breast collar, without the pressure, blood flowed freely down the front of her legs.

"How long has she sat in harness?" Josef demanded. "More than seven days?"

Tears welled in my eyes. I couldn't bring myself to answer.

"Grab that sack and the bucket of water."

I quickly complied and started to let her drink.

"That water is cold. She'll drink better if you make it warm. The cold water will help to stop the bleeding. Grab another bucket and go outside. There is plenty of snow for you to heat over the fire."

When I returned and had set the water on the stove, he called me to his side. He took two huge handfuls of what looked to be finely ground salt from the sack and poured them into the cold bucket of water, mixing it with his hands. Suddenly he grabbed my hands and immersed them in the freezing brine, holding them under.

"Grab the salt. Grab it in your hands," he commanded.

I did as I was told. Slowly he pulled my hands from the bucket and placed them on her wounded body. A salted wound can be a terrible pain, so immediately I drew back.

"Her suffering cannot be ignored. You will find that the salted water pains her less than water alone and will begin her healing."

Josef ran our hands all over her body, guiding them into her deepest injuries.

"Rid the wound of any dirt and debris. Flush it out. Don't leave anything, even a piece of her own flesh."

Again I recoiled, pulling back. But he firmly held my hands as I cried, pushing them through the cuts and over the abrasions. The flick of her ears and tail, and the deep laboring of her breath were the only signs of her discomfort. And as I worked along her side, I could feel her lean into me, just lightly.

Though I was not conscious of it, cleansing the atrocities done to her body was a form of purging for me, a kind of absolution for what I had done to her. I had not dealt with the loss of my family and would not for some time. Somehow a form of healing had begun at the rough hands of this old carpenter. As I cleaned her injuries my tears slowed and eventually subsided.

"She is lucky. Though some wounds are deep, the worst are on her hips and upper thighs, not her abdomen or chest."

First with just my hands, then later with a soaked cloth, I cleaned every wound.

Josef cleared the snow from the door of the carpentry shop, which he simply called the carpentry, and ushered me inside. Candles were lit and the fire stoked. It was definitely warmer than the barn. Josef called to his wife as he removed his coat and hung it near the furnace to dry.

"Gabriella, we have a new apprentice who will work with us to repay a debt and earn his room and board."

I believed he said it for me, reminding me I was welcome, a worker earning his keep, not a burden.

"Josef? Josef?!" a woman's worried voice called.

Josef took me through a dark hallway at the back of the carpentry that opened up into the most glorious little kitchen. I say little because it was smaller than the carpentry, about the size of a bedroom. But it was the first kitchen I had ever seen that was made for cooking, or baking, or something to do with food. I didn't know. But it smelled fantastic.

Then the most adorable fleshy young grandmother entered the room from the opposite doorway. I didn't know if she had grandchildren. It didn't matter. I didn't even know if she had children. It didn't matter. She had the spirit of a grandmother. It was in her eyes. I learned later Gabriella was never blessed with a child of her own but she radiated unconditional love. This of course, did not keep her from berating Josef.

"Goodness, where have you been, Josef? You knew there was a blizzard coming. You had us scared half to death. If I wasn't so happy to see you, I would smack you in the head!"

From behind Gabriella stepped a girl. Her hair was strawberry blonde. Her eyes, sparkling in the flickering firelight, saw me. The world held its breath. Or maybe that was me. She was lovely, and I knew in that moment I would love no other.

Josef talked as if Gabriella hadn't said a word, as if he had just walked in from a refreshing spring day of work.

"Sold most of the chairs. Not all, but most."

Gabriella saw me.

"My God!"

It was the closest I would ever hear her come to swearing. And truth be told, she may have been praying.

Gabriella pulled me to a seat by an open oven fire that bathed the room in oranges and reds. She removed my jacket and vigorously began to rub my arms and hands. But all the while I couldn't take my eyes off the girl. Ensnared, I stared at her. Openly and serenely she looked back. I began to think she was an angel or something from my imagination since no one had acknowledged her existence.

"Josef, what were you thinking? Now I know that you think those horses are more important than your worrying old wife. But they could have waited."

"Gabby," Josef began.

She shot Josef the meanest, cutest, angriest look. The girl and I laughed out loud.

"This is not funny. This poor child needs attention," she said to the girl, who shared a small smile with me over the absurd cuteness of Gabriella's vehemence.

"I mean you, dear," Gabby said to me, cupping my face. "You are, of course, welcome to laugh, and I hope you do."

"Gabby," Josef tried to interject again.

"No offense, dear, but you need a warm bath." Gabby whispered to me. "Josef, warm up some water for a bath."

"At this time of night?" he asked.

Another stern look from Gabriella and Josef gave up the losing battle. Shaking his head, he exited the door. Gabriella took my old tattered coat and looked closely at it and then at me. She placed the coat on a hook next to the door.

Again she took my icy hands and began to massage them.

"Dear child," she exclaimed, "you are nearly frozen. We'll warm you up soon enough, and I am sure you will feel better."

Again the angelic girl stepped out from nowhere, this time holding a basket. Inside were the most glorious golden loaves of bread. I could smell them from where I sat, and my mouth watered as my stomach made a series of embarrassing rumbling sounds.

"Go ahead," the girl encouraged, speaking for the first time. "These are for you. Eat until you are full."

"Right you are, Sarah," Gabby said. "We must get you some food and something warm to drink. Sarah, bring some honey for the bread. And I'll get you a tureen of hot soup to accompany it."

Her name was Sarah. She was fourteen and the baker's girl. She visited the carpentry each day to bring Josef and Gabriella and their apprentices delicious baked goods and to enjoy Gabriella's motherly company and loving friendship. Her family frequently used these baked goods in barter for Josef's carpentry services, and he had helped them by building baking racks, cabinets, and tables for their bakery. Sarah would often stay with Gabriella if Josef was away to keep her company and make sure she was safe in case of any crisis. She and Gabby were the best of friends, and although not their daughter, she was more than family.

Sarah seemed to glide across the room as she retrieved the bucket of honey and the honey dipper and brought them to where I sat.

"Water is on," Josef announced as he reentered the room and sat at the table.

"Sold most of the chairs," Josef said again, "not all, but most."

The women ignored him and went about their work.

Sarah selected a small loaf of bread from my basket, tore it in half, and coated it with honey oozing off the dipper. As the bread overflowed with the sweet nectar, Sarah licked her fingers and then handed the dripping bread to me. I had never tasted anything so glorious, so sweet.

Sarah watched me with delight as I ravenously ate the bread and started in on the hearty soup, which Gabriella set beside me in a steaming bowl. As I continued to eat and revel in their kindnesses and generosity, Gabriella and Sarah brought trays of meat and cheese and still more food until I could not eat another morsel, having consumed a magnificent feast that I would remember for all my years.

They had rescued me.

They had taken me in when I had no place else to turn. Josef realized this when he looked into my eyes. Gabriella and Sarah were equally wise.

I didn't know it then, but I was still in shock. That night I was more alive than I would be for most of the coming year. Even with love, these things take time.

Josef began to gather bedding from a lower cupboard. "You'll get a bed in the carpentry," he said. "The mornings are early. I expect you working by first light."

Gabriella stepped in front of Josef, cutting him off as he piled up the blankets and grabbed a lumpy pillow. "There's time enough for that," she said. "How about we begin with a name?"

"KRIS!"

Trees loomed in the darkness. Small feet ran through the snow. Through the trees my brother Owen slowly walked up the steps of the roadhouse. People poured out of the roadhouse, standing at the door.

"Who's he?"

"Sniveling brat!"

"Abandoned!"

"I don't want him."

"I'm not taking care of him."

"He's from the sickness!"

Owen stepped onto the porch. The roadhouse giant stepped forward from the crowd, placed his foot on the chest of my brother, and gave him a mighty push.

"Leave him to die!"

Owen turned his head and looked straight at me. His violet eyes pleaded for help. Silently, his mouth called my name.

"KRIS!"

I jolted awake. Another morning had dawned.

Light poured through the doorway of my makeshift room. At Gabriella's bidding Josef had boxed in my cot at the back of the shop with standing shelves so that I might have some place of solitude.

I poked my head out and could see across the room to the windows. The storm had broken and departed. Josef was busy examining a piece of lumber. Silently I set about organizing my sleeping space and putting it back in order, folding my bedding and stacking it in a corner so that it would not be an obstacle.

"KRIS!" Josef yelled as he began sawing into the lumber.

I moved in front of him to gain a better view and watch him work, unsure what else to do.

Markus, Jonas, and Noel, who were busy with various tasks, eyed me with disdain. I felt embarrassed for having slept so long, vulnerable. This would be the first and last day I overslept. I only hoped I hadn't spoken in my sleep. Their eyes were upon me as I helped Josef anchor the piece of lumber at his instruction while he continued to finish off a clean cut.

The carpentry was filled with the tools of Josef's trade, a wide assortment of unusual saws, knives, chisels, punches, hammers, mallets, gougers, planes, wood-turning lathes, and various other implements used to measure and hold wood, including a collection of ingenious grips and vices, which Josef had no doubt devised and fabricated, along with drafting tables, cutting tables, storage bins, and shelves that contained scrolls of drawings and plans, sawdust-covered books, and small carved cornices.

The carpentry itself was shaped like a large, open barn, twice the length of its width. At the far end were two swinging doors that opened to the outside, which allowed room for the larger finished pieces to be carried out. To the left of the barn doors were stacks of raw, uncut wood and scraps. To the right lived a very organized system of separating wood based on size and shape. Along the length of the rest of the right wall, above a working counter, hung most of the tools of the shop. On the counter, a grouping of small baskets was filled with screws and pegs of varying lengths and sizes. The space itself was broken up by three long tables. Just to the left of the counter, two tables ran end-to-end. I could tell by the mess that this was where the apprentices worked. To the left of the length of tables set the third workspace. This table was neat and organized. I could almost tell the logic of the intended undertaking for the day. These pegs, these pieces, would become an arm. These screws, these pieces, would become the back of a chair. I could see how they would be assembled and where the worker would position his body from one task to the next. Josef had set out his day's work.

On the right wall, in the back of the carpentry, sat a large furnace surrounded by neat stacks of split logs. Just to the left were the shelves that framed my sleeping area, a cot with just enough room to walk around. In the back corner, opposite the furnace, was the doorway into that glorious kitchen with its delicious smells, promising breakfast. High along the left wall ran a series of windows that cast light throughout the carpentry. Beneath the windows sat a few large lathes with dowels in various stages of crafting and completion. A single door split the wall to the outside.

Markus stood at a small table by the stack of raw wood, sanding boards. His sanding created a fine dust that he occasionally blew at Noel as Noel walked by, carrying bundles of wood cut into standard shapes and sizes.

Jonas was sweeping up the sawdust and debris in a constant state of frustration due to the new piles of sawdust Markus made each time Jonas got closer to completing his task. Markus seemed to hesitate and hold each new release of the pilings until just after Jonas had swept up a hefty batch and dumped it in an old wooden barrel by the scrap heap.

Throughout the day I watched with fascination as Josef transformed pieces of raw wood into strong and useful objects, both functional and beautiful expressions of his craftsmanship and artistry. His instructions to me were filled with depth and life—words which, throughout my training, would shape and hone my being.

This was the solution to reuniting my family. If I could learn this trade, I could take care of my brothers and sisters. And in that moment I decided I was going to master this craft. One year, I gave myself. If they could only survive this one year, I could save them. This was the pact I made with myself on my first day as an apprentice.

I studied each of the boys as they engaged in their tasks and every move Josef made as he sliced and trimmed pieces of lumber or sawed massive boards into sections or shaved the bark off thick logs that might soon become pieces of elegant chairs or sturdy tables.

Josef wedged his saw into a log and then instructed me. "Remember. Measure twice, cut once. Now, two-foot lengths until I tell you otherwise."

The other boys had stopped working and were watching me and waiting to see how well I would proceed, snickering among themselves in hopes I would miss a mark or rudely cut a piece of fine lumber.

"None of that," Josef barked at his apprentices. "You each have many tasks ahead, and I am watching your work."

Josef turned to me and poked me in the chest with a T-square. "Think you can handle that?" he asked.

I took the tool in hand and began measuring the logs and marking them. I measured each of them again and again and again, until any doubt of error was erased. And I began to cut with slow, meticulous strokes of the saw. The backward cut was easiest. It seemed the direction the teeth cut into the wood with less difficulty. Once a deep enough groove was made, the forward motion was less jumpy, more even. With greater confidence I began leaning into the work, pulling and pushing, a slow and continuous movement working the saw steadily through the wood.

Markus was beveling the edges of a table with some kind of cylindrical knife. He giggled to the other boys over the simplicity of my task. They responded in kind to his prompting and distracted me from my efforts.

It wasn't that their teasing affected me. I was too deep in a world filled with greater issues for me to be aware or care about such things. I was looking to their actions as examples from which to learn. I was hungry for knowledge, and I wanted to understand how the knife in Marcus's hands functioned.

"Focus, boy! Keep your eye on the wood," Josef snapped. "It'll be months before I put a knife in your hand. I've no patience for mistakes."

I did as Josef directed.

"A carpenter is useless if he doesn't cut his own wood," Josef said to me intently. "Start by knowing the saw. You must use it like an extension of yourself, and guide it with a dedicated focus that will bring you mastery over the raw and wild nature of the wood."

Josef's powerful words would remain with me throughout my life. "Use it like an extension of yourself." That was his first instruction to me on my road to becoming a master. The tool responds to your thought without the mental distraction of figuring out how to make it function. The truth of this I have seen again and again throughout my life, from great musicians to gifted cooks and bakers. Art, I have come to believe, means the excellence of a thing. It is also, I imagine, how we were made in God's image. The creator gave us the great ability to create with the talents bestowed upon us and with craftsmanship earned from learning and hard work. It is in our small creations that we resonate the power of God.

Jonas nicked his finger with a knife and let out a whimper. I glanced over to see what had happened. Josef grabbed me by the chin with his rough, scarred hands and glared directly into my eyes. "Focus!" he commanded.

I looked down at the wood I was about to cut. The saw blade was resting on my thumb. Had I started to cut the wood, I would have injured myself, delaying the plan that was taking shape in my head. Shaken, I lifted the blade off my finger and reset it upon the mark I had made in the wood. As I began to saw, Josef took hold of my elbow, moving it to a steady pace. At first I fought what seemed an awkward action. But once I caught the natural flow, I felt the blade move more smoothly through the wood and the effort lessened for the muscles in my shoulder.

"When you are out of tune or out of rhythm, the teeth will skip and catch on the wood," Josef said to me. "There is a place where the saw works with your arm. With proper practice, tools will do their job cleanly; with mastery they will obey your thoughts."

"You will have repaid your debt once I have two sets of quality chairs," Josef said as he walked away.

"How will I know they are good enough?" I asked.

"When I can't tell the difference between the chairs you have made and the ones I have made with my own hands."

I threw my focus into measuring and remeasuring, cutting and trimming.

Later that week, several men from the village approached the carpentry in an old and battered wagon. Josef greeted them outside. I listened as one of the men told him of a body found along the roadside on his journey back from trading at the coast. The woman seemed a victim of illness and the recent storm. They wanted Josef's help in collecting the remains and tending to their disposition.

The other boys were filled with morbid curiosity, for they were not experienced in death. I remained quiet, pretending to be focused on my work.

Josef instructed all of us to continue our tasks and hastened to add that he would not accept any misbehavior. Then he ventured off to help the other men tend to the body they had discovered. For me there was no doubt who they were intending to bury, and I was thankful.

These are good men, I thought. But I could not reveal to them the awful road I had traveled. "Never let them know where you are from," my mother had told Garin. Was she right? Would I find myself cast out again into the cold relentless winter? I decided to practice silence. It was a habit that I came to rely on.

In the evening, I was sitting alone at a small table in the carpentry eating a hearty soup and bread when Josef returned. From the darkness I listened closely as he told Gabriella what had transpired.

They had found the woman, frozen by the roadside. They knew she had been looked after in some fashion since she was laid in a sleeping position with her arms crossed about her breast, and with her head supported by a pillow of snow and ice. Her suffering and struggles were revealed by the look upon her face and the evidence of illness left upon her body.

"It seems to me she may have died before her body froze," Josef told Gabriella. "She was laid to rest there, no doubt, because the building storm and bitter cold made it too difficult to take her any farther."

"And, what became of her body?" Gabriella asked.

"We found the ground too hard and solidly frozen to bury her with dignity," Josef said. "Since the others were fearful of the disease, we built a large fire and placed her body upon it, until it was fully consumed by the flames."

Gabriella comforted Josef, "May the Lord bless her soul and those who loved her."

I watched the flames leaping and raging in the furnace of the carpentry. I thought of how many times over the past year I had seen such fires consume the memories of friends and neighbors. My mother's departure in this way gave me final assurance that she would not be further abused and that my duty to her was finished. I was finally and fortunately released from her control over my life and of my destiny, I told myself. I was free to do what I thought best.

A plan had taken hold in my mind, and I was committed. In a year's time I would reunite my family. I mentally retraced my steps, creating a picture in my head of the journey back to find my scattered siblings. I would be fourteen years old, a full-grown man, no matter what she had said, ready to take care of all of us.

May our mothers forgive the arrogance and insults of our youth. There are some of us to whom telling is just not enough; we must learn through the pains of experience.

That night, when I returned to my bed, the little toy wooden bear that my brother had left behind was resting on a table near my bedside.

I did not know when Josef placed it there or how he understood what it could have meant to me. Though we never spoke of it, I knew he had discovered at least a portion of my secret story. I laid the wooden bear near my pillow as I went to sleep and tried to cry. I had cried for the abuse endured by our horse, Gerda. I had cried and cried in unstoppable

rivers of tears that overflowed their banks and streamed in burning chan-
nels down my cheeks until I could not cry another tear, until my breath
had been sucked from my lungs. But when I thought of the weight of
suffering and misery my father and my mother, my brothers and my
sisters and I had been crushed and splintered by, I could not summon
a tear.

Gerda healed well, and on off days I would spend long hours brushing
her and grooming her or simply sitting in her stall splitting hay. My
work, my focus, my dedication to carpentry, to Josef and to Gabriella,
carried me forward hour after hour, day after day, week after week, as I
slowly increased my skill and confidence.

Sometime during that year, my fourteenth birthday came and went.
At the carpentry shop, I experienced generous growth and built myself
up from the scrap of a boy that I had once been to a young man of
greater strength and value—and girth due to the glorious pastries plied
on me by Gabriella. Stocky, well, even hefty, I may have been, but I
could lift more than all three boys together, even Marcus.

I worked by Josef's side whenever he would allow and captured
lessons regarding his techniques, which were by now instinctual to him.
When I measured and cut piece after piece of raw wood, he would stand
nearby to lend a helping hand, a watchful eye, or a terse direction. When
I missed a mark or hesitated to complete a difficult task, he was beside
me to help me rethink my approach and regain a solid footing.

Josef created finely formed and durable carpentry in great measure,
each piece bearing a special accent or signature that gave it uniqueness
and meaning. He would delicately carve these rich-grained woods with

geometric patterns or elaborate flourishes and dust the pieces with a soft-bristled brush to survey every groove and cut. He would fit these pieces together into glorious church pews, benches, chairs, and other valued furniture that he would create on commission or sell to those who encountered him at the market.

I helped by applying fine finishes and oils to pieces once assembled or by building simple tables and doors, which became increasingly sophisticated as my skills improved.

One afternoon as I raised a nearly finished door to a standing position and was blowing sawdust from its panels, Sarah breezed through the carpentry. The dust swirled around her vibrant green dress and framed her like a living work of art. She stole my attention. I knew she had been in the carpentry often during the many weeks of my training, but I was so consumed with my work I could not remember actually seeing her. So beautiful she was that I knew if I gave myself opportunity, I would fall victim to distraction each time she came into a room. At some point I realized I was staring.

Though polite in her greeting and ever so friendly, touching my arm as she walked by, she didn't look directly at me or notice my attentions.

But Markus, Noel, and Jonas did. Their jealousy was obvious when they saw how Sarah affected me. And I knew they would do their best to make me look the fool and embarrass me before her. Noel glared at me from behind a stack of boards and tossed a chunk of wood onto a scrap pile in the corner.

Over the coming months, I would continue with my tasks as Sarah came and went each day to steal a glance at projects I was struggling to master. She tried so hard to appear detached, as if she did not care what I was doing, but when I would look away or return to my work, she would sometimes sneak behind me to lightly tap me on the shoulder or brush past me when she left for home. Her playfulness made her all the more beautiful to me, but I could not easily release my guard and speak with her freely. I thought her so kind to take an interest in a broken soul like me. But she didn't know the horrible things I had done. I was sure if she looked into my eyes she would discover the truth, so I maintained a distance, telling myself that any distraction would keep me from attaining my goals. But she kept coming, and, in secret, I took comfort in her presence.

Gabriella, too, would watch us work from time to time, and on special days might bring us muffins or a plate of cookies to reward us for our efforts. The other boys would race to snatch as many cookies as they might, but I refused to fight them for the crumbs and pieces they would squabble over and stayed focused on my duties.

One day, as Gabriella noticed this, she called me aside and handed me a small platter of frosted cookies all my own. Markus was jealous, envious that I received this special attention. Jonas smiled at me. We shared a similar status, and he understood how significant these small joys were. But Noel was furious in his resentment as I took a generous bite and proudly set the platter near my workbench. And how utterly aghast they all were when Sarah entered the room and I proffered her my plate.

"Would you share these with me?"

Sarah looked at me in surprise. I had never before spoken to her. In all this time, and under her subtle attentions, I had never said a word to her. She paused and looked at me to consider my offering.

Somehow I found myself talking: "You brought me bread and honey. Now I would like to share with you."

Then Sarah smiled. Her eyes sparkled. She reached out and took the frosted cookie I was holding. She was supposed to take one of the cookies from the plate I held out to her. But as she grasped one side of the cookie, I held the other firmly, almost not knowing what to do, and neither of us released our hold. That awkward moment was one of the most wondrously embarrassing of my life. And when I finally snapped out of my delirium, watching her take a bite from the cookie was a fourteen-year-old boy's dream.

Marcus dropped a log on Noel's foot, and his piercing howls made Sarah laugh. I had forgotten how lovely the sound of laughter could be.

"You don't talk much," was all she said as she turned to leave.

There were always chores for us to do at the carpentry, and we stayed forever busy organizing supplies, cutting wood, sharpening tools, and cleaning up debris. Josef taught us to keep an orderly shop, to value hard work, and to dedicate ourselves to a job well done. He demanded that we put forth our best efforts at all times and increase our skills and productivity. The work was satisfying, and we were well looked after.

I went about my duties each day in silence, though the other boys often bickered or taunted one another as they carried out their tasks. I did not have a need to talk and rarely spoke, as my thoughts were occupied by the projects I worked on and the objects I helped Josef create.

One day, while I was sitting at a worktable eating a delicious and generous lunch that Gabriella had brought us, she surprised me as she placed a crisp, leather-bound journal near my side and set a small piece of charcoal atop it. "This is for you to practice your letters, dear," she said to me. "You do know how to read and write, don't you?"

I nodded. My mother had taught me my letters. It had been very important to my father since he could not read.

"You might want to use this to keep notes about your work or drawings of plans, or you may want to write down what you are thinking."

I knew the value of milled paper. This was a gift of immense worth, a personal treasure beyond any monetary value. It was leather bound, with a cover that wrapped the book once over again and then tied with a leather cord. Books were rare, and it reminded me of the Bibles carried by the traveling holy men who would visit our village church. But this journal was empty, awaiting my life to fill its leafy pages. And as I sat there gently holding it, running my fingers along its rich texture, I gained a friend. When I wrote inside this book, I was speaking to a lifelong confidant, a companion who was always there to listen and who never judged. We explored thoughts and ideas. We spoke about my darkest secrets.

I am not sure Gabriella knew the gift she was giving me. Maybe she did. She and Josef had a wisdom all too often absent from this world.

On one quiet afternoon while taking a short respite for lunch, I sat looking through a window at Josef and Markus outside. They worked together to load a sturdy table into the back of a customer's wagon. Josef had finished the table a short time ago and was delighted with the results. So proud was he of his work that he had described and demonstrated to us the quality of the joints and the ways they fit together almost seamlessly. Josef was never boastful, yet he wanted us to learn and appreciate fine craftsmanship, to take joy in our achievements, and he used examples such as this to illustrate how superior results were achieved. And although our customers lavished praise and thanks upon all of us for the works we created, it was important to Josef that we learn to evaluate our own results.

"Confidence comes from within," he would say to us. "A man who places his personal value in the hands of others will find himself begging for approval."

He inspired me to complete tasks. Not only did a realized project fill me with gratification, it also served to reinforce my feelings of self-worth.

Each day the carpentry tools were responding more easily to my bidding. A technique once taught became a building block as I began to combine them into uses I had yet to learn. I studied the carvings in the legs and arms of the chairs Josef had created and did my best to reproduce them. When time permitted, I cut and assembled sections of a new chair similar to the ones I had broken on my arrival. Frustration! I knew it would be some time before I could match the quality of Josef's work. My failures fueled my dogged tenacity.

But all was not without a cost. Josef might have been caring, but he was a stern taskmaster. When I carved too deep or left a sloppy edge, he would admonish me in front of whoever was there to listen, making me redo entire pieces for the smallest of mistakes. On the rare occasion that I nicked or cut my hand with a tiny slip of the knife, he always seemed to be right behind me with a terse corrective slap on the back of the head, a reminder to take my time and focus. In those fleeting childish moments, I hated him, threw unspoken expletives in his direction. But once the sting to my ego had worn off, I strove twice as hard to earn his respect.

The world itself spoke to me of methods and mechanisms, and I began to consider new designs of my own. When I observed a small child playing outside near the wagon, rolling a rusty round iron band from some discarded barrel by prodding it with a stick, I saw the crank, I saw the lever, and I saw the wheel and pinion that would give life to otherwise inanimate wooden objects. I looked to Garin's wooden bear for inspiration and thought, "What if it could move? What if it could bend, or walk, or dance?" A dancing bear? Perhaps I could make a toy for each of my brothers and sisters and give it to them upon our reunion. If I did this they would surely know that I had never forgotten about them. I grabbed a warped piece of lumber lying on the ground, a handful of pegs, and began creating gears.

When time allowed and I was not with Gerda, I sketched designs for toys I imagined and began the creation of a playful toy bear that would move and dance as its parts were manipulated. Cutting pieces to fit precisely was no easy task, and I practiced on small joints at first to improve my techniques and gain a tighter fit.

Josef saw the bear one day in its earliest form and picked it up to examine it. As he moved the pieces of wood, the little bear came to life. Josef immediately laughed in response and made playful growling noises like a bear cub as he danced with the toy in the workshop. The four of us boys watched, mouths hanging open in surprise at his unexpected playfulness. I suppose that was the day I first realized we are all children at heart. When he was through with his amusement, he looked around at us awestruck boys, set the toy gently on the shelf, and gave me a little wink.

Markus craned his neck to see what Josef had enjoyed so much. Later I caught him carving a poorly formed neck of a wooden duck, which could have doubled for the neck of some misshapen mythical creature. As Markus carved, its over-shaped and malformed head snapped off in his hands. He violently chopped away the identity of the wooden figurine so no one would see his degree of failure. Looking back, I should have helped him. But I was too young to understand the envy he had over my deepening relationship with Josef or his fear of losing his position as lead apprentice.

Oblivious, I continued developing my new inventions and found myself in love with each new toy. Long hours were spent each day completing the chores Josef would assign to me, and at night I worked by the light of a single lantern to improve my sketches and toy designs. I was not deterred from my mission, no matter how dark or cold the night, or how fiercely the wind might threaten outside. I carried on until I could not work another moment, and when sleep overtook me and demanded I surrender, I drifted off in chaotic dreams upon my cot with the few toys that I had made resting beside me.

Sometimes in the night Gabriella would leave a tiny cake or a freshly made cookie near my cot in case I should awake and choose to return to my efforts. But if I was so fast asleep that even a tempest might not rouse me, she would extinguish the lantern and leave me to my slumber, hands hanging off the edges of my cot, holding my open journal or clutching the beginnings of a wooden snowflake I was making for Nikko. He was going to be a year old and ready for something to shake, so I made a ring with little snowflakes—copies of my mother's pendant for him to rattle and to prove our relation to the old couple with whom I had left him since he would have no recollection of me.

Birds and bears were my inspiration as the other gifts began to represent their intended loved ones. The dancing bear was of course for Garin, a reminder of a connection to an earlier life and a whimsical promise of joys to come. For Tomas, I created a woodpecker that would peck its way down a wooden pole anchored to a base painted to look like a tree. When placed at the top of the pole, the weight of the bird would create a rocking action as it slid down. For Talia, I made a climbing bear that hung from two separate strings connected to a small horizontal stick attached to a hook. As the strings were pulled first to one side and then the other, the bear climbed from one arm to the other till it reached the top. Jess was still young, so I made her a goose that, pulled with a rope, would waddle behind her as she walked. When it came to Owen, I wanted something that would inspire his imagination. I came up with a wooden carousel of flying swans that carried little boys on their backs. The swans hung from strings attached to a central pole, and as the top of the pole was turned, the birds would fly in a circle.

Kendra, alone and old enough to remember our loss, deserved something special. I drew up plans for a beautiful toy duck whose head and wings would move as a simple lever was pulled and twisted in her fingers. With the exception of the bear, all the other toys relied on tricks. This required real ingenuity. I lost myself in the mechanics of the turning wheels and axles. As I worked assembling the puzzle pieces of the toys, the other apprentices watched with much fascination, though they tried to pretend they were busy with other tasks and had little interest in what I was creating.

Sarah watched me too from a corner of the room, and when I held the duck aloft and made its wings flutter as if to fly, I could hear her gasp behind me.

"It's magnificent, Kris," she whispered into my ear. Her hand rested on my shoulder. I am not sure what was more thrilling, the triumph of completing the duck or the warmth of breath from her whisper. As I turned to look at her, our noses bumped. I was mortified. In her embarrassment, she grabbed her breadbasket, skipped out of the carpentry, and closed the door behind her.

Markus, Jonas, Noel, and I continued to learn and develop under Josef's direction, but the other apprentices took many opportunities for granted and wasted chances to enhance their skills where I did not. They had full lives and families and little joys that came from both. I had the blessing of learning and building to occupy my mind. Lack of focus left room for troubling thoughts to enter my days and nights. Work was my weapon against those unwanted ghosts.

I enjoyed designing and sketching plans for new chairs and tables and sometimes worked on several pieces at a time to help Josef complete the orders he had on hand. It was time-consuming work, especially since Josef wanted each finished piece to be of his standard.

Often I would ready several sets of legs for chairs or tables and pile them in stacks until they could be joined with chair backs and seats the others might be working on.

Josef's skill at wood engraving was well known, and I delighted in watching him work with delicate, firm strokes as he cut with a burin, a small knife with a V-shaped tip, into the wood. With that knife he could capture anything, from landscape and animal to the most elegant scrollwork. My favorite was the Borre knot work, reminiscent of our lost Viking heritage. One day, as he was engraving the sides of a pew for a church in our district, he called me to his side.

"Kris, I want you to try your hand at this," he said as his hands unconsciously continued their masterful work.

Josef selected the precise chisel for each task and set about with it and his mallet to cut and score the wood. Periodically he would blow away the fine shavings and brush aside the dust to examine the lines he was cutting. Halfway through he handed the mallet and chisel to me.

"Make sense to you?" he asked.

I could only nod my head affirmatively, as I wondered whether I would ever be able to make such a glorious pattern as this.

Josef pointed to one of his finest masterworks and challenged me. "Now, do the next six of those. And don't mess it up. They're coming for them in two weeks."

What? I fumbled with the tools as I considered the significance of the task at hand and the importance of the work Josef had directed me to do. The pews were all but done. Any error would destroy weeks, maybe months, of work.

Josef laughed gently at my hesitation. "Go on, boy. Take your time. See the image in your mind as you set about engraving. If you can see the results you desire clearly in your thoughts, you won't fail." Then he chuckled as I swallowed hard and set the chisel to the wood.

Jonas laughed as though he understood the joke and then yelped as a small block of wood hit him in the back of the head.

Noel stood next to Markus on the other side of the room with a scowl as Markus juggled another block of wood from hand to hand and looked for me to make a blunder as I set about my assignment.

Gabriella interrupted the awkward scene carrying a tray piled with breads and pastries and a pitcher of fresh milk, which she invited us to come and enjoy.

"All right, my busy bears." Gabriella chuckled. "Time to reward you for your hard work."

She laughed even harder as the boys rushed to the platter, eagerly grabbing at the food.

Josef wiped the dirt and wood shavings from his hands with a cloth lying nearby and went into the kitchen.

I stayed at my workbench and studied the engravings I was about to continue.

"Strudel! Fantastic!" Jonas shouted, as he and the other boys ripped into the food.

I set the chisel and mallet aside briefly and picked up Kendra's mechanical wooden duck, setting the gears into motion, and the duck into animated life as a boost to my self-confidence. I could do this.

Gabriella patted Jonas on the cheek and then looked over to my workbench. "Now Kris, don't forget to eat," she said as she followed Josef inside.

Noel snickered under his breath. "Forget to eat." He elbowed Markus, who was busy stuffing his face. "Guess he thinks he's too good to eat with us!" Noel scoffed.

As I got up from my work and dusted myself off, I was hit hard in the side of the face with a roll that Noel had thrown.

"Bop!" Noel laughed.

"Oooooooohhhhh!" Marcus teased.

"I'll feed you, piggy!" Noel shouted at me.

Markus cautioned him sarcastically. "Noel, Kris looks angry. He might come over here."

"Like to see jelly belly try," Noel mocked.

"Did you hear that, Kris?" Markus said loudly.

I tried to ignore their insults and went back to studying the engraving.

"Hey Kris, where's your family?" Jonas asked innocently.

"Yeah Kris, where is your family?" Noel taunted.

"Away," I replied.

"Do you miss your mother?" Markus taunted. "Hey Kris, what happened to your parents anyway?" he continued. "What's wrong, didn't they have enough food for you?"

Markus and Noel broke into uncontrollable laughter as they approached me. Markus came around in front of me, and Noel approached me from behind, picking the roll off the floor that he had thrown at me. Threateningly, he tossed the roll from hand to hand.

"What are you working on over here, Kris?" Markus asked.

Noel jumped forward and snatched the toy duck from my work table. "It's a stupid little toy," Noel mocked.

"Let me see it," Markus demanded.

"Give it back!" I shouted at Noel as I tried to take the toy from him.

Noel jumped aside and threw the toy to Markus.

"He speaks!" Markus laughed. "We don't get to hear his silly voice very often."

"Give it back right now!" I said firmly, the boiling anger building in my words of warning.

"It's not like I'll break it," Markus said patronizingly. He held the toy duck out to me. And as I reached for it, Markus smashed the duck on the edge of the table, shattering it.

Snorting like a pig, Noel jumped on my back and tried to shove the roll into my mouth. Markus kicked the pieces of the toy across the room and laughed at the sounds Noel was making.

I was a dam bursting from of all the anger I had held inside. I wanted someone to hurt. I wanted someone to accuse. By breaking that toy they had injured one of my family. Worse, in that moment, they became responsible for every wrong I had experienced over the past year. Unwittingly they had given my fury and anguish a focal point.

Noel hurled off my back and into the workbench, where he landed with a crash. Markus tried to back away; he could see the vehemence and insanity in my eyes, but too late. I grabbed the front of his shirt and cracked him across the temple with the heel of my fist. His legs went limp and he slumped to the floor. Without hesitation I was on top of him, pummeling him relentlessly. Blood began running from his nose and the corner of his mouth. He flailed his arms at me to no avail as he tried to issue a weak defense.

Josef yelled to us as he came quickly into the room. "All right! That is enough!"

But I did not hear him.

"How could you?" I screamed. "How could you leave me?"

"Enough," Josef bellowed.

But I could not stop myself.

Josef grabbed me by the collar and snatched my arm as I tried again to engrave my impassioned message on Marcus's face. As Josef pulled me away from my bloody target, Markus jumped back up, ready to fight. Josef stepped between us and grabbed Marcus by the shoulder. "This ends now! Have Gabriella clean you up. Go home. All of you! There's nothing more here for you today!"

Noel and Jonas quickly followed Markus through the door, scared. Josef watched me as I scrambled frantically to collect the broken pieces of the duck from the ground.

"Kris," Josef said sternly to me—though I was blind and deaf to him. "Kris!" he roared as he seized both my shoulders and my attention.

As I looked at Josef, seeking both his understanding and forgiveness, he began to take the broken pieces of the toy from my hands.

"The world hurts us all, Kris," Josef said. "None of us gets to own pain."

And with that, he snapped the last pieces of the duck together and handed me the toy.

Chapter

Expectations

As Christmas approached, I replaced the broken chairs asked of me, taking pride in the craftsmanship and the knowledge that my debt had been paid. I set them side by side in the carpentry shop for all to see

The next morning I collected my belongings and wiped the wood shavings and dust from the toys I had created. I placed them carefully in a large sack that would protect them from the weather on my long and difficult journey ahead. I organized my bedding and left my sleeping area neat and clean, then set my journal in the center of the cot and was ready for departure.

The journal had been a gift for me, of that I was sure, yet I couldn't bring myself to take it with me. Deep down, I now believe, I left my writing for someone to read and to discover the painful circumstances that I had faced and lived through. It was selfish. I wanted someone to feel for me, to understand.

As I looked back over my shoulder, I found Josef watching me from the doorway. I turned to him silently, and we remained silhouetted in that awkward manner, each waiting for the other to speak. Neither of us quite knew how to acknowledge the relationship that had been forged or give voice to the blessings born of it.

Josef walked over to the eight chairs, which I had positioned in a line along the left wall in front of his workstation. One by one, he inspected each cut and curve, each joint and finish. With eyes and with hands he explored the strength and balance of all.

"I cannot tell," he said, almost to himself. Then, as he smoothed his hands along the sanded silken surface of a varnished seat, he announced, "I cannot tell the difference between the chairs that you have crafted and the ones I have made with my own hands."

"That is because I have made each one. "

When he looked up at me, it was with pride and respect.

"Clean. You have a knack for it," he said with approval.

As I moved across the room carrying my sack of toys, Josef stepped aside to let me pass. "You haven't left any work unfinished?"

I could only shake my head no. If I had spoken I might have lost the nerve to leave the love this home had given me. So I shuffled past, staring at my shoes.

A teary-eyed Gabriella hurried from the kitchen and into the carpentry bearing satchels of food for my travels. "Tomorrow is Christmas. Can't you stay until after the Christmas feast?" she asked. Again I could only shake my head "no."

"This will hold you over 'til..." Gabby threw her arms around me and pressed a kiss on my cheek. As she did, she stuffed a few more small bread rolls into my pockets, which now bulged with food.

I almost faltered.

Josef interrupted. "Keep that on ice. If it's frozen it will be harder for the wolves to sniff out."

They followed me outside where I greeted Gerda and stroked her neck, then loaded the sleigh. When all was set, I climbed on board.

There was nothing to say—or there was too much to say. I gave Josef and Gabriella a silent nod and was on my way.

This was the culmination of all that I had worked toward. In the journal I had drawn a rough and clumsy map of my first delivery, the harrowed journey along the road where I had deposited each of my brothers and sisters. The journal was back in the carpentry inside the cubby on the cot where I had made my home. But the image of the map was burned into my thoughts from nights of staring and dreaming and falling asleep to the promises I was determined to keep.

Lord, hold them safely this last day till I can reach them. Forgive me for who I am and what I have done. See me for who I want to be and what I strive to become. With all my heart and all my soul I want to bring joy to my brothers and sisters. Give me the opportunity to care for these children. And I will give them my life.

On the Eve of Christmas, one year to the day of my first delivery, I set out to reunite my family.

Great expectation coursed through my veins and filled me with a growing excitement that I could not now contain. I was at last off to find each of the beautiful souls I had dispatched into the world unprotected and gather them once again as a family. My skills and strengths were now such that I knew I could provide for them and harbor them. I could comfort them and dry their tears and ask their forgiveness for having forsaken them to the harsh unknown.

As we raced ahead through the snow-blanketed terrain, I imagined what I would find when I discovered my brothers and sisters. How they would shriek with joy to see me! How their eyes would sparkle with delight! How thrilled and excited they would be, just as I was, to meet again.

Just a few hours. If you can survive a few more hours, I can save you from whatever trials or neglect you might be suffering. Seven children to remake our scattered family. By Christmas I would have a new life and new challenges to address. I was exhilarated with anticipation over the trials I would face as a surrogate parent and protector.

Time became the watcher that day as I moved through, past, and around it, the same as it would with every delivery in years to come. Time stretched as I looked for the signs I had marked in my mind, indications that I was on the right path. I didn't notice the passage of the day, so deep was I in my thoughts and imaginings. In my daydreams, time gave up its hold over our sleigh as it traveled great distances, negotiating the tangled paths of my memories, leaping chasms in the forgotten terrain I encountered along my journey, until by some miraculous inter-vention I came finally to the roadhouse where I had last seen Owen.

I cleared a space on the seat of my sleigh and rummaged through the sack of toys. Excitedly I withdrew the carousel of flying swans and little boys; I was sure it would delight Owen's heart.

But then a child's shriek pierced the day's chill air.

"Just a few seconds," I begged, "give me a few more moments, and I will be there to protect you." I sprinted to the roadhouse, fearful some tragedy had just befallen my young brother, gripping the forgotten toy in my left hand. Remembering the roadhouse giant, I swept up a fist-sized rock from the frozen earth with my free hand. If need be I would fell this Goliath on my own.

Skidding to slow my momentum, I reached the front steps of the roadhouse and leapt onto the porch. I was struck by what I spied through the windows of the door. Completely unaware of me, the giant and my brother wrestled and challenged one another on the floor. Owen continued his shrieking, which grew into fits of laughter as the man lifted him and roared, then set him once again on the floorboards and stomped away playfully.

From another room, a woman called in the sweetest voice, "Come here, Jonathan, darling. Come here."

Owen answered her call without hesitation and stumbled into the kitchen out of view.

Truth hit like an avalanche. Sweet, violet-eyed, toddling Owen had become a boy.

"This cannot be!" I said to myself. This is not the Owen I knew and loved, but another boy! I wanted my soft, innocent baby brother back. I wanted time to give back what it had taken—not this new boy, some

Jonathan, who had been bewitched and charmed into submission by this roadhouse giant and his unseen wife!

But even as I floundered in bewilderment, I had seen the delight in Owen's eyes and clearly recognized he had found a pleasant home and a fresh new life.

Just then the man pushed open the door, backing out with a half-barrel in his massive arms. He grunted as he swung around in the doorway, looking for a place to set the barrel on the porch and registering genuine surprise as he encountered my wide-eyed gaze. Retreating, I fell backwards off the porch and scrambled to my feet still clutching the wooden carousel with its dangling pieces, but to my dismay I had dropped my invincible rock.

The man gave another push at the door, to open it even more widely, and watched me as I stood like an animal that had been cornered and trapped. Instead of confronting me or moving to capture me, he gave me a small, friendly smile and tilted his head to one side as if to invite me into the roadhouse. I cautiously approached until I was close enough to place Owen's wooden toy on the steps before him. Then I turned and sprinted away.

After gaining some distance, I looked back and saw that the man's wife had joined him near the steps. She picked up the gift I had left and admired it curiously, turning the center pole and sending the swans into flight.

Owen had found a new identity and a new home. And I realized I was no longer even the smallest part of his young memories.

I also knew he would only suffer the deep and crippling pain of loss, once more if I were to rip him away from his newfound family. So I ran.

The man shouted after me, "Young fellow! Halt! You won't be harmed. Come sup with us!"

I ran back to my sleigh, red-faced and out of breath as the tears streamed down my cheeks and froze to them. I had not considered that Owen might forget the life he had once lived. But as that certainty gripped me. I knew Owen was much better off than he had ever been. He was free of the burdens life had cast upon us and the tragedies we had faced. In their place, he had found happiness and protection. It was this consideration which upended me.

I hopped into my sleigh and vaulted ahead to find the others, who I longed so much to see. I could only wonder what they would say. Resolute, I decided I would convince them that Owen was safe with a new home, a new family, and new memories that we could not provide.

> *Snowflakes floating down to earth*
> *all forget their place of birth*
> *and drift to where the winds will go.*
> *As they swirl across this world,*
> *the things they felt, the ways they melt,*
> *are secrets they will come to know.*
> *But others never will.*

Awake! I shook the lonesome flurries from my brooding thoughts. "Rejoice!" I shouted to myself as much as to the wind. My brother was safe and happy and healthy. Life was good. He had survived. More than survived, he had found a home. I struggled to keep my heart light, speeding to what it longed for—the comfort and security of an understanding heart. I needed my brothers and sisters. I allowed Gerda to sense that need, select my path, and lead me back to the places where my heart beckoned.

Eventually we came upon the baker's house, where Tamas and Talia had first felt, and later endured, the wrenching disconnection from our family. How would these two now fare? I fought back my fears. We would overcome whatever scars this year and separation had left. We would heal and care for each other. We would survive this tragedy as families do, with time and love and new memories to build new hope, new promises, and a new future.

Perhaps we could not patch every wound opened by time and distance, but our blood was the same blood no matter that our severance had been deep and long.

As I stood upon a small pile of logs stacked beside the baker's house to chance a glance inside, my reflected image looked back at me and challenged me from the glistening frost-edged window.

"What are you now?" it asked me curiously as I studied my own questioning eyes in this ghostlike, mocking reflection. Was it man or boy who brought these toys and snuck about to avoid detection?

A sudden cacophony erupted from inside and commanded my attention. I gazed beyond the glass into the baker's house and saw my lovely twin siblings throwing lumps of dough and flour at each other as they ran around furniture and used it to shield themselves. Their faces were as white as dough-kissed seraphim, and they snickered and chuckled in what seemed to be endless peals of laughter as they plastered each other with big, doughy chunks and dusty clouds of powdered flour.

The baker's voice shattered the moment, booming from an adjoining room, "How many times have I told the two of you!"

The twins froze, dough in hand, and looked to each other for strategy as the baker stomped into the room with her hands on her hips.

"You've got to wait for me!" She laughed as she plopped a handful of flour into each of the twin's faces.

How they giggled and chortled and ran as the dough chunks soared and flour flew from their hands.

I cautiously withdrew from the window and collected the pecking and the climbing wooden toys from my sack in the sleigh and placed them on the windowsill for the playful twins to find when the dust was cleared and their games were done and they looked at last outside.

By now my lonely heart was settling into a dark and quiet solitude. With little personal satisfaction I knew with certainty the twins and Owen were all right. Gerda and I sped on through the breeze, and from a great distance the sound of the lumberjacks called out to us long before their camp came into sight.

> *When springtime comes, oh, glad will be its day!*
> *Some return to home and friends, while others choose to stay.*
> *The sawyers and the choppers, they lay their timber low.*
> *The swampers and the teamsters, they haul it to and fro.*

It was by now late afternoon as I walked cautiously around the edges of the deserted woodmen's camp. The wind whistled through the trees and made them shiver and dance with nearly as much anticipation as I now possessed. I heard the distant sounds of jovial men close now as they returned from a hard day's work. The song of a solitary axe rippled on the blustery winds, and I saw my brother Garin, a youngling of ten with shoulders only half the breadth of my own, splitting logs with the passion of the sturdiest of men.

A tall, powerful lumberjack approached Garin and stood off to one side in admiration of the sureness of his strokes. Garin finished the final split and looked to the lumberjack with pride. The man raised his fist and held it aloft in a show of strength and testimony to Garin's skill. They both had a hearty laugh.

"That's enough for now," the lumberjack said as he ruffled Garin's hair playfully. "Carry some of this wood to the fire and stoke it well. It will be a cold and breezy night."

Garin plunged the axe blade into the chopping block, scooped up several sections of the split wood, and headed to the fire pit with his arms fully loaded. The men shared the chores of their evening ritual and sang songs as Garin fed the wood into the fire.

I studied the toy in my hands and wondered how I might deliver it to Garin. I did not have the courage to impose upon this happy group. He had walked away, taken fate into his own small hands, and not looked back. Who was I to force Garin back to his long-forgotten memories of the last horrible days and nights we had shared? I left him the toy dancing bear near his axe so he might know how much I cared.

Gerda and I left that day to the singing of the jacks—the absence of their axes left the song solemn almost holy.

> *All stay we here with a welcome heart and a well-contented mind!*
> *For the winter winds blow cheerfully among the waving pines.*
> *The ringing of saws and axes halt as the sun goes down.*
> *Lay down your tools, me weary boys, to Elysium we are bound.*

Gerda pulled me earnestly over the winding trails as my thoughts carried me back to other times and other places. I lost myself in those bygone days among the smiles and memories of my family's faces.

All the world was quiet and serene as we reached the country inn. I crept up to that familiar window's snowcapped sill to steal a gaze within, in hopes of finding how my sweet, red-headed Jess had been.

She sat teetering if not tottering on the bar crying and holding out her little arms. "Momma," Jess cried, even though there was no one else in sight.

But like the others, I could soon see she was safe and loved, as the bar matron quickly approached, lifted her up, and headed for the stairs at the back of the tavern, as I imagined, to tuck her into bed before the ribald holiday crowd arrived for the night's festivities.

"You little scoundrel," my sister's adopted mother teased her as they walked up the stairs. "I don't know how you get up there, but if I ever catch you climbing I will redden your bottom. Hear?"

"Yes, mama," my darling sister replied and then shrieked as her new mother commenced a series of belly blows that sent her wriggling and squirming for freedom.

"Mama, mama,' she begged between gasps and giggles, "I wanna stay up. Please, Mama, pleeeaassee!"

"Not tonight, love. Tomorrow is the Christmas feast, and you will want your rest or you'll get grumpy. Sleep tonight, love; the sooner you sleep, the sooner you wake up."

And my sister looked like she was on her way, head lolling and bobbing as she fought the losing battle.

I snuck inside and smelled the rich, yeasty sawdust spread across the tavern floor, which mixed with fragrant smoke from the fading flames in the hearth. I placed the wooden duck on the bar where Jess had sat and drifted once more through the door and out of sight.

We arrived sooner than I expected at the churchyard and its adjoining cemetery. The church still beckoned like a private beacon as I urged Gerda to shelter in a safe spot just beside the sanctuary.

In the distance, I could see candles lit and placed near the small gravestone of a child. As I approached and watched them flicker and glow in the deepening twilight, I felt some tragedy had surely befallen my dearest gentle sister Kendra. Grief and distress pierced my heart, and my breath came in gasps as I struggled to swallow the lump rising in my throat.

The gravestone had no inscription I could read, as its edges were worn and shadowed in the quickly vanishing light. I lost myself in the desperate contemplation of how foolish I had been to leave her here unattended on such a cold, cold winter night.

Whispered voices taunted me, first from one direction and then the other. My sanity seemed lost as I heard Kendra's loud breathy whisper brush past me from the trees. "Here. Come here. I am over here."

"Where are you?" came the whispered reply from the other direction. But this time I was sure it was another girl.

Just then a white rabbit bolted from the underbrush, followed by the snapping of branches and twigs and the tromping and crunching of clumsy feet.

I hid behind another gravestone and waited there to see what was to come, less fearful of an apparition than moments before. From beyond the distant monuments, a young girl emerged, followed shortly by my freckled sister Kendra. Her long auburn hair flowed freely from beneath her woolen hat and caught glints of moonlight as she danced and chased the rabbit and her friend into the churchyard.

Kendra stopped suddenly, twirled, and fell to the snowy earth. She moved her arms and legs in a gentle wave as she carved an angel in the finely powdered snow. The rabbit stopped for one moment as if confused, then thought better of it and leapt for the trees. Kendra's blonde companion laughed and plopped herself down beside my sister and joined her in the fun.

The church groundskeeper shouted out to them from his modest stone cottage nearby, "Come inside girls. Mama says your supper is hot!"

As the girls quickly hurried into the cottage, I ran back to the sleigh and to my nearly empty satchel of wooden toys.

Inside the church vestibule, I found the table where one year before I had left Kendra sleeping and the mat I had placed her upon. The old stone nativity scene had been set upon it, just off to one side. The figurines had nicks and scratches born from the momentary anger of my last visit. One of the gift givers had a chipped piece missing from its shoulder. I felt terrible, knowing now the work, love, and craftsmanship that had gone into that creation. And in one selfish outburst I had tainted their beauty forever. Nearby, a small woven offering basket stood waiting for church donations. I placed the carved toy wooden duck inside the basket as my simple gift to Kendra.

A firm hand took hold of my shoulder, startling me. But another strong, weathered hand clasped my elbow and held me for a moment.

Then, strangely, the hand walked one finger at a time down my arm to the hand and the table and the basket to discover the wooden toy.

"Interesting," the holy man said.

I jerked to free myself from his hands.

"Please," the tall, white-haired man said to me, still holding me gently if firmly. Then he reached up to explore the contours of my face. "Let's see who I have come to visit."

"You are blind," I blurted out. His eyes were solid white from cataracts, worse than any of the elders I remember from my village mountain home.

"For men at first had eyes, but could not see," the holy man said simply. "You are cold." Then he patted me on the cheek.

I stepped back and released the breath I had been holding.

"Come. What would ease your travels?" the holy man asked.

"A miracle," I said to him.

The old man turned and walked to a large fireplace glowing on the far wall of the stone church within. "What makes you think a miracle is not happening right now?"

"There are no miracles."

"Ah, no miracles! I see," said the holy man. His fingers stumbled across the mantle above the hearth to find a porcelain mug left resting there. "It has been hard for you."

"How would you know?"

The holy man smiled softly, ignoring my insolent tone, and reached over and found a wooden ladle hanging by a leather lanyard beside the hearth and dipped it into a kettle of steaming liquid suspended from an iron hook above the flames.

Again I asked, yearning for something hopeful, "How would I know if a miracle was happening?"

"Hmm, that is difficult," he said. "Miracles are revealed one secret at a time."

A mocking grunt escaped my lips in response to what I felt was a useless comment, but he was not finished.

"When you cry through the night and wake up with the dawn asking God for comfort."

I watched him in silent wonder as he reached his unprotected hand into the hearth of the fireplace.

"When you give away all that you are," he continued.

Deftly he lifted the ladle that sat inside the boiling cauldron.

"When you sacrifice your belongings, your sleep, your health."

Slowly he poured the steaming hot liquid from the ladle into the mug.

"When out of helplessness, you choose to act."

His hands went on another cautious march to find a small jar and remove its lid.

"And when those acts of helplessness become habitual."

I watched him place two teaspoons of sugar into the cup and then hesitate before deciding to add a heaping third.

"Those acts are the signs of a miracle."

He stirred the liquid and then set down his spoon on the mantle.

"Do you think He was ever lonely?" I asked, looking at the small stone manger with the infant inside.

He lifted his head and looked directly at me. If I didn't know differently, I would have thought he was staring into the depth of my eyes, looking for something. Still, those eyes held me.

"Of course," he said plainly. "Loneliness is a part of suffering, which is simply part of the human experience. But He had faith."

I looked up at the little wooden cross hung above the table in the vestibule.

"If He had a choice, why go through it all?"

His short answer sent me into a torrent of guilt and action. "So that no child is forgotten."

"Nikko. I almost forgot Nikko."

He reached over to pinch the edges of a small plate containing shortbread, which rested on a large flat stone near the hearth.

But I had no time. Again, I had almost forgotten my infant brother. "I am so sorry. I can't stay. I have to go."

I stuttered as I looked around to gain my bearing and moved toward the door.

The holy man walked to the table then stood there holding the plate of shortbread and the mug of warm liquid.

"May you find your miracles," he called after me as I ran through the door.

As I vaulted down the steps of the church and leapt into my sleigh, I imagined him sipping the tea casually as if he had knowingly made it for himself.

He was a mystery to me then and is to this day, but at that moment I was too occupied to give him further thought. Unknowingly I was to begin my greatest act of helplessness, spawned by my search for the one who had most needed me in his innocence, whom I had left with some nameless old couple one cold Christmas morning.

There was no road to the old cottage. No easy access. I found the place where I had laid my mother to rest. She was gone, of course. It was haunting yet comforting to stand where I had left her. I held Nikko's rattle with its clinking snowflakes.

"I almost forgot him, Mama. But I didn't. I am going to leave him this gift. It is a rattle to entertain him. I made it myself. Look how I made each little snowflake like the one that hung around your neck. I was going to use this to prove my relation. But I have come to find each of your children has found a new family, and I expect no different with him. I miss you and Papa. I don't suppose the others will remember much of our lives together, maybe Garin and Kendra. But I don't wish that on them. I hope they can release their past so that they may embrace their new future. From what I saw today, it looks to me they have already begun to do so. As for me, I am lost. I will leave this rattle on Nikko's door and leave to some unknown future. They are safe. You were right, they do not need me. I would only have been a burden. But what about me? I needed them, and you took them away from me. How could you put me through this? How could you let God put me through this? I hate you! I hate you, Mama! I hate you!"

I had fallen to my knees, punishing the snow-packed earth with the butts of my fists. And I placed my forehead to the earth, ready to cry, but the tears would not come.

I eventually found the old cottage after walking and walking once again over the snowy rolling hills to where I had deposited the infant Nikko what seemed a lifetime ago.

As I arrived upon the fateful scene, all seemed so quiet and unnatural. Time had become frozen like the world around me. I was by now tired and world-weary as I trudged onward through the snow.

When I eventually reached the cottage I hung the rattle of snowflakes over the great knob on the weathered and splintering wood plank door. I was committed to leave my infant brother in peace with his new family as I had left the others. But as I released the rattle, the door creaked slowly open. Inside, the dark and lonely shell revealed the tale of a home long abandoned to the elements. I pushed harder on the door.

Old, discarded broken furniture littered the cottage floor. There was evidence that life had indeed prevailed here some time in the distant past, but the cottage now was mired in disregard and decay as if forsaken ages ago.

Fury and pain burst from my lungs and ignited explosively, shattering the silence with my shrill cries. I smashed and destroyed the tables and chairs; I beat the walls and ripped the mantle from the fireplace. I wailed in my suffering and self-condemnation.

I had lost Nikko. She was right. I couldn't take care of them. She was right. I wasn't strong enough. I did not deserve them. She had been right!

Gerda received me without judgment as we reunited. Soon, I settled upon a course of action and headed out for the only place I knew to turn.

When I reached the carpentry, I put Gerda to rest and quietly slipped inside to announce my presence. The shop was empty. The apprentices would not arrive, for it was Christmastide, and I knew Josef and Gabriella would be together still at breakfast as the morning came alive.

But I could not bring myself to interrupt their privacy and intrude upon their gentle sanctuary.

I sat alone in frustration and embarrassment for quite some time, running my fingers along the smooth curves of a set of chairs in front of Josef's workstation. I thought about that fateful day when hunger and a growing storm had first driven me there, how Josef had insisted that I replace the broken chairs. And in anguish and desperation, I lifted a chair and smashed it in to the others.

I could hear Josef's hurried footsteps as he rushed into the carpentry from the house. He was holding a large, sharp knife and stood ready in the doorway to defend his home and life.

He slowly began to relax as he saw me sitting slumped over amid the remnants of the chairs I had shattered, and he watched me for a moment without uttering a word.

"I broke the chairs," I confessed.

"I see," Josef said. He walked over to retrieve one of the sturdy chair legs I had shattered.

I followed him with my eyes to see how this would finally matter.

"This is not the scrap wood you broke last year," Josef said.

I pointed to the area where Josef kept his stock. "It's just common."

"Sha!" Josef interjected. "This is carving you haven't learned yet." Then he looked at me for another long moment and offered his consideration. "I could teach you."

Josef walked closer and stood looking down at me with kindness. "It might take a few months, perhaps longer, years, as slow as you learn."

I reeled up and threw my arms around Josef's waist, and he awkwardly held me, placing his hand upon my head. And I cried. For my mother and my father, for our village, for my brother Nikko, and finally for myself, I cried.

When I was all cried out, Josef slowly lifted me to my feet.

"Let us see if we can convince Gabriella to make you some breakfast."

As I walked with Josef into the kitchen, he placed his hand upon my shoulder and softly said, "Next year, son—you don't have to break the chairs."

Chapter

Home

I returned to my chores as an apprentice and to the daily lessons Josef provided at the carpentry. The other apprentices looked at me in a new light after my surprising return, though I do not believe they were altogether happy to see me. I also think my fierce outburst from the prior year had left them a little hesitant to push my patience, lest they again release my demons. I grew even stockier or stouter or huskier or however nicely you would say it: I got a tad fatter. Gabriella's food only tasted that much better as I became more present to life. Of course, this did not go unnoticed or without endless comments from Markus and especially Noel, which sent them tittering and laughing like schoolgirls. Nonetheless, I went about my duties with renewed vigor and continued to advance in my skills and knowledge. Thankfully I had lost some of my single-minded obsession, which allowed me to see the world again for its beauty and possibility. Sarah was in no small part a glorious object of that awakening. Now that I was more aware of my surroundings, it also meant that I felt more of the sting from my fellow apprentices jibing.

How thankful I was to be home, here in this place of good work and industry, and to have such generous souls as Josef and Gabriella to look after me. As I began to lose details from the memory of my earlier life, the carpentry shop felt more like home than any I could recall. A child's memory can be like that. Even so, my existence was not complete, not yet. I knew there would always be a gnawing emptiness inside where I had once felt the love of my brothers and sisters, whom I thought about during every passing day. There still lived a guilt and pressing responsibility over the loss of my infant brother Nikko.

Projects and orders came to us with regularity, and if we were not always burdened with commissioned work, we generated a steady flow of well-made pieces for Josef to peddle to his appreciative customers abroad.

The church pews Josef built were given extra care, made of strong and lasting materials of beauty, as fitting a house of God. We worked together under Josef's guidance to assist him in finishing these finely crafted pieces, and with great pride we prepared to deliver them into use. They would add a significant beauty to whatever church gave them a home.

I remember clearly the day we carried the last of those fine pews outside, loading them into an old and beaten flatbed wagon. Noah, a man of some girth and substance, had arrived to collect the pews on behalf of the district church. He delighted in coaching us as Josef, the other boys, and I struggled to lift the heavy pews into the wagon bed.

"Lift! Careful, now!" Noah exclaimed as if we needed his constant direction and warnings. "Take it easy, Josef. Make sure the short one doesn't get himself crushed under that thing!" Noah pointed to little Jonas. Then our rotund supervisor laughed at his own statement as if he had hit upon a point of humor all of us should relish.

Jonas looked about curiously to question why he was being mocked.

"Gently, gently—all right. Good!" Noah encouraged us as we finally got the pew into the wagon.

"You could help lift, you know," Josef retorted.

"I could, yes," Noah chuckled, and he began to pick at the gaps between his teeth with a small splinter of wood.

"All right, boys, we're almost done. Grab that last one, and we're finished!" Noah said with encouragement. And he grinned a big toothy grin.

"Lift!" Josef instructed.

"Watch the edges!" Noah warned. "If that pew is scratched, it won't be worth a tinker's fiddle to me. Easy with it. Whew!"

We all stopped to catch our breath, and Josef wiped his brow with an old, worn towel as Noah slapped him on the back.

"See! That wasn't so bad, old boy. That's what we call teamwork."

Josef twisted and stretched his back to relieve the pain. "Okay, boys. Take a few minutes to rest. Then get started straightening up the workshop."

"Hold there a moment," Noah demanded. He reached into his pockets and pulled out rock candy suckers for each of us boys. This was an unheard-of treat and made all his japing and cajoling worth the experience.

"Now, get on!" Josef commanded.

As the others went inside, I drifted out of sight and lingered just around the corner of the carpentry so I could observe the men and listen to their conversation. Josef obviously treated this man as a friend, and I wanted to hear how friends spoke to each other. I had never yet had a close friend and confidant, someone my own age with whom to compare and share experiences and perspective.

Noah began to rub a mild scratch off one of the pews as Josef watched him. "Yes sir, Josef, I am most pleased," he stated with appreciation.

"They turned out good, didn't they?" Josef said. "Strong, sturdy. Of the finest quality."

"So, what's your guarantee?" Noah asked.

"I don't see you needing a new batch while I'm still in business. Not if they're treated right."

"Good man! That's what I like to hear," Noah exclaimed emphatically. He continued to examine the workmanship of the benches and rubbed his plump fingers across the fine grain of the wood.

"So, that will do it?" Josef asked.

"Um. Come to think of it, not quite," Noah confessed. He began to search his large pockets for something and then waddled over to the wagon and rummaged through a sack stashed underneath the driver's seat.

"It's the funniest little thing." Noah grunted. He struggled to find the object with great determination. "Never seen anything like it. It was left for Kendra last Christmas, and she and Leah just would not stop arguing over it."

"Kendra?"

"My daughter," Noah said proudly.

"Noah! You and Layla risked another one?"

How I now struggled to restrain my interest. Kendra? Was this my Kendra? Of course! This could be the church that had so miraculously appeared out of the night. I inched closer and strained to hear what they were saying, trying to capture all the news of my sister.

"No, of course not," Noah chided him. "You see . . . this is why you should show up to service more often. You might stay more up to date on current events!"

"I will follow that advice when you do!" Josef laughed.

Noah looked at Josef with a crooked smile. "Listen, God and I have an agreement. I tend to His house six days a week and He gives me Sunday mornings off." Noah stopped for a moment to catch his breath, as all the activity and talk had tired him. "I'll tell you about Kendra," he said. "It's a story though. A strange one, too." He stopped again upon locating the desired object and signaled his success. "Found it. Take a look at this." He tossed Josef the wooden mechanical duck I had carved and left for Kendra in the church donation basket.

Nervousness and fear washed over me as I saw the wooden duck in Josef's hands, and I was sure I would soon be found out. So I hurried into the safety of the carpentry to rejoin the other apprentices.

Markus was organizing tools as Noel stood behind him, sucking on his candy. Jonas was engaged in cleaning off Josef's workbench and collecting small, leftover pieces of wood. He spun around and sat down as I came into the room and made loud, sucking noises on the hard candy in his mouth.

I grabbed a broom as if preparing to sweep, but in my abject panic I continued to watch the men outside through the window.

Noel began to complain to the others. "He gives us these stupid suckers. Does he think we're babies or something?" He pulled the sucker out of his mouth for a moment and looked to the other boys for response. "Almost killed us with those ugly benches. You know what I mean, Markus?"

Markus tried to ignore him. "Noel, would you just shut up and try to get some work done?"

"Huh? All I'm saying…" Noel began, but he stopped short as Sarah entered the room carrying a basket loaded with fresh bread and muffins. Her silhouette broke the light pouring through the carpentry doors. She didn't walk, she flowed. Sometime over the days since we had last seen her, she had gained curves that we had not perceived before. If we hadn't noticed them previously, with all certainty we noticed them then.

I tore my eyes away from Sarah to watch the exchange between Josef and Noah. It was one of the few times in my life that I was able to deny her my attention.

Sarah swooshed by, gently brushing me with her dress as she passed, and approached the other boys, dragging my attention back to her.

"What have you got there, Jonas?" she said coyly.

Jonas smiled broadly while sucking loudly on the candy. He seemed to swell with pride because Sarah had addressed him while ignoring the others and me.

"Jonas is still sucking on his pacifier." Noel laughed.

"Looks as though you have one, too," Sarah said to him. And as Noel tried to respond, Sarah slapped him on the back as she walked by. He was cut short by the impact of her hand and began to choke, coughing the candy up and spitting it out and onto the dirty, dust-ridden floor.

Markus thought this was hilarious and pointed at Noel and laughed. Jonas also started to chuckle.

Noel retaliated by stealing the sucker out of Jonas' mouth and shoving him off the bench he was sitting on. Jonas hit the floor with a thump as Noel bit into the stolen candy. Markus shook his head in amazement and ridicule and then returned his eyes once more to the newfound swing in Sarah's sashay.

Sarah quickly tired of their foolish behavior and approached me as I once again gazed outside through the window, watching Josef and Noah in their continuing discussion. Sarah set her breadbasket beside me and strained her neck to get a glimpse of what I was looking at so intently. She smelled of lilac water and honey, and her hair brushed against me as she leaned to get a better look through the window.

"Do you know that man?" I asked her.

"Yes, that's Mr. Keplin. He's the groundskeeper for the chapel a few towns away."

"Have you met his family?" I asked.

"No. But, I've heard him talk about his daughters."

I looked at Sarah with great interest to find what more she might tell me about Noah and his family, but she disappointed me by brushing off the subject with a sly comment.

"They're far too young for you, Kris, still just children."

Her teasing comments were interrupted by Josef's loud voice, which called to me from outside. "Kris!"

I hesitated for a moment and then forced myself to walk outside, terrified to see what Josef wanted of me. Sarah followed at a distance, curious to see why Josef had called.

"Kris?" she said to me softly, but I ignored her and went out into the yard. As I approached the men, Noah watched me intently, still picking at his teeth with the piece of wood that he held between his fat fingers.

"Kris, come here," Josef said. "There is something Mr. Keplin and I want to talk to you about."

My fear now completely triggered, I stopped several feet from them and kept my eyes focused on the ground.

"Come here," Josef repeated.

As I got closer to them, Josef held out the wooden duck Noah had brought with him. I could quickly see that mishandling had damaged it.

"Mr. Keplin says this toy was left last Christmas for his daughter, Kendra," Josef said.

I looked at each of the men and at the toy and then back to the ground, unsure how they wanted me to respond.

"Kendra?" I asked finally in a desperate attempt to make the name sound unfamiliar to me.

"Yes," Noah said. "She and her sister loved that toy to death."

Noah tried to reassemble the toy to show me how it had been damaged. "I told those two to stop arguing over it and to take care so as not to damage it. But they wouldn't listen to this old man, and finally the toy was broken."

"I'm sorry," I said to him.

"I asked throughout town if anyone knew what to do with it, and how it might be repaired," he said. "But, they were stumped when I showed them which parts had once moved."

"They wounded it," I said unconsciously.

"Wounded?" Noah exclaimed, laughing. "Yes it does. It looks to have been wounded. Well, that's a good one. Wounded! Ha! Clever boy you have here, Josef."

Noah flipped the toy back and forth in his hands.

"Well, what do you think? You're the toy expert. Least that's what Josef tells me. What do you know about a toy like this?" Noah asked.

I remained quiet as I looked at the men, not knowing what they wanted me to say, and afraid to reveal too much to them, too soon.

"Well?" Josef asked.

"Wa-What?" I stammered.

"Think you can fix it for him? Apparently, it is his daughter's favorite toy."

"Ahhh, yes. I see. Yes, I can fix it."

"Well go take care of it before he has to go home," Josef said as Noah handed me the duck. "Hurry on!"

I hastened back toward the workshop to see how I might repair the broken toy.

"Thanks, ma' boy. My daughters will love you for this!" Noah shouted after me.

I stopped and turned to Noah, meaning to say, "Thank you, Sir," but I heard Josef question him.

"So, you said you do not know who left Kendra or the toy at the church?"

"Nope," Noah said. "I saw him the first time, but he was at some distance, and a scarf covered his face."

"How do you plan to find him?" Josef asked.

"Don't think I want to," Noah grunted. "Better off not knowing some things."

Josef looked over and saw me watching them. "Get on!" he said. "You have work to do. Now hurry. But make it right! You'll know what you need to do."

I raced into the carpentry with the broken duck. Its wings had been chipped and cracked, and it no longer was free to fly. Time and rough circumstance had taken their toll upon this gentle winged creature, but it had been loved as well. It had been treasured, held closely. And now that it was injured, it had winged its way back to me so I could heal its broken parts, and return it to the place where it had nested, to bring joy and play again.

I rummaged through the pieces of wood I had practiced on while first building the toys and found an earlier version of the wings I had set aside in dissatisfaction due to their crude form. The earlier design was slightly simpler but sturdier, and these would surely work as surrogate parts with some gentle shaping and a loving touch.

Sarah watched me as I set about to repair the toy duck, but I ignored her as I worked and focused on finishing off the replacement wings and reconnecting the pieces so the toy would be whole once again.

Jonas, Noel, and Markus continued with their assignments at the back of the carpentry, oblivious to the enormity of what I was living through.

After some time, Sarah interrupted my silent work.

"Kris?" she asked.

I continued to ignore her to discourage her from pursuing idle talk.

"Kris," she said more emphatically.

"What?" I asked her sharply.

"Are you all right?"

"I'm fine."

"Are you sure?" She pressed. "What was that all about?"

I was so obsessed with my work that I was annoyed by her interruptions. Couldn't she see I was busy? This was important.

"Don't worry about it. It's nothing. He just wants me to fix a broken toy."

"I heard. But why are you acting like that?"

"What? Like what—what are you talking about?"

"Why didn't you tell him it was your toy?" she whispered to me pointedly.

By the time I realized what she was asking me, my fear of her discovery, ruining everything, made me rude.

"Why? Because it isn't!" I said to her.

"Why are you trying to cover it up, Kris? Didn't you hear that his daughters loved it? He probably would have paid you to make more of them."

"Well that's just great. But I didn't make this toy," I said again.

"I remember seeing you work on it, Kris. You held it up to me and made its wings move."

"Do you think I am the only person on earth who makes toys?"

"Like that one? Yes," she said.

"I don't even know that man. Why would he have one of my toys?"

"I don't know, Kris. I'm sorry. I guess I was wrong."

I returned my attention to the toy and tried to block out Sarah's accusations. Sarah wandered over to another window and gazed outside for a few moments, seemingly at the barn. I thought she had relented, moving on to other thoughts, but then she asked, "Why do you think Josef keeps that old horse?"

I knew she realized I was troubled by the events that had just unfolded, and would not yield to her curiosity. She was trying to put together the pieces, and then I would lose everything, even her warm if distant attentions.

"He doesn't," I said to her curtly.

"She seems awfully old to be lugging that sleigh around by herself. Poor girl could keel over any time. Especially if she's out trudging all that distance across the snow."

"Sarah. Please stop."

"Are you making toys for the chapel orphanage or something?"

"Sarah, stop!"

"I just think it's nice," she said.

"Stop talking! Would you please just stop talking and leave me alone!"

I returned to my work, but I could tell I had hurt Sarah deeply. She quietly backed out of the room without notice, and when I looked up again, she was gone.

I glanced over at Markus, Noel, and Jonas, who were staring at me in shock. When they saw me returning their stares, they jumped back to their tasks at hand, looking all the more bewildered.

Some weeks later, I was out collecting firewood to stoke the morning fire in the carpentry. We had more than enough beside the furnace but Josef made me begin each morning replacing what we had used the day before. Chopping wood on a cold morning can be miserable, and all I wanted was to crawl back under warm covers. When I at last returned to my cot, I found a neatly wrapped, sizable gift resting on it against my pillow. This surprised me considerably. I ran my fingers over its decorative covering. I decided, finally, Gabriella must have left it, since she was the one who usually brought me special treats and items she felt would be of use to me.

I opened the wrapping, touched by its attractiveness, evidence that someone had spent considerable time decorating the gift in such an elaborate way. As the wrappings were peeled back, I saw thickly padded, deep red fabric neatly folded. I removed it from the package and held it aloft to discover it was a fine-looking big, red winter coat.

Red. I had never seen anything similar to it. I knew that women would dye their yarns different colors and that socks or scarves or hats of each village had a pattern of colors that would delineate their origins. I didn't know how red was created. Some kind of berry, I imagined, or a specific type of tree root that would soak for days. Either way, she must have used a tremendous amount of it to die the entire coat.

But why red? The boys were certain to laugh at me. To be sure, the color was strange. But I didn't care. I thought the coat magnificent.

How wonderful it was. Gabriella truly must have labored over it. How incredible it felt to receive such a fine gift, so thoughtfully and lovingly presented!

Gabriella had commented many times about the old and dilapidated coat I had worn since I first came to them. What special feelings it brought that she would attend to me so.

I hung the coat on a large hook near my cot and ventured over to my workbench.

The toys I worked on had become more detailed and inventive over time. And before me now I studied the moving parts of a toy wolf, which I held inches from my face so I might inspect every edge and fine feature.

Sarah entered the carpentry, carrying her usual delivery of freshly baked goods. We hadn't spoken in weeks, not since my rude outburst. I was embarrassed and didn't know how to heal the divide without addressing her earlier dangerous questions.

Sarah placed her basket on the counter, not looking at me. Turning to leave, she adjusted the cloth covering the bread in the basket, making sure there were no openings to let out the heat. Then I saw her fingers. They were stained dark red, and I knew it must be from the dye. It was she who had made the coat. It was she who had spent hours cutting and sewing. It was she who had lovingly wrapped the wondrous gift and laid it against my pillow.

A surge of awareness stole my breath. She had already forgiven me. In that moment I fell in love with her.

I had longed for her and thought about her, but this was different. She had forgotten herself and instead focused on her uncanny under-standing of me. Without words or explanations, she knew me. She was the angel I had imagined that stormy night a lifetime ago when I had first laid eyes on her.

When she noticed I was studying her, she quickly hid her hands behind her back then stood awkwardly, waiting for me to do or say something.

I did not know how to close the gap. Words did not come easily to me. I looked down at the toy in my hands, considering all the ways I might apologize, all the ways I might say thank you for her precious gift. I sat there trying to appear occupied with the toy wolf while stumbling through my thoughts. It was Sarah who first spoke.

"I just came by to deliver bread," she said defensively.

She lifted the basket of fresh bread and walked out the same way she entered. After about five steps, she realized she had mistakenly picked up the basket and turned back around. A little shaken and trying to hide her mistake, Sarah walked back to where she had first put down the basket and began taking out loaves of bread and stacking them into some kind of pyramid, as if this is what she had intended to do the entire time. Unfortunately for her the bread structure tumbled with each new loaf she placed on top. I could tell it was frustrating her, but I was fascinated by the absurdity of what she was doing. Finally, on the verge of tears, she grabbed all of the loaves with the cloth they were initially wrapped in and stuffed them haphazardly back into the basket. Left that way they were certainly going to go cold quickly. I could tell. And I started to point that out to her when she rounded on me, planted her foot firmly on the ground and announced vehemently to the empty carpentry, "I won't bother you. I promise."

"No, please!" I said, "I'm happy you are here."

I jumped up in my very clumsy way to clear a place for Sarah to sit with me nearer the furnace.

"Don't," she said.

What a curiously beautiful girl she was.

"That really isn't necessary," she continued.

I ignored her and continued to clear a place so she could join me. "I wanted to thank you for the coat. Please warm yourself" I said.

Sarah looked away without speaking, crossing her arms as if to feign indifference.

"It's really so soft and comfortable," I said to her. "And I know it will keep me warm."

"Which coat?" Sarah asked. She looked at me defiantly, feigning innocence as if she had no knowledge of what I was speaking about.

"The big red one. I wanted to thank you for it. It's so beautiful."

"I'm sorry?" Sarah continued, unwilling to take credit for the gift.

"All right," I said as I turned away, surrendering to the discomfort of the moment.

Then I heard a small giggle and turned back to see what she found that was funny. She melted me with the warmth of her gentle smile.

We looked at each other for a long time before she walked to me, sat down, and took my hands in hers. "I didn't want you getting lost in a snowdrift delivering toys. That's why I decided it should be red. To stand out against the snow." Then, almost embarrassed, she added, "And because it reminded me of your big heart."

"Well, you aren't a very good liar," I said, but as I heard the words spill from my mouth, I realized they had come in far too abrupt a manner.

Sarah ran her red-stained fingers over the toy wolf in my hands as if she were petting it. "I guess we have something in common," she said coyly, reminding me of my denial and obvious lies regarding Kendra's wooden duck.

Now it was my turn to be embarrassed, and I was curt with her as I tried to deflect her comment. "I thought you promised not to bother me."

"I guess I am just a bad liar," Sarah said, smiling. She held up her stained fingers with a smile and wiggled them as if the dye had made them sticky or stiff.

If I told her what she wanted to know, I would ruin everything. Even if the town didn't make me leave, Sarah would never see me in the same way again. "I don't want to talk about this with you," I confessed. But I instantly regretted my words and I could see they only compounded the hurtful things I had said to her earlier.

"Fine," Sarah said as she rose and took her leave.

I stood up as I called after her, "I'm fully capable of caring for myself." But we both knew that too was a lie.

Fiercely she looked back at me and then stormed right up to face me. "Yes, I know," she said coldly as she lifted herself on tiptoes. "That, of course, is why you stay here."

Her statement stung me sharply, but I could not contest the truth. In an effort to regain the upper hand, I challenged her again. "And I am supposed to trust you? You just lied to me."

She took a breath. With Sarah on her toes, her eyes were only slightly beneath my own. "And I would lie just as hard to keep your secrets safe," she whispered.

I could feel her breath's warmth on my lips. She looked through me as if to penetrate my heart. Yet I found myself still desperately unable to lower my defenses.

"Don't worry, you won't have to," I said and sat down.

How I dreaded those words that escaped from my lips and tore at Sarah like the teeth of my saw.

"I'm warm enough now," she whispered to me. There was a sense of deep hurt in her voice as she lowered herself to her heels.

Somehow I needed to stop her. "Sarah?" I said gently.

She looked down at her feet like an injured bird. "What?"

"Do you promise?" I asked.

"Do I promise?" She looked up at me as quiet tears washed her face. Then her eyes transformed with realization. "Yes," she said solemnly and sincerely, "I promise."

I could not continue to look into her tear-filled eyes. So I turned my back to her, placed the toy wolf away from me on the table, and nervously began to whittle with a knife and small flat piece of wood that had been left lying on the worktable.

I could feel Sarah behind me, watching, waiting.

Hesitantly, I started. "Josef and Gabriella took me in . . . because . . . my own father is gone."

"And what of your mother?" Sarah asked.

There were no words I could find to sum this up simply, directly. How could I begin to tell a story that I did not fully know? How could I venture down a path where my heart did not wish to go?

I could hear Sarah as she pulled the stool behind me and quietly sat. She placed a hand gently on my back, and I knew my secrets were secure with her and that here my heart was safe.

"She is gone with him."

I ran my fingers along the edges of the wood, felt the roughness and unfinished nature of the cuts I had made, and thought about the ways I would shape the wood and smooth its coarseness to complete it.

"I'm sorry," Sarah said, and she waited patiently for me to tell her more.

"He was the first," I said to her, haltingly.

"Your father?" Sarah asked.

"We thought it would pass," I said. "But after the elders, it took the babies and children, and then everyone. Our world was filled with the constant toil of disease and loss."

I spoke to her softly. Carefully. With painful breaths that stabbed at my weakened spirit. I spoke about the terror that raged through our village and the dangerous and perverse fears that fanned the growing fires of destruction. I spoke of the times when logic no longer prevailed, when illness consumed the feeble and vulnerable, and brought once strong and vital men and women to the door of death. I spoke of all the pain and suffering the fires were meant to eradicate and the towering columns of smoke that climbed the sky. But we had not triumphed over the disease as we had wanted. We had not cleansed our lands. The fires had only taken our homes, not the illness.

And in the silence that followed, I thought about the words forgiveness, giving, and living, and how elemental they were. And I thought giving must be the essence of our lives. Could a soul once broken be made whole by giving of itself?

"You are from the mountains?" Sarah said to me, breaking the silence.

I nodded quietly in response and listened for a moment, awaiting some condemnation or other, but none followed.

"We tried to burn the sickness behind us," I said. "My mother was weak. She could barely feed Nikko."

"Your brother? You have siblings?" Sarah asked softly, slowly. "Were there others? Other brothers and sisters?"

"I was the oldest. I wanted to take care of them. My mother did not believe I was strong enough. I begged her and argued with her, but she wouldn't listen."

Sarah gently placed the side of her face against my back, rubbing her hand back and forth as if to wipe away my pain.

What carpenter had carved a heart like hers? I wondered, as I leaned slightly back against her hand.

"I put them all into the sleigh," I said. "I was the one who found them homes. The one who left them there alone. My mother didn't care. She was dying and didn't want to know what became of them. I was the one forced to make those choices."

I sliced at the strip of wood before me, making deep gouges and ripping at its edges.

"Be careful with that," Sarah said.

"I abandoned my brothers and sisters. One after another. My brother Garin jumped off the sleigh, and I didn't stop him. The others I left stranded before strangers that I prayed would take them into their homes and shelter them from the bitter cold."

"Kris," Sarah said softly in an effort to comfort me.

I carved with unconscious hands that moved of their own volition.

"We ran from the flames we left behind, but we could not outrun the sickness in my mother. I carried her with us in that sleigh until she died, and left her body in a snow bank to decay."

I cut and punctured the wood against my hands.

"This Christmas I couldn't find Nikko. The family that took him in when I left him at their cabin had vanished. He's gone."

I looked back at Sarah to share the fullness of my regret. "I lost him. It was my fault. My mother was right. I was weak and could not be trusted to care for them. They were only children, and I abandoned them. Left them to survive alone. That is who I am, Sarah. I am sorry, but that is who I am."

"You gave them a chance to live, Kris. What more could you or anyone give?"

I held the scrap of wood in my hand, now a delicate wooden snowflake, like the one I had left with Nikko. And as I ran my fingers across its edges, blood trickled onto the wood and dripped onto my worktable. I snapped the stained snowflake in half and let it fall to the floor.

"Your hand!" Sarah exclaimed. She took off her scarf and wrapped it around the palm of my hand, tying it in place to stop the blood from the cuts unconsciously left there. When the bleeding had finally ceased, Sarah stooped to pick up the broken snowflake. "These carvings." She looked to the wooden wolf on the table, "these toys, they are for them, aren't they?"

"That's all over now."

What do you mean?" Sarah inquired.

"They fought over it. The girls fought over my duck and broke it. They aren't my brothers and sisters anymore. They have new families now. It's wrong of me to remind them they are any different."

"Your toys are special, Kris," Sarah said to me soothingly. "Why not make toys for each of them?"

"Each of them?" I asked, trying to understand her point.

"Your brothers and sisters have new families, with whom you share a common tie and a common love. These other children, Kris. They are your family now, too."

Sarah stunned me with her words. Then she continued.

"You have given the most precious thing you have, your love, in sharing your brothers and sisters with those who embraced them," Sarah said. "You are part of that love, part of that family just like your brothers and sisters are. You have a talent, Kris. Your toys are special. Now even more children can find joy from those gifts."

Sarah had turned me inside out cutting away my pain and doubt. To offer such a stunning notion, wrapped in a simple solution.

I laughed. Then I kissed her.

There are some moments so sublime in life they transcend the ability to describe. So I will refrain from trying. But I will say this. Kissing her was the best and smartest moment of my fourteen-year-old life.

When we stepped apart, she looked at me in stunned silence.

I looked at her in stunned silence.

We looked at each other across that space which just short moments ago had contained both of us.

And softly, all she said was, "You should laugh more."

And I did laugh more. I made a habit of it. It took time for the boys to get used to it, but laughter is infectious. Josef and Gabby were the first to catch the symptoms, then Jonas, and lastly Marcus. Noel never seemed appreciative of the laughter, unless it was cruelly inspired, no matter how hard we tried to include him.

Over the coming seasons I attained my fifteenth year and grew more than a hand span taller. I was thick as an old oak and could have lifted one of Noah's church pews by myself if I had to. And in the middle of one irregular night I sprouted hair everywhere: my chest, my arms, the back of my knuckles and, most annoyingly, my face.

Sarah found no end of delight in teasing me over the red fuzz that covered my cheeks and chin. At first I tried to shave every day with my knife, but time and the drive to avoid cutting my own throat finally convinced me to leave the growth.

Sarah and I hadn't kissed again since that glorious moment. Not that I didn't want to; I dreamt about it every day. First, I really wasn't brave enough to try again. Second, we never found ourselves alone, which was probably due to the brilliant and watchful eyes of Josef and Gabriella.

More importantly, if we had been caught we would have been kept apart. It was too much to risk, for a day without Sarah left me aching and feeling hollow.

Another year had passed and found me healthy as a lark and happy as a bear. Some people would say it's the other way around, but here's something I have learned: waking up at the break of dawn singing keeps you healthy, and if you have ever watched a lazy old bear, they sure look happy. I was aware that Sarah still cared for me from the thousands of slight and small touches we would sneak in our passing. Looking back, I think the only people we were fooling were ourselves.

In the early morning light I reached for the red coat Sarah had made with so much love and wrapped it around me. How proud I was to wear it on this year's delivery, and how comforted by its warmth.

It was a glorious morning, and my heart was filled with joy as I sang the holiday carol my brothers and sisters knew so well. "Counting snowflakes from our sleigh, count the hours till Christmas Day. Drifting snowflakes, tumble down, lift your head and spin around. Falling snowflakes, count them all. A Christmas wish as snowflakes fall."

Inside the barn, I found Gerda waiting for me, loyal, snorting in her excitement and devotion, her coat glistening in the morning light that spilled between the barn planks and through the opening high on the roof. Then Gerda shuffled, and much to my surprise, out from the other side of her stepped Sarah with brush in hand.

"I must be sure to stay in her good graces," Sarah proclaimed. "Otherwise she may not bring you back."

With Sarah there and no one around, I didn't know what to do with my hands. They kept reaching toward her as if they had their own mind. I wanted to squeeze her until she yelped. I had done that with a dog once when I was very young. It took days and a full meal of table scraps to get him to come near me again. So I crossed my arms and held my hands captured in my arm pits to a make sure I didn't make a fool of myself.

Sarah leapt into my arms. Thankfully I was quick enough to catch her. And she squeezed me until I yelped. And I did YELP. I don't know what that dog's problem was; Sarah could have done that to me every day of my life.

Then she broke away and ran over to the small counter where Josef kept the clamping iron and other tools for the barn. She snatched up a small bag and held it out to me. Inside were the most delicious gingers. The only person who made better cookies than Gabriella was Sarah. And she knew that gingers were my favorite.

"I'm sorry I didn't get you anything," I said.

"That's all right . . ."

But before she could forgive me, I lifted her into the air, tossing and teasing her. "I could never forget you!" And I did my best to give her that full squeeze.

"Never?" She wrapped her arms around me, holding me tight. And again I YELPED!

"Did I hurt you?" She pulled back in concern.

"Never!" I leaned my head against hers, closing my eyes, smelling lilacs and honey. Then I remembered my surprise. "Oh, your gift! I hoped to show it to you yesterday, but I can never seem to get alone with you without Josef around. I was afraid I wouldn't be able to give it to you until I returned. And that may not be for some time."

I walked over to the stacks of hay and pulled from behind them a large device. On the bottom was a small box with a lever. Suspended above the box were seven large gears, the likes of which I used for the internal mechanics of my moving toys.

Kneeling, I placed in on the ground and motioned for her to turn the lever. "Go ahead. See what it does."

No one was more fascinated by the mechanics of my creations than Sarah. She turned the lever with childish trepidation and sent the gears into motion, moving and cranking against and through each other.

"Kris, it's wonderful," she exclaimed.

"Watch," I said. And as the gears moved, twisting and turning, seemingly expanding and contracting, they came together as one, almost magically, into the shape of a large heart. I had seen Josef carve the design into cabinetry intended for a distant client once, and it seemed appropriate.

"Kris. I love it." She wrapped her arms around me and held her face to mine. "I will miss you at Christmas feast," she whispered.

"And I you."

She moved her chin teasingly against my rough and scraggly beard. "I like it," she said thoughtfully.

"Good thing, I don't think it is going to stop growing." I lifted her as I stood and placed her on her feet. "Don't show this to Marcus and Noel. I will never hear an end to it." Then I yelled, "Ouch," as she pinched me. Then she reached up, grabbed my beard, and pulled me down to her eye level.

"Don't show this to the baker, or he will have us wed!" she said with a smile.

It was the first time I saw her eyes that close. If you ever have an opportunity to watch two people in love gaze at each other in a private moment, they don't smile. All tension is released from the face, and they are completely open. This was the moment I remember having with her that Christmas Eve morning.

"Sarah…" I started, but she put her fingers over my mouth.

"Come home to me."

"Once I deliver the toys, I am going to find Nikko."

She began buttoning up my jacket. "Don't get lost."

"I think you have made that impossible," I said, looking down at the red coat.

We laughed, and I kissed her for the second time.

I leaned up against Gerda and gave her a gentle hug. She nuzzled me and pressed her soft face against mine, and I asked her, "Will you take me out into the world again, my girl?" And she snorted and whinnied and shared her tender reply, signaling she was once more up to the task.

"And bring him home safely?" Sarah added and joined me in my embrace with Gerda.

I loaded my sack of toys into the sleigh, and in the wink of an eye we were off.

We set about to deliver our simple toys to my distant and growing family. Gerda led the way with a newfound pride and strength of purpose equal to mine. As we sped across the countryside with happier hearts, I sang the songs of Christmas I had always cherished.

We passed as ghosts through time and space as we delivered the tokens of our love, our secret gifts, to my brothers and sisters, to their brothers and sisters, and to those who comforted them all. I secretly observed them and witnessed all the joy and love in their hearts, I was no longer sad to see them in these far off places where they had been replanted. I could see the growth and blossoming of each and laughed with their newfound joys. Owen was three and walking and talking and laughing and falling. Jess was five and already helping with preparations for the feast. Tamas and Talia, at seven, still carried that bond I hoped would last their lifetime. They had grown in responsibility, this year making and rolling the traditional pastries for the Christmas feast with only a random thrown dough ball or brief flour fight, unlike last year's all-out baker's brawl. I heard but didn't see Garin this year, leaving a small carving knife on what was obviously the only boy's bedroll of the camp. And Kendra had become a little lady. Most importantly, and by the grace of God, there was love.

But I thought of Nikko too and wished I could discover with certainty that he had lived and found the same rich soil in which to grow. This was the journey I set my feet upon that Christmas morning.

As daylight began to fade, we came at last upon the place where I had left my mother to her peace. There was no grave or marking for anyone to know or find her resting place. There was but a small clearing in the trees beside the road.

I stood in the middle of that empty space imagining a closeness to her. "There is a girl, Mama. Her name is Sarah. She's not like you. Which is good, because I am like you. Which is good.

"I am a carpenter, Mama. A very good carpenter. You and Papa would be proud of what I make.

"I have lost Nikko, Mama. All the rest are safe for now, and I promise to keep watch over them, but I am going searching for Nikko. And I promise I will never give up on him. I am sorry if I have let you down.

"I wanted you to know that you were wrong, Mama. When you said, 'Never tell them where you are from,' you were wrong. There are some who you can tell. I just wanted you to know."

There was no short or fast way to the cabin where I had left Nikko. So I did what was required. I walked.

The cabin was lonely and gray from the old, weathered wood. From a short distance I could tell that no one had entered since my last Christmas visit. The rattle encircled with small snowflakes still hung from the knob of the door, which stood ajar to the approaching night.

Once inside, I looked around at the destruction I had left behind. I unrolled an oiled cloth onto the ground which protected a small set of tools from the damp cold. First the table, then the chairs, then the mantle, I fixed in turn. A few small candles, which I had brought with me for the purpose, lit the darkness. Then I went outside, looking for wood to cut and split for the fire. Purposely I had worked into the cold of the night without warmth. I bound thrushes to a stick and swept the hearth and the cabin of all debris. Once the cabin was restored, I sat in front of the cold and empty fireplace listening to the wind outside.

To the sides of me I had amassed a small stack of various branches, split logs, and kindling. From my pockets I withdrew a handful of dried fungus and a small tinderbox. The fungus I piled into the center of the hearth. Inside the box was a piece of quartz that I held in my left hand over the fungus tinder and a thick iron hoop that I laced the fingers of my right hand through. Striking the iron against the stone sent sparks flying, igniting the tinder. I broke the broom into its smaller and larger pieces, blowing the fire into ever growing life as I added the soft woods, the pine twigs and sticks, then the branches, and eventually the harder wood logs I had split that night.

Once the fire was raging, I pulled out the small bag of cookies Sarah had given me and broke my fast.

"Joy to you this Christmas, Nikko."

That night I slept beside the warmth of the fire, and the next day I set off on my quest. Over hills and through ravines, into towns and valleys I searched for a child I wasn't even sure I would recognize. In the faces of strangers I looked for hope and was warmed by what I found there, even if I wasn't successful in my search. People took me into their homes and listened to my story and held my hands or touched my shoulders in sympathy. And though they didn't have answers, their hearts shared my burdens, and in those brief moments they would come to be like family. They fed us and sheltered us and would hear no argument. They mothered and cared for Gerda and me as if we were dear, long unseen relatives. I showed them the toys that I had made for my growing brother should I find him. And my hosts reveled in the toys' ingenuity and uniqueness. These newfound families I added to my list of deliveries for the next year. I allowed myself the twelve full days of Christmas, and then I gave twelve more before I succumbed to the impossibility of the task I had set for myself.

Nearly a month had passed when Gerda and I turned our sleigh and began our trek, now in the fullness of winter, home.

So much time had passed that it soon dawned upon me how I missed my own new family. Spending time alone requires a precarious balance.

If you are never silent to your thoughts, you will never hear the deep resonance of their mysterious wisdom. If you live there too long you may begin to believe some of the illusions and lies you whisper to yourself. Thankfully my journey had produced new friends and new perspectives. How I wanted to return and share my stories with Sarah if I could find a solitary moment alone with her. I thought of her so many times each day on my road home and longed to look once more into her eyes, watch her smile, and feel her warmth near me. I dreamt of how we would all live together.

These dreams and images filled my thoughts so fully, I could not think of anything beyond. I was consumed with a new sense of purpose.

I had come to believe that it was possible I could help shape and contribute to our lives and build our futures in the same way we had planned and built so many fine objects of well-formed wood, finished and polished to perfection. I was excited to reunite with my friends and family at the carpentry and share the lessons I had so fortunately stumbled upon. Somewhere along the road of the past month, I had met the man I was becoming, and he had taught me something. As acquaintances became familial friends and I watched them play with the toys I had left over from my Christmas delivery, I grew to believe two truths. One, all the children on the earth are our family. And two, we are all children.

My heart beat with anticipation as Gerda and I at last approached the lane leading to the carpentry.

Immediately I knew something was wrong. My mind raced back through images of sporadic clusters of homes as we approached the village. And there it was. One of the homes on my journey toward the village had not lit its window candles for the night. This could have been in error, but for some reason I doubted it. People were vigilant about those candles. They told the world that all were healthy inside and that none need fear contact with the inhabitants. No one wanted the stigma of that mistaken message.

I lit my lantern and held it out in front of me as I drove the sleigh toward the rear of the carpentry. It was then I witnessed Noel throwing stones at the dark windows of Josef and Gabriella's house.

"Stay inside and rot," Noel yelled as he launched a stone into the night sky. True to its purpose, the stone found its mark and shattered the window high on the side of the wall.

"Take it!" Noel shouted at Jonas as he pushed a large rock into Jonas's hand and encouraged him to throw it.

"Noel!" I yelled at him, seeking some explanation for his hostile behavior. "What are you doing?"

"Look! Jelly belly has come back!" Noel yelled. And he threw another large rock, which landed with a loud thud against the side of the building.

I jumped off the sleigh and started toward Noel in an effort to stop him from damaging my home any further.

"Did you come to see him die?" Noel shouted, taunting me. "Or, maybe you wanted some more food from the filthy fat woman!"

I was distracted for a moment, as Markus now moved through the shadows near the carpentry. And, while I looked in Markus's direction, Noel hit me with a large stone that glanced across the side of my head, and I went down. The lantern hit the ground, spilling its liquid flaming content across the snow. Dazed, I had enough awareness to roll away from the fire. Then hazily I watched Noel bend down to pick up a thick branch and heft it like a club, wrapping both hands around the end for greatest power. He began swinging it at the air with great fury as he shouted, "I'll bet you have it too! Get inside, fatty."

Noel charged. And he laughed. He knew he had me. Though stronger, I could never outrun Noel. Stunned, I tried to shake the cloud from my thoughts in preparation for the impending attack. I struggled to my feet, desperate to master my unbalanced equilibrium; then the world faded and tilted as I fell to the earth in failure. My vision cleared a little, just enough to see Noel rear back on the branch, barreling down on me in his final assault.

"Go rot with them!" he screamed.

Then a blur from his left took him out at the knees. Markus tackled Noel and sent him sprawling to the ground with a large thud.

Markus and Noel continued to struggle as I tried to make sense of what was happening, and I looked about to see what other damage might have been done.

Noel shouted at Markus, "What are you doing?"

And Markus pushed him to the ground.

"What's the matter with you, Markus?" Noel asked in his angry confusion. "Are you siding with piggy now?"

"Go home, Noel!" Markus shouted.

"What?"

"I said, get up and go home," Markus yelled even more forcefully. "You're not wanted here!"

"Why are you getting into this?" Noel demanded of Markus. "He's trying to get in to see that dirty—"

And Markus hit Noel as he shouted, grabbed him by the collar, lifted him into the air and threw him to the ground once more. I wasn't the only one who had grown stronger over the year.

"I'll say it again, Noel," Markus shouted fiercely. "Get out of here. Go home to your mother."

Noel backed away in defeat but cursed both Markus and me as he retreated from us. "I hope you burn with them, Markus! You and that fat, piggy friend of yours. When you have caught it, too, we will burn you all!"

Markus took a threatening step in Noel's direction, and Noel ran off into the night.

I was bewildered by what had come over Noel and Markus and also fearful of what I might learn now that Noel's assault had ended.

Markus anticipated my concern, but decided to challenge me in other ways. "Where were you?" he asked, in an accusing fashion.

"I had work to do. I was looking for someone," I said defensively. I was still confused and unsure about what had transpired here in my absence. The rock hadn't done much more damage than a momentary stunning, but I was still getting my bearings.

I looked to Markus to see what he might tell me and noticed Jonas as he moved forward from the shadows where he was hiding.

"What happened here?" I asked.

But they did not answer me. It didn't matter. Jonas's eyes always told the truth.

"Tell me!" I yelled at them, not wanting to acknowledge the reality I already understood better than I should.

"Don't go inside," Markus said solemnly. "It's too late. You can't do anything to help them." And he began to walk away from the carpentry.

"Markus!" I called to him.

But Markus ignored me and said to Jonas, "Come on. It's time for us to go." And he continued to walk off into the smothering night.

Jonas gave me a gentle wave as if to say, "I am sorry. Kris." And he ran to catch up with Markus.

By now, of course, I knew that plague had come to the carpentry shop. Desperate remembered anxieties threatened to seize my body, first squeezing my heart and then capturing my ability to breathe. Slowly I took back my body. I fought back the destroyer, fear. I must go inside. Despite the warnings of Markus and the ones ringing in my own head, I had to find Gabriella and Josef. With a snort I shook off the debilitating grip that held my life hostage and headed for the side door to the carpentry.

As I entered the kitchen, I saw the broken shards of glass littering the floor, and furniture broken and tossed in disarray. Gabriella startled me as she entered from another room carrying a tray of medicine and damp rags.

"Gabriella, what has happened?" I blurted out to her. "Did Noel do all this damage?"

Gabriella looked up at me in shock and terror.

"You need to leave here," she entreated.

"Where is he?" I asked.

"You can't see him now," Gabriella weakly commanded. "Go, Kris. Please go. You must go."

A blood-soaked handkerchief fell from Gabriella's tray and plummeted to the floor. She bent to pick it up and tried to place it in her pocket, but the tray slipped from her hands and crashed to the ground.

I ran to her and led her to a chair by the fire. "You must sit and rest a moment," I said to her gently. "I'll take care of it. I'm here."

She crumpled into the chair behind her that rested against the wall. I collected the spilled and broken items from the floor. I could hear Gabriella softly weeping and my heart filled with great sorrow for what she had undergone.

I crossed to her and wiped her tears with my handkerchief. I knew the depth of her pain and the suffering she would endure ever more, as I would, when Josef finally was lost to us.

Gabriella at last caught her breath. I placed my hand upon her shoulder, and she reached up slowly and placed her hand upon mine. I stood with her in that way for some time to share my deepest sympathy for her suffering and sorrow.

Then I said to her, "I will go to see him now. You stay here and rest. I will look in on him and try to make him comfortable."

And Gabriella quietly nodded as she began again to weep.

I left her there to rest and release her stream of despair, and I quietly walked through the house until I arrived at the bedroom where Josef was sleeping. I listened at the door for a moment, but it was quiet inside. Though I did not want to disturb his needed sleep or impose myself upon his time of suffering, I knew I must enter, no matter what I might find there, and help him as I could.

I opened the door slightly and pushed upon it gently so its hinges would not creak and so I would not startle Josef by bursting in upon him.

An oil lamp burned on his bedside table, emitting black smoke. It gave the room a hazy patina that washed over Josef and the objects in the room, making them appear more distant and otherworldly. The dimly lit haze flowed to the corners of the room and blended with the darkness of the shadows that lurked there unmolested. In the weak light, it seemed as if the darkness itself was watching and waiting, preparing to creep in on Josef to consume him. He had wasted away quickly in my absence, only the shell of the man he had been weeks ago. He was lying in the bed with an expression of agony on his face. It was a look I knew too well, seared into my memory and the weakened walls of my heart so many times over.

I moved to the fireplace and laid a fresh log upon the fire. It instantly brightened the room and generated greater warmth.

"You should not be here," Josef said from behind me. Then a wet cough rumbled deeply from his chest and continued to roll until he was required to pull in breath.

"I have nowhere else," I told him. Then I stoked the fire with a poker until the flames surged again.

Josef watched me from his bed, and I realized that my life was now modeled on his. He had cut me away from the rotting bark which had once covered me, trimmed my coarse edges, sanded me to a greater smoothness, and shaped me into one of his works by providing balance and strength, then clever design and a carefully layered finish that changed my rawness to something of greater value.

As I watched him, our eyes locked in silent understanding of the certainties we now faced. It hurt me so to see him dying in this way. But I also knew his spirit would not be lost because I now carried it inside me.

I pulled a chair to his bedside, and together we stared into the fire and sat in the comfortable silence of old friends who didn't need words to share in each other's company.

When he finally spoke, his words were low and gravelly, allowing himself just enough energy to convey his thoughts.

"I've always loved wood, working and shaping it in my hands. When I was a young man, I was to be a fisherman," he said. "Have you ever watched the fish along the mountain rivers?"

"No," I answered simply. But as I looked into his eyes, I knew there was more he wished to say.

"My father's fish. I would often watch them," Josef said. "In leaps they cut the air, fighting the current, moving against the stream."

He looked at me as he spoke, but his gaze passed through me, and traveled deep into the past and the days of his youth.

"As a young man I thought their triumph was their struggle. But I was wrong. It is in their acts of helplessness that they triumph," he said.

"What is an act of helplessness?"

"It is a choice when there are no choices. It is to laugh in a moment of despair, to walk when there is nowhere to go. It is to make toys you will never play with for brothers and sisters you will never know."

Josef stunned me with these words that revealed just how well he knew the secrets of my heart. "You should just rest," I said. "You will breathe easier if you are not trying so hard to talk."

But, he ignored me and continued as I wiped the sweat from his forehead with a soft cloth. "Those fish were going home, Kris. To that place of connection," he said, struggling. "That's the gift you give. Not the toys. It's the connection.

"Your gifts tell them they are not alone," Josef whispered hoarsely. Then he shuddered and hacked uncontrollably, and his breathing became more forced and painful.

"What can I do?" I asked. "How can I help you?" I wanted to calm him and let him know I would do whatever he asked of me, if it would improve his circumstances or remove his suffering in any way.

"Pack up the shop. Everything. Take care with the tools. They are irreplaceable."

"And what should I do when I have packed them all?" I asked. I looked at him in my silent desperation, for I did not know how else to respond.

"Go deep into the Northlands," he continued. "They say people live forever up there."

"You will get better," I told him.

"Listen to me!" Josef said forcefully. "Do not stay here. Do not return to the mountains where you came from."

"Sarah told you," I said to him.

"No Kris. You wore it in your eyes when I first saw you."

"I could have brought this sickness into your house. This is my fault."

"Sha! Carriers do not live. They die quickly like those who are consumed. We have been well a year over. You are no carrier. This did not come from you. But others will fear you. The villages nearby are no safer. People will hear of your story. They may say this disease has followed you. They will blame you in their ignorance. They will hurt you if you do not go."

He watched me quietly, for a moment as the significance of his words registered with me.

"Sickness is not the ugliest of killers," Josef continued. "Fear is."

Josef pulled me close to him. His hands were thin and weak, and his skin resembled yellowed and torn parchment. Then he whispered to me and shared his final words.

I closed his eyelids, pulled the blankets over him, and retreated to the carpentry, overwhelmed with sadness. I collected Josef's engraving tools and laid them out on a fold of cloth. I wrapped them carefully, quietly in thought.

As I began gathering additional tools, knives, and many of the special rigs Josef had created to shape and carve delicate wood, Markus returned to the carpentry. He watched me for a moment as I categorized the tools, and he began adding chisels, mallets and other useful items to my collection. We worked together in silence, for it was clear it was my mission to assemble all of the important tools and prepare them for travel.

"He was good to me," Markus said sadly. And his eyes began to water.

"He knew how you felt about him," I said.

We continued to pack and wrap the tools securely, placing them in large satchels that I would carry with me in the sleigh.

As we finished, I walked through the carpentry, looking for any useful items I might have left behind. The carpentry seemed hollow and empty now, except for the piles of wood stacked in bins and on the floor. So many finely crafted works had been created here. So many delicate pieces of richly grained wood had been transformed into masterful furnishings, long-lasting benches and cabinets, and other functional devices and products. It was no surprise to me that Josef's works would last beyond his lifetime, or mine. They were made with so much care, so much skill, so much passion. They were extensions of Josef himself, representative of everything he was, everything he shared, and the goodness in his life.

"Gabriella told me you spoke with him," Markus said. "What did he say to you?"

And I thought back to the painful image of Josef dying in his bed, and his final words to me as he prepared to leave.

"Burn us down."

Markus stood beside me as the light of the flames reflected on our faces and as the night began to glow with raging fire. I could feel the intensity of the heat and knew the wood and scraps piled throughout the carpentry would fuel this inferno, which would burn long into the night.

I had maneuvered Josef's horses and the wagon into position away from the carpentry, tying Gerda to the rear. Markus helped load the satchels of tools and supplies and stowed them securely. I assisted Gabriella as she climbed into the sleigh with her eyes somberly diverted from the house and from Josef's room. I am sure she was occupied by the lifetime of memories that flooded her thoughts and the relentless pain that tore at her heart.

The blaze burned so fiercely that it cast a glow up into the sky, and I imagined it might be seen for great distances. This was a fire that was as powerful and as passionate as Josef had been in his life, and it radiated nearly as brightly as he had for so many who had known him and benefited from his goodness.

"You put yourself in danger," I said to Markus.

"No direct contact," he replied. And he loaded the remaining tools and supplies into the wagon as I thanked him and climbed on board.

"It's good it was us and not the others," Markus said.

His words took me by surprise. "The others?" I asked with apprehension.

Markus paled as he looked at me. "Then you have not heard?" he asked.

"Heard what?" I said impatiently as worry began to sweep over me.

"It was the baker's wife who first fell victim to the plague. Josef caught it there when he went to be of service to the family."

"What?" I shouted. "Why didn't you tell me this before?"

"I thought you already knew," Markus said weakly. "Many frightened villagers are gathered there demanding the bakery be destroyed."

"What of Sarah?" I asked intensely.

Markus looked at me, as if his mouth had lost the ability to speak.

"What of Sarah!"

I snapped the reins before he could answer and drove the wagon forward with Gerda pulled behind. Markus stumbled in the wake left by the surging cart.

The wagon threatened to tear apart as I pushed it and the horses beyond their proper usage. When I at last approached the bakery and Sarah's home, the outlying buildings were already in flames. A mob of people had surrounded the bakery and its living quarters and had boarded the doors and windows shut from the outside in an effort to trap those remaining within. Enraged villagers threw rocks at the bakery and yelled insults and curses at its occupants.

I reined the horses in hard and pulled the wagon scraping and jumping to a stop. I was horrified by the scene before me. I saw Noel standing in the crowd near his father, who was lighting the ends of a wet rag hanging from the mouth of a large bottle. He tried to force Noel to take the bottle and instructed him to throw it at the bakery.

"No, Papa, no," Noel said, shaking his head in response. But his father was wild-eyed and caught up in the excitement of the crowd that continued to shout curses and work itself up into a rage.

Noel's father grabbed him by the back of the neck and screamed, "Boy! I won't have weakness." His father shoved the bottle into Noel's hands and made him hold it while he instructed him again. "Now, do it!" he yelled.

I tried to stop Noel by shouting over the crowd, "Noel!" But he did not respond to me, so I continued to scream at him, "Noel, don't do this!"

Noel jerked his head in my direction and looked me in the eye. His hesitation vanished when he saw me, and his anguish was replaced with a cruel smirk as he took delight that I would see what he was about to do. The crowd continued to shout and jeer and encourage him to take action, and Noel lobbed the burning bottle onto the roof of the house, where it shattered and exploded into flames on impact.

I vaulted from the sleigh and went for Noel and his father swinging. If I could get through the crowd I might make the bakery before it became consumed by the hunger of the fire spreading across the roof. Villagers who got in the way or tried to block me were slugged aside in my fury. Noel continued taunting me as I ran toward him. His father tried to stop me as I rushed forward, but I quickly knocked him to the ground and turned on Noel, whose expression had changed from gloating to fear. I drove my fist into Noel's face, and he crumpled before me. As others reached out to stop me, I lashed out at them and struck whoever might be so bold as to interfere, and I broke through the crowd with a clear view of the cabin ahead. A hand reached out to grab my shoulder, and I turned quickly to push away a man I did not recognize who was intent upon stopping me. Just then the flat of a shovel hit me in the face, and I fell.

I had no recollection of where I was when I awoke from the darkness with my head split and my vision blurry. Soot-covered fingers reached out and grabbed me by my coat, and I looked up to see Sarah pulling at me, trying desperately to drag me back away from the mob and her burning home and toward my wagon.

"It's the child," somebody yelled.

"It's Sarah!" shouted another. "She has it too!"

"We've got no choice," pled yet another desperate voice.

"She has the sickness," shouted an ugly woman from within the mob.

As one the mob surged forward, threatening to take us.

"Stay back!" I heard yelled from the direction of the crowd. And a long torch swung the length of the compressing mob, scattering them in an arc out and away from the wagon. Marcus stood with brand in hand, holding the mob at bay like some hero of old might have held off a starving pack of wolves.

"You are her neighbors!" he screamed at them.

"You have no right to judge us," others replied. "We won't die from her sickness!"

"They're unclean," screamed a man from the crowd.

"You are the filth!" Marcus yelled in response. "These people called you friends." The crowd hesitated in their approach as they seemed to dread the truth of his accusation.

"What do you want of us? Shall we give up our children for theirs?"

"I pray I do have it. So I can give it to each one of you," Sarah screamed, spitting at them through her tears. The throng pulled back in fear.

"Hurry, girl!" Gabriella shouted. "Hurry! We must leave quickly before they kill us all."

Sarah again fought, with Gabriella's help, to lift me into the wagon. With whatever faculties I could muster, I assisted in pulling myself up and throwing a leg over the side, and with one last grunt and a mighty shove, Sarah and Gabriella boosted me onto the wagon.

Just then Marcus's father rode up with a group of men on horse.

"You'd best be going," he said quickly. "We can keep them from following, but we can't protect you for long here. And there are others worse off than the likes of you. Godspeed."

Then they rode to confront the mob, and I watched Marcus leap onto the back of a roan his father pulled alongside.

Sarah jumped up beside me while Gabriella climbed up and onto the rear bench. Sarah took control of the reins, gave them a powerful snap, and launched us safely into the night.

We could hear the fire raging and feel its heat as we left the bakery compound. Villagers yelled after us to defend the hateful sins they were committing. Thankfully there were men of sound enough mind and strong enough will to bring logic and order to bear.

With Sarah's snap of the reins, we had moved beyond that world. We became like ghosts among the living, passing unseen through the most northerly towns and villages and beyond. With little protection and less knowledge, we ventured to a place unknown.

Chapter

The North Pole

Terrain shifted and changed under the legs of our tired horses. Each night I would remove them from harness and rub their sore bodies down so as not to repeat the negligent injuries that, as a child, I had allowed to befall Gerda. We covered so much distance that many days had passed into night and back.

As we moved north, we experienced a cold never before imagined. Our pace became more labored as we searched for a gentle place of opportunity where we would attempt to make our home. The wind howled ceaselessly, and we began to doubt the choice we had made to pass this far north. Still the horses' hooves continued to crunch their way through veneers of ice and snow, leading us forward.

I sat in lead of the wagon now, and Sarah and Gabriella huddled together on the rear bench in an effort to stay warm. As I looked back to judge their condition and their determination to continue, I could see their lips were chapped, and their cheeks burned red from the bitter cold wind that whipped at us. I began to seek any place of shelter, for we could not continue exposed as we were to the elements without fresh food and warmth to return us to a reasonable strength.

The endless forest surrounding us was nearly silent, except for the wind still whistling through the trees. Its somber song lulled me in my weariness and declining energy.

I imagined other sounds carried on the wind, the song of birds, or the muffled laughter of children lost in the dense forest. But then there it was again, the giggling or gaggling of cooing birds. I looked through the trees on either side of the clearing through which we rode, trying to find some source for the sounds. After a moment or two I decided my tired ears must have deceived me due to the enchantment of the wind's unwavering melody.

Movement caught my eye as a glimpsed shadow leapt though the trees. And I heard it again, but this time distinctly and unmistakably: the laughter of children. I picked up our pace to match the moving of the shadows as I squinted to look about to see what I might find. With careful study I was able to capture fleeting glimpses of some powerful, stocky, furry deer with mighty antlers that ran silhouetted within the surrounding woods. Once again came the unmistakable laughter of children. And then the silhouettes in the forest became the movement of a child darting behind a tree. And then another. And another. Children leaping and laughing and playing through the trees. But as I looked to be sure they were not merely my imaginings, the images emerged again from behind the trees as those strange, stocky, majestic deer. I was caught between some fantasy or childhood anxiousness as my mind imagined these wild deer children as a kind of mysterious changeling.

Quick motion caught my eye from beyond the wagon as dozens of those deer began to lope from the trees and across the snowy earth, kicking up a spray of snow that flew around their hooves to encase them like a low-lying fog. As I watched them leap and sail across the powdery snow, their graceful movements added to the illusion that they were skimming across the surface of the earth or flying.

We had accomplished some speed as I strove to keep pace with these phantasms. Then, in a rush, a herd of children broke through the trees, more than twenty, running directly in front of the wagon. I fought to bring the wagon and horses to a stop as the children ran by laughing, unaware of the danger. It was then I saw the magnificent antlered deer running through, around, and with them. There was a sharp sound behind me, like the pounding of a drum, and I quickly looked back but could not determine its source. Gerda whinnied, as if to signal me.

Frozen in front of the lead horse was a small native girl standing in the path of the wagon. She stared up at the horse in fearful fascination. The horse snorted, steam escaping his nostrils. The child screamed and bolted into action as she dashed back to watch me from the trees.

I winked at Sarah and Gabriella to suggest they stay quietly in place, and I gestured for the young girl to come closer. She stuck her head out and shook it in what must be the universal signal for NO, then yanked her head back behind the tree, peeking with one eye to see what I would do next. It was all I could do not to laugh.

I handed the reins to Sarah and jumped off, cautiously venturing toward the small girl. As I slowly moved closer to her, I again tried to signal she should not be afraid, but she shrunk back into the deeper shadows.

I was certain she would still be watching me, and so I reached into my big coat pockets and pulled out a wooden toy duck. I held it out for her to see and tugged on a string suspended from the toy to make its feet paddle in the wind. In a moment the girl came forward with wide-eyed amazement as the small duck swam through the air. I set the duck down in the snow between us and slowly backed away.

She approached my offering cautiously and picked up the toy, holding it to her chest to claim it as her own. I nodded my approval and smiled at her. She shared an enormous grin in response.

Abruptly, a bearish voice bellowed from the trees. Behind the little girl a short, stocky native man marched toward me with authority. His legs were bowed as if he had ridden on the backs of large animals for many years. His older, muscular frame revealed his physical prowess, but he was slightly stooped in response to his advancing age. He was dressed in colorful attire with shiny metal clasps that began at the high collar of his coat and trailed down in a wide, decorative strip to mid-chest.

As he walked forward, he called again to the young girl, who ran to his side. He put an arm around her protectively and barked at me in a language I did not understand.

"I am sorry I don't understand what you are saying."

Again he spat angry words at me, gesturing to the horses and wagon and the children that surrounded us.

"We meant no harm. We are just cold and in need of shelter."

This time I understood his meaning and his forceful words, as he swept his hand away, ordering us to leave.

I was fraught and at the end of my patience. "I will not go! These hills and these trees are not yours!"

The man pulled the girl to him protectively, and his eyes grew fierce as he growled something undeniably menacing at me.

Then the young girl did the unexpected, she held up the toy duck for him to see. Curiously if firmly he took the toy from her hands and upon inspecting it pulled the string. The ensuing duck paddling brought him to uproarious laughter. The powerful little man continued his rich expression of amusement as he pulled the string again and again, causing it to swim freely in the air.

Just then, the clutch of children emerged from the trees. Sarah pulled upon the reins to hold the horses in place. The children were clothed in animal skins that had been tinted with colorful pigments and accented with bright strips of red cloth.

The man bent down to the little girl at his side, spoke gently, and handed the duck back to her. She quietly bowed her head and ran back to join the other children. Their animated voices greeted her with excitement as she held the duck with pride.

I could see more shadowy forms in the dark spaces between the trees, and some of the children at the edge of the shadows began to emerge to get a closer glimpse of the magical present the young girl had obtained through her courage in coming forward.

The stocky little man looked past me to the sleigh where Gabriella and Sarah huddled together freezing. He smiled at them and looked again to me, hitting his chest with the palm of his hand as he spoke.

"Pel," he said. And he pointed to himself to make sure I understood this was his name. "Pel."

Then he pointed at me.

"Kris," I responded, gesturing in the same fashion to let him know my name.

Pel laughed and he repeated, "Kris," and then he smiled.

He pointed to Sarah and Gabriella, and I gestured toward them with my arms.

"Family," I said slowly. "My family."

Pel said, "Good family, Kris."

I laughed to discover he understood my language, if only slightly. And he laughed again too.

Pel looked to the trees and with a vast wave of his arms said, "My family. Sami people."

From the trees, as if on command, many young children emerged with their older brothers and sisters and mothers, and they all moved closer to us and began to form a group around our wagon, to see just who the strangers were that had come to visit this day.

These were a people who had warm expressions of welcome, and their eyes lit up with excitement as they gathered nearer to us.

Pel let out another cry that startled us all. Sarah and Gabriella looked to me for reassurance as the sound of Pel's voice echoed long and deep through the woods, bouncing from tree to tree.

Almost magically, a slew of Sami hunters stepped from the woods and into the clearing. Some carried bows. Others held strong wooden staffs. At their sides, all wore large knives with ornately carved bone handles and elaborately decorated sheaths. Several of the men led huge, powerful reindeer into the clearing. It appeared as if these mighty creatures had been harnessed as beasts of burden to assist the Sami men in hauling logs or carts loaded with other heavy goods.

Pel signaled to a few of the men, who approached me while the women made their way toward Sarah and Gabriella, and a young Sami woman took the horses' reins.

Pel spoke to them again in his native tongue, and many of the others laughed. He tugged at the sleeve of my big red coat and made another joke, and then he patted me heartily on the belly. I laughed at his antics. As I did so, Pel puffed out his own belly and patted it too, and all the people had a good laugh as he compared our girths.

The girl leading the horses smiled and said to me, "He tells the men, 'at least you not starving.'" And with that, some of the Sami men also patted me on the belly and indicated with a smile that I should follow Pel and the others.

Pel led his people and my family along the trail that bordered the tree line. In little time we came upon what appeared to be a small Sami village in an area that was dotted with strange snowy hills of varying sizes. As I studied the curious shapes and placement of the hills, a woman emerged from one of them through a canvas piece that covered an opening leading into the mound. I realized then that these mounds were their homes.

More families and children came out from the mounds as we approached. And as Pel called out to his people, it seemed as if they all wanted to get a look at the weary travelers who were escorted into their village as friends.

The young Sami girl who had received my gift of the wooden duck ran up to Sarah as we walked among the earthen homes. She had the toy duck carefully tucked under one arm, and in her hands she held a small doll made from cloth-bound straw that she proudly handed to Sarah. It was a simple but beautifully handcrafted toy which she took delight in sharing. Sarah thanked her with a smile, and the little girl laughed and danced where she stood, then ran to her friends who joined her in her excitement.

Pel indicated we should lead Gerda and the other horses and wagon to a quiet spot out of the way. He had his men unharness them and walk them into a giant mound, which served as a stable where they would be given food and shelter.

Pel soon brought us to another snowy mound, and we all laughed when, as we followed him inside, each of us had to duck our heads significantly to pass through the low entryway.

I was the last to enter Pel's hut, and before I did so, I turned to acknowledge and thank the other members of this gentle village that was to become our new home, though I didn't know it yet.

Once inside Pel's living quarters, I could better observe the manner in which the unusual Sami dwellings were constructed. They were framed by thick, curved tree branches, shaped to absorb the weight of the exterior walls and positioned in such a way to fashion a living space and entry large enough for a man Pel's size to walk into easily. Birch bark, sticks, and branches covered the sides of the hut in alternating patterns woven to form the curved walls, and deer pelts layered the entire structure, creating a base where heavy bits of snowy turf were fashioned into a thick final outside layer that was encased by the falling snow. It was an earth home. The living area was built around a large fire pit, and the floors were covered in furs and hides for comfort. An opening to the sky was left in the roof to allow smoke from the fire to escape and to provide some illumination during the daylight hours.

Pel and his Sami people were a friendly and hospitable group. On our first night they prepared a welcoming feast that Pel delighted in overseeing. We were served large portions of stew made from the strange deer that Pel called renkok, and a heavy, dark bread made from rye flour and deer blood, along with fresh cheeses, hearty broth, and big chunks of dried meat, which we washed down with milk of the deer mixed with a pulpy liquid made from boiled mountain sorrel, crushed cloudberries, and bilberries. The men handled the cooking of the deer stew and prepared various dishes as if they were tending to a sacred ceremony and its secret recipes.

As the ceremonial dinner concluded, Pel had some of the women lead us to an empty hut, which Pel offered to us as temporary living quarters. "Someday," he said, "you make new home. We help."

Pel was clearly the master of his world and the leader of this village. I found myself constantly entertained by the tall hat that he often wore. He would stuff it with hay or straw for insulation, which made it stand straight up and gave me the impression that he walked around wearing a steeple on his head. It also allowed me to identify him from great distances. Despite his often comical appearance, he commanded his people with a sense of leadership as pure as his strength. His every wish was met with an unspoken response and immediate action. The Sami people seemed to know their duties and carried them out faithfully. In such a harsh climate, cooperation such as this was no doubt necessary even for survival.

Pel became our guardian and provider. He opened his village with generosity and good will. He was forever fascinated with the toys I made and the tools I carried with us from Josef's carpentry. Again and again, he would study the mechanical toys in my satchel and pull on levers or strings to make the toys dance and fly and paddle as they were designed to do. He asked me to show him the ways I had created these objects of his fascination. In return he would teach me about the land and deer that he called boazu, upon which their entire society and survival were based. We came to call them "reindeer" because the Sami people would halter them and attach them to small sledges like our own horses.

So many times we laughed as we spoke together. And though Pel did not always understand my efforts to communicate with him, he was adept in understanding our needs and helping to see they were realized. He loved to tease me about my size, using the word ruoidnadit, which suggested I shrink what I eat. He would often greet me with the playful question, "Is possible you are larger?"

And I would respond in kind, "Is it possible you have gotten shorter?"

I thought back on Josef and Noah and how they had bantered almost insultingly with each other. And I knew it was a statement of acceptance. We had become friends.

Over the lifetime to come, Pel would remain a loyal supporter and stalwart champion. His mysterious, almost magical, quality was born of his closeness to nature and the spirit of the world, for he was said to be a noiadi, wise man or shaman, by others in the village.

At times when we were alone Pel taught me and offered to confide great secrets, if I would only remain patient and dedicated enough to learn. He spoke constantly of the reindeer, as he instructed me, and told me they shared the earth together. Shared the sky. Shared the spirit of the world.

Every piece of the reindeer became a useful part of the life and spirit of the Sami people. Reindeer were important to their food supply, but they also were put to good use in hauling wood and building shelters, in working as beasts of burden to transport other heavy loads, and in the creation of garments to protect the Sami in this harsh and sometimes unforgiving environment.

Pel showed me how the hides, hooves, bones, skulls, blood, and sinew of the reindeer served as sources for tools and utensils. These elements also were used in making drums and instruments that bridged the spaces between this world and the supernatural, through their ceremonial and mystical practices.

One day during his teachings when we were alone beside a raging fire, Pel said, "You see many Sami. We move across the land like reindeer. We are the reindeer."

I remembered what I had said to him in anger on our first meeting, and I realized that I had been right; the hills and the trees did not belong to him. He belonged to them.

The Sami village was made up of a hundred members, or perhaps a few beyond, of all ages, and each with something to contribute to the others and a job to complete. The village was a busy hive of activity necessary to sustain a nomadic lifestyle. They moved about to follow and herd the reindeer through different seasons. They hunted, fished, and collected the wild herbs and berries they desired. Pel and his people remained separated from the rest of the world.

It was not unusual for them to have occasional contact with outsiders, as traders sometimes appeared and brought them cloth and tools, rare foods, or weapons and supplies, for which they exchanged dried reindeer meat, hides, antlers, carved bone knife handles, and the simple toy dolls made of sticks and straw that were wrapped and tied in pieces of torn cloth.

Pel and his people moved with the seasons. They saw time as a spiritual entity and cyclical journey governed by changes in the visibility of the sun and moon, the weather, and the migration of the reindeer.

The Sami people were an inseparable part of nature, like the animals they herded and hunted and lived among—reindeer, wolves, bears, birds, and fish.

All living things were treated with respect because each had a spirit, just as we all do.

The Sami had so many words for snow, I could never hope to master them all. Snow was named for its freshness, or its age. Its density. The way it fell upon the ice. Or melted and refroze. Or the sound it made as you walked over it, or as the reindeer hooves cut into it. Reindeer, too, were described in countless ways, based on their age or sex, their disposition, the shape and spread of their antlers, their size, strength, and speed, or the color of their coats. Each aspect of their nature and condition received a special name. As with the naming of the snow, I learned the reindeer had so many different names because they had so many different purposes and spirits.

One afternoon I came upon Pel grinding reindeer antlers into a fine powder as he squatted next to a blazing fire. I sat near him and watched in silence. At times he looked up to point at me and laugh.

I had grown accustomed to Pel's laughter and cherished it. His laughter revealed his strength of spirit, his warm heart, and the humor he found in almost everything.

When he finished his grinding, a large pile of powder lay before him and he let out a YAWP that startled me. Then he looked me in the eye.

"This for you," Pel said. "You stir this in reindeer milk. And drink. Two days. Then you have big love." Then he laughed and laughed and whistled and sang in his native tongue.

I was horribly embarrassed by his knowledge of my thoughts and desires and he enjoyed my discomfort immensely.

"If it has not happened, it will. Soon enough. You do plan to make her a home?"

I nodded in reply.

"Good. I do not want to dislike you. I will make preparation." He arose to walk away.

Preparations for what? The wind whispered at the powdery mound and carried breaths of the powder off into the sky.

"She lives in your home. Now is time."

What did he think could happen? With Gabriella living with us, Sarah was the safest maid in the village.

"Will she have you?"

I nodded in reply.

"Have you asked her?" He stopped.

"No."

He smacked me in the back of the head as he walked away.

"Ask!"

The memory of Josef brought tears to my eyes. Yes, of course, it was time. If she would have me.

When I turned back to look for Pel, he was gone.

Sarah was grinding nuts with a mortar and pestle when I entered the earth home. The loss of her family hung heavy on her. We were so occupied with surviving that memories of our past were more easily ignored. It was a blessing that her family had passed before the mob had come: otherwise, I believe the horror would have been more difficult for her to live with. They had said their good-byes, even though there is never enough time when the end comes for those you love.

"Kris?" The way she said my name held all the care and compassion in its question. It was also delicious just to hear her speak it. Kris. Who thought my name was so glorious.

Gabriella stepped from behind her, smiled, and lightly touched my arm as she walked past me out the door.

We were alone.

"Sarah." I handed her a box I had carved from a white ash tree. She took it from my hands and sat down on a mound of reindeer pelts. She opened up the box. Inside was a strip of finely woven leather, and hanging from the leather was a piece of wood made up of consecutive circles that formed the most elaborate snowflake. There was never a break in the design, so it was impossible to tell where I had begun and where I had ended. It was the finest work I had ever created. It was the only thing I could think of giving. It was a connection to my past and my hope for the future.

"I do not have anyone I can ask for your hand, so I ask you."

Then we kissed for the third time. But that is none of your concern. Within a week, before God, Gabriella, and our Sami people we announced our marriage. And it is still the best decision of my adult life.

A reindeer dashed from among the trees and raced up a hillside, where it stood upon a large rock and stared down at me.

Reindeer represented life for Pel and the Sami and served as undeniable evidence of the direct connection of the Sami people to nature. The Sami also excelled at hunting in the rugged terrain and fishing in the numerous frozen lakes and inland fjords.

Pel showed me how his people followed the well-known paths of the reindeer migration, which were almost the same each year depending on the harshness of the weather or the quality of the grazing land available for the herd. He also demonstrated how each member of his village, according to their age and ability, assisted in herding and caring for the reindeer as they traveled across the wilderness and how they learned from experience as I was learning.

When they traveled with the herds to grazing lands far away from their village, they would construct new portable homes, which they called laavu. These were made from large forked branches angled together in the shape of triangles, which supported each other. Other sticks, branches, and pieces of canvas or reindeer hide served as walls. A canvas sheet was hung as the doorway to these dwellings, whose floors also were covered with piles of hides and furs for comfort.

When it was time for the herds to move again, the Sami harnessed the largest and most powerful reindeer to pull the sleds that carried the parts of their moveable homes and necessary supplies.

Herding required a deep knowledge of the reindeer, including their ancestry, strengths, and capabilities, for it was these factors that helped to determined how the reindeer would serve the Sami people and how the Sami would engage with them.

The animals often were allowed to roam as freely as they wished within some limits, though the Sami watched them closely through every season.

In the same way Pel and his people were obligated to know the nature of the reindeer, they also were required to know the nature of the land and the weather and the conditions of the pastures and foraging areas they might cross and depend upon.

Through every season Pel and his most trusted men would cull the herd and select reindeer that would supply their meat, those to be used for breeding, and those for work as draft animals. They regularly reviewed the size of the herd to be certain they could provide sustenance for the large number of reindeer they managed and all the people who were part of their ritual migration. They gave careful consideration to the lands they crossed and the conditions they faced, often speaking about these topics for hours at a time around a ceremonial fire.

The seasons here were frequently harsh and challenging, but they also brought lush blessings to the Sami people. In the spring and in the summer, the herds would journey to lands nearer to the coast to benefit from robust grazing in the fertile grasslands. Food supplies not found inland during more severe weather and more punishing seasons of the year allowed time for the reindeer to gain size, weight, and muscle, and for the Sami to store food that could help them survive the long and hostile grip of winter.

In the richer pastures, Pel and his people allowed the reindeer more freedom to roam and forage as they wished while watching them closely to be sure they did not stray too far or become separated from the herd.

Pel gave me the task of looking after several prominent reindeer stags selected for mating in the rutting season. I followed them with the other men to be sure they did not break away from the herd or succumb to other dangers. They were considered of great value, for they would propagate the herd and assure its continuance. I was honored Pel had awarded me such a position of importance while allowing me to learn from the men I accompanied.

May and June brought the promise of new life to the reindeer herd, as many calves were born and welcomed by the Sami people.

Sarah and Gabriella helped other women and some of the younger men and children look after the calves, which were valued not only for qualities that would help to build a strong and lasting herd but for the nature of their soft coats, which could be used in the making of clothing. Only those calves that had lost a mother or were too weak to survive the harsh surroundings were taken from the herd.

Occasionally, I spotted reindeer perched high upon the cliffs and on dangerous precipices and could not determine how they might have executed such a difficult ascent. When I ventured to discuss this with Pel, he took a long draught off his bone pipe and blew the smoke from it out into the air, wafting it on the breeze, as if to say the reindeer had crossed the sky as the smoke did.

Summer also was the time of the midnight sun, when for seemingly endless days the sun would stay visible without pause, depending on the weather and the clarity of the sky. The sun's unyielding glow, even while we slept, made many of us more irritable and often brought to surface our lesser qualities. Pel would sometimes throw handfuls of snow into the wind in an effort to chase the sun away in his ceremonial wish to have a shorter day.

In the dawn of the autumn season, we began our journey back to the territory closer to Pel's village. This was the time, as we moved farther from the sea, when we were most able to see the radiant dance of the magnificent northern lights rippling across the sky. Pel told me these colorful displays were blessings sent to signal good fortune ahead. They shimmered in airy flows of many colors, vibrant reds and greens with alternating waves and sprays of gold, blue, pink, and violet. They were said to be powerful spirits dancing in delight as they observed the goodness of the world.

During one vivid display composed of shimmering curtains and waves of red and blue colored lights, Pel took us to the edge of a meadow. "The spirits talk to us," he said as he pointed to the sky.

"The colors are the same as your clothing," Sarah said to Pel. He smiled at her and laughed softly.

"They happy you are here," he said to Sarah. "They want to give you long life. Many reindeer. And big love."

Sarah blushed and I blushed with her.

Pel laughed and pointed back to the sky. "The colors dance with many riches," he said. "We share with you. With everyone. These are our gifts."

"Can we somehow thank the spirits and the Sami people for these beautiful gifts?" I asked Pel.

"They know your heart," he said. "They say your heart is strong and will bring joy to many people."

Along our pathway home we collected and stored mushrooms, fresh berries, herbs, and plants that we would use to sustain ourselves throughout the winter months.

Winter was a challenging time, and overseeing the herd became much harder. The reindeer wished to move about as freely as they had in milder seasons and in open grazing areas, but the unforgiving winter weather demanded we keep them near us for their safety and survival.

Pel commanded his clever dog Enok to chase the straying reindeer when they began to wander off and redirect them toward the herd. Enok was a massive dog that more resembled a bear than a canine, but he could run swiftly and maneuver better than many of the reindeer. His powerful authority helped to keep the herd close and well contained on the journey home.

If a reindeer strayed too far from the herd or refused to return at his urging, Enok would leap into the air and wrestle the reindeer down to the ground, holding it there with his powerful jaws until it relented or was captured by the Sami herders.

One day I asked Pel how Enok had come to be a member of his family, and told him I was curious about the meaning of his name.

Pel looked at me and flashed his infectious smile and said, "One day trader come, bring many dog to chase reindeer."

Then he lit his pipe and took several long draughts of the aromatic smoke that he released to the sky before he continued.

"Trader tell me Enok fast dog. Strong dog. He say Enok run like bear. And when he jump on you, Enok you over."

Severe winter was hard for both the people and the reindeer. We lived in almost total darkness, as the sun did not appear in the sky at all except to sneak a little closer to the horizon, where it leaked a bit of twilight for brief periods each day.

The reindeer survived on the lichens they would dig up from beneath the snow, and we lived on our stores and reindeer, fish, and other animals that could be hunted or trapped. Pel and his people often conducted ceremonial activities to honor the spirits of the plants and animals that sustained them.

When the heavy snows began to fall again, we found it somewhat easier to follow the herd due to the well-defined hoof prints the reindeer would leave as they wandered.

The great challenges of winter brought the herd always closer together, just as it brought Pel's people together. It was the time of mating and "big love," as Pel would tell me with an air of seriousness and a hint of laughter.

It also was the time when wolves would follow and stalk the herd as it traveled and foraged.

When the harsh winter closed in upon us, the wolves became more prominent, and they searched for weak calves or strays to attack and feast upon.

As we drew closer to Pel's village, the weather grew much more punishing and the wolves sensed we would now be all the more vulnerable. They stalked us relentlessly and began to attack the herd whenever they could. Pel could feel the fear of his people. He rallied several of his best hunters to defend the herd, but even they were not enough to stop the attacks once the wolves decided they were ready.

Wolves ran at the reindeer from many directions, frightening them and causing them to scatter. Pel's men tried to contain the reindeer and chase away the wolves, but the wolves were too numerous and too threatening in their persistent and savage assaults.

As one reindeer fell, Pel charged the attacking wolf, trying to drive it away or kill it. Other wolves moved in, and one leapt at Pel, knocking him to the ground. I ran to his assistance and struck the wolf many times with my staff, forcing it to back away, so Pel could escape. Then more wolves began to surround us. We held them off with our staves, knives drawn, as they circled us, snarling, preparing to attack.

Another wolf lunged. Enok charged the savage animal and grabbed it by the throat, throwing it to the ground and snapping its neck. More men raced to our aid, and we were able to force the wolves to retreat into the woods. But we knew they would continue to follow us and wait for another opportunity to score a fresh kill. We could feel their eyes always upon us.

Pel sent the women and children ahead to the village on the sleds. Several of the men accompanied them to provide protection.

Pel skinned the wolf Enok had killed and gave Enok the victor's prize of fresh meat to reward his heroism.

We traveled later that night when the snow was solid and easier for the reindeer to cross, and in time we approached the village compound, which the earlier arrivals were preparing for the celebration of our safe journey home.

The reindeer were herded nearer to the village huts and watched constantly to prevent another attack by wolves. Pel told me the wolves were frightened to approach the village, so he felt we would be safe from further intrusion.

He also showed me the large stone pits that had been sunk into the ground and hidden to trap encroaching wolves. The pits were positioned in strategic places around the village, deep enough and large enough to prevent a wolf's escape once he was trapped. The pits were covered with branches to disguise them. The intestines of small animals or other bits of food were placed in the center of the covering to lure the wolves. When a wolf approached and tried to claim the food, he would fall through the leaves and branches into the pit, where he might be captured or impaled on sharp sticks lining the bottom of the pit.

The Sami respected the wolves but knew how deadly they could be to the reindeer herds. Thus the wolves became their adversaries in the struggle to live within their natural surroundings.

The fur of the wolves, along with their hides and carcasses, were used, as the Sami used all things, to make tools and protective garments and as food for themselves or their animals.

On the night of our return from the great reindeer migration, large fires were built, and a feast was prepared. They lit braziers of Agarwood, a rare evergreen that grew in the sacred places of the Sami. When we stopped by one of these sacred groves where no trees should grow this time of year, Pel led me into its heart and taught me its mystery. The ground was strangely warm with no or little snow, and the air was heated with a damp mist. Pel warned me away from places that spat scalding water to the sky. From time to time the whole area would rain large drops of tepid water. In the grove there were a few trees that had been attacked by mold. Prior to the effect of the mold, Agarwood is pale. Once infected, however, the evergreen produces a dark, aromatic resin that permeates and transforms the tree into a very dark and dense resin embedded heartwood. I had never heard of or seen anything like it. Pel explained to me that the transformed Agarwood was then used as an incense and that it held unique mental and physical healing properties.

The Sami men sat near the fire, and many held drums made from reindeer hide stretched and laced across oval birch frames. The drums were decorated with a symbol of the sun in the center, which was surrounded by the representations of the animals and sacred places revered by the Sami. Each drum was different and designed to tell the story of its owner and the world surrounding his family and his life.

The men held small hammers made from bone or antler, which they used to strike the drums and make a rhythmic, enchanting music. It reminded me of how we would gather as a community to sing Christmas carols, and I told them as much.

"Juovllat," Pel said, and others in the circle nodded in agreement.

"Juovllat? Christmas? How do you know of Christmas?" I asked, confused.

Pel took the drum from the closest man and showed me once again his story, how it began with a star, a crude drawing of a small child and two lines that formed a rough cross. As the men passed around their drums, I saw that every story began with these three symbols.

"He is the tree that was cut down only to grow again," Pel said.

"How do you know this?"

"It is part of our story." He shrugged. "Many moons ago, before the memories of our grandfathers' grandfathers, a great noiadi leader of the Sami followed a star to the child's side. He watched the tree grow until it was cut down, and then to its rebirth. We did not see him again."

"If you did not see him again, how do you know this?"

"His spirit speaks to us," was his straightforward answer, and I was never to learn more. To him it was just a simple truth.

The Sami sang through the night, and the music put us in a wistful mood. When the music faded to completion, Pel moved near the heart of the fire, lifting his drum and striking it slowly as he sang in conversation to the spirits of the animals, so he might travel in their ethereal world. He sang about the wanderings of his people, the beauty of the world, and their place among all things. He thanked the animal spirits of those sacrificed along the way and said they were now part of our spirits as we were part of theirs. He thanked the reindeer that had always helped the Sami in their spiritual quests and formed the basis of their lives.

As Pel passed deeper into his ritual drumming and song, he began a long and colorful Yoik, which I learned was an improvised song known to bestow upon its subjects a greater strength and blessings, as it described their personalities and important characteristics.

What I did not know was that the song he was to sing that night was mine.

He spoke of the way I had come into their world, and the magical gifts I had made and shared with his people. He sang of my journey with the Sami and my help in protecting and providing for the reindeer. He sang of my big love and devotion to my family and my bravery in fighting off the wolves that had attacked us so fiercely. And he sang of my efforts to save his life and protect all the Sami people.

When he finished, he told me this song was not about me. It was me. I was its owner. Forevermore his people would sing my song and remember how I had become a part of their world, of the earth and the sky, and the places reindeer fly.

Pel placed a silver ring on the skin of his drum and watched the way it moved and danced and spun on the drum when he struck it with a small hammer made from a reindeer antler. When the silver ring at last completed its journey, Pel said to me, "We are children to the father of miracles, we shelter beneath the tree that grows again, we are reindeer herders. Will you walk the snow with us?"

It had been difficult to make toys during my first year in the village, when I was learning so much from Pel and the others. Pel could see I was determined to get back to my calling and one day as the spring thaw was underway, he came to me to discuss an important matter.

"Now time to build home," he said. Then he looked me over with a studied eye. "Must be big home, for big family and big love." Then he laughed to the point of falling and rolling on the ground.

Pel assembled his best craftsmen: Haakon, Eilif, Baldur, Roald, Vidar, and Flem to assist me in collecting the large and thick tree limbs and sticks we would need to support the walls and coverings of our dwelling. He showed me how to clear and prepare the ground to make a proper base. Then he decided I should have a specially designed home that combined adequate living space with adjoining rooms for Gabriella, a carpentry to house my tools, a barn for Gerda, and windows so I could always see the beauty of the world.

"You have learned way of reindeer," Pel told me. "But this no job for you." Then he picked up a toy wolf lying on a flat board where I had carved it. "This your job," Pel said. "We make reindeer. You make toy."

"That wolf is my gift to you," I said to Pel. "It is the sign of your power over them. They may threaten others, but will never harm your spirit."

Pel and his men helped me collect the materials necessary to build our new home and carpentry. They taught me the ways to bend the key supporting branches so they would continue to hold their shape as they dried and how to interlock them to add strength to the wall supports. They showed me all the types of sticks and tree branches that would serve to make the best wall panels and how to peel the birch bark needed to fill in the spaces in the walls that reindeer pelts and the turf would eventually cover.

They also emphasized the importance of the fire pit and the circular opening above it, which was our doorway to the spirit world and the place through which our smoke would rise into the skies. This was the center of our home, like our hearts that glowed warm to sustain us.

When the frames had been constructed and the wall sections detailed, the men began to cut and brace the windows and their shutters and roll large sections of turf, which was applied in sheets and chunks to coat the outer walls. It was monstrous. The main room had a tunnel with bedrooms on either side which opened up into a huge space larger than Josef's carpentry. The stables were at the back end with a huge tarp covering a hole large enough for a horse. One day I will build a door large enough for a sleigh. I needed to start with something smaller until I figured out how to unify our village design structures with the Sami's earth homes. So I fashioned a large door of wood planks which I had cut large enough to accommodate my own comfortable entry.

Pel was impressed when he first saw the door, which was the only one of its sort in the village, where canvas was the covering of most entryways.

"You wise like big bear," Pel said to me. Then he laughed as he opened and closed the wooden door and brought many people to see the ways I fitted the wood together, with strong joints and polished panels. His greatest joy of all was the image of the flying reindeer I had carved into the center of the door as a symbol of the reindeer people who had shared their homes and village with my family. It was also part of a joke between Pel and me because he often described the reindeer as flying, which I had taken to tease him over.

Pel held a ceremony to welcome my new home and carpentry to the village, and the people who came to visit and inspect the home of the flying reindeer brought us furs and hides to comfort us and keep us safe as we journeyed into the night-land of our dreams.

Pel and the men pounded on their drums and sang a song of the powerful reindeer that transformed their lives and traveled as spirits above the earth and below. They sang of the blessings they would bring to all the reindeer people.

When the song was finished, I surprised Pel with a gift to thank him for his instruction and guidance in building this home and for the way he had opened his heart and his village to us. Sarah and Gabriella had wrapped the gift in soft animal furs and tied it with birch bark bows and sprigs of flowering plants and herbs, which delighted Pel beyond our expectations. He walked among his people and held the package out to them so they could see the beauty of its presentation and the pride he felt upon receiving the gift. The villagers crowded in to share his delight and gaze upon the wondrous gift. Then Pel placed it on the ground before them to unwrap it. The villagers pressed in again to see what was hidden inside.

Pel held his people in suspense as he folded back the layers of the wrapping slowly and carefully to preserve them. Then his face took on a glow as brilliant as the northern lights as he threw back the covering to reveal a glistening bowl drum, which I had carved from the heart of a beautiful burl wood knob I had discovered in the forest.

In the center of the drum's bowl, I had carved the sun and surrounded it with the Sami's symbolic images I had learned from questioning and study. Beginning with what was intended to be the top, I placed the star and began the story of the three wise men as I imagined it. Beside the star was a mountain. Atop the mountain sat a great noiadi shaman in view of the star. Next I had carved a sacred grove and the noiadi picking the sacred wood. This I now believed to be the holy incense brought to the feet of the Christ child. I showed great stretches of strange terrain and two occasions when the noiadi gained the company of a fellow follower of the star. When the great journey ended, I showed him kneeling as one of three gift givers at the feet of an infant surrounded by animals who lay about the child. This completed the first half of the drum, and at the bottom I bisected the drum with the two rough lines of the cross. I then told the story of Pel and his people, their village, and the reindeer that are the essence of their lives. Next to Pel I had carved the image of his beloved dog Enok, standing over the wolf he had conquered.

"It is as we see it," Pel said to me, filled with the solemnity of the night's experience. "How do you know this to be true?"

"The spirit speaks to me," I replied, which was the simple and honest truth.

Pel sat before us all and made music from the drum and sang a song of the reindeer flying and of me upon their backs. He sang of toys, and he sang of Juovllat, and he sang of all the blessings and big love his people would enjoy in this world and beyond.

Chapter

The Great Delivery

One day, we awoke to find Pel and the Sami villagers gone. They had moved out to follow the reindeer on their ritual migration path.

Pel was adamant that I spend my life and time creating the toys that he knew to be my passion, yet I could not help but feel a deep sense of loss due to his absence and the separation from our people and the reindeer.

As the months and years went on, Pel and the Sami and the reindeer would return to our village and depart again in a constant process of change and growth that reflected the cycle of life around us.

I worked to establish my carpentry and build the toys I wished to share with the children in a similar cycle of giving and exchange.

Sarah and Gabriella learned the lore of the land and excelled at gathering the plants and materials we would need. The carts, sleds, and furniture I built we shared with Pel and his people and the traders who would on occasion visit us and restore our supplies.

Time passed in the wink of an eye and before I knew it I found myself a man of nearly 34 years, blessed with many new and fruitful memories to replace the dark and distant days of my youth.

Each year, like the trees around us, I seemed to grow in size as I added to my experience. I was by now a broad man with a full, red beard and ruddy cheeks kissed by the cold wind that danced across the snowpack.

Throughout the years, in addition to the objects I crafted and carved to trade with others, I built fine chairs and tables and other essential furnishings, which stood in stark contrast to our earthy dome-roofed home. Of course, I also made as many glorious toys as I could produce to share with others in many faraway places.

As I entered our living quarters on one blustery day after a long and busy journey, I kicked the snow from my fur-lined boots and hung my heavy red coat on a wall peg. Sarah had looked after me with such a passion and wished me always to stay warm, and each year she made me a new coat of bright red fabric lined with thick, warm fur to protect me from the elements.

I warmed myself briefly by the fire and settled into my sturdy rocking chair, which was positioned in such a way that I could bask in the warmth of the hearth and read and write in my journal by the light of the fire.

After reviewing some of the most recent journal entries, I held it close to my chest and rocked slowly in the chair until I closed my eyes and drifted off to sleep.

I awoke to feel the slender fingertips that slipped across my shoulders and chest, then up to my beard. I let the fingers roam, then snatched the hand and tossed my journal next to the inkwell on the table. Like a bear fishing in a mountain stream, I reached around, grabbed Sarah from behind, and pulled her onto my lap.

"Kris!" Sarah screamed.

I chuckled and held her close, cuddling her and cherishing her warmth.

"You have to be careful with me," Sarah admonished.

"Do I, now?" I said.

"Yes."

"What happened to my rough, wild girl?"

"You spoiled her and made her civil."

"Shame on me. Perhaps I should take you out to follow the reindeer once again?"

Sarah brought her face near mine, and we rubbed our noses in a gentle show of affection. Then she turned away from me and scooped up my journal from the table.

"You write more every year," she said.

"There is more to write every year," I replied as I playfully snatched the journal from her.

"What will you do when the pages are full?" Sarah asked.

"I'll have to write on you," I told her as I dipped my fingertip in the inkwell.

Sarah giggled and ran from me, shrieking as I chased her threateningly with the dripping ink.

Triumphant, I trapped her on the other side of the room.

She gently caught my hand as I held my ink-stained finger out to touch the tip of her nose. "If you want to write on me, you'll have to take me with you when you go to check in on the children."

"Then you'll have to wake before the sun tomorrow!"

"Tomorrow? You have more to do?"

"Well, the family is getting bigger. Yesterday's babies are today's fathers and mothers, and we are spreading farther along the countryside."

"I was worried, Kris."

"Sorry I was so late."

"Well, as long as you keep away from the dangers of the mountain passes."

"How many times must I promise?"

"How many times will you leave me?"

Our eyes met and I could see her genuine concern for my safety.

"I'm preparing a gift for you, and you have to be around to claim it," she said. Then she pushed my ink-stained finger back onto my own nose and escaped as I trailed after her.

"What is the gift?" I asked as I pursued her.

"A secret."

I grabbed her again and held her close. "Give me a hint," I said as I tickled her with my inky fingers.

"Stop it! You're ruining the dress."

"Then tell me," I said warning her.

"It will be ready by Christmas."

"Christmas?"

"I think so."

I lifted her from the ground and tossed her up into the air as our play continued.

"Stop, Kris. You'll hurt the baby."

I let out a gasp of astonishment then set her down very gently. "Oh, Sarah," I muttered softly.

"As I said, you'll have to be careful with me now."

Gabriella peeked in from a back room. Her snowy white hair and wrinkles born of infinite smiles had transformed her now completely into the grandmotherly figure I had first imagined. "Does he know?" she asked with excitement.

"Gabriella!" Sarah said, playfully cautioning her.

"How long?" I asked.

"Three months. I wanted to be sure."

I rested my hand on her belly. "That leaves six months, mother. I have six months. He'll need a crib. You'll need a changing table. And his toys, oh, the toys!"

Sarah fluffed my beard with her hand. "One thing at a time, that's how we get things done."

Gabriella reemerged to lure my dear Sarah away so she could learn how I had responded to the news.

"I could use some help with the baking," Gabriella said to her with a wink.

"I'm coming," Sarah sighed.

"Oh, no hurry," Gabriella chortled with a smile.

I stroked Sarah's face, and she gave me a little kiss on the cheek and then skipped off to assist Gabriella.

I crossed back to the table where my journal rested and picked it up, slowly flipping through the pages. Then I closed its cover and placed it on the stone shelf, which rested near the base of the wall.

Sarah spent many more hours at home as her pregnancy advanced, and she would watch me from time to time through our shuttered windows as I worked to haul logs and branches that I later would transform into sleds and products for the traders who visited us.

Sarah's belly was beginning to grow now. One morning, I saw her standing near our hut sipping a warm drink from a wooden cup. A blanket was wrapped around her shoulders. She held my journal in her hands. As I looked across the field, she set her cup down on the workbench beside her and opened the journal to the ribbon marking the place where I had last finished writing.

I watched her as she looked down the long list of names until she came to the end of the list, where I knew the name Dahlia had been crossed out. Sarah paused for a moment and looked up at me. She went back to the journal and shuffled to the next page where I had listed the names of towns, with numbers beside them: Roppland 34, Tillehammer 42, and so on. Then, she closed the journal and went back into the hut.

Later, when I had finished collecting and stacking the wood, I went into my workshop, where I began reviewing the plans for our baby's crib.

I worked at my drafting easel experimenting with designs, and in a short while, Sarah appeared at the entryway to the workshop, holding the journal.

"You didn't tell me about Dahlia," she said.

I looked up at her, forlorn, and returned to my drafting. "I didn't want to upset you. I saw you looking at the journal and knew you would discover the news yourself."

"You have listed many more children than your family, Kris."

"It was just an idea. These children, they deserve the effort it takes us to bring them joy."

"But, gifts to entire towns?"

"Gifts for the entire countryside. Every child! As I said, it was an idea."

"You haven't built a single toy."

"There is other work to be done first, my love."

"No. I do not accept that," Sarah said emphatically. "I do not need your help to carry this baby, Kris."

"Sarah, I'm doing what you need me to do."

"No, you set out to do something, and you will do it," Sarah said, as she set the journal down firmly on my easel.

"I've waited too long, Sarah."

"And I've known you to do the impossible," she replied stubbornly.

Sarah reached for the snowflake pendant hanging from her neck and ran her fingers across it. "You have work to do."

I looked up into those knowing eyes of hers and saw the rightness of her conviction. What was I to our child if I was lost to myself? I had never forgotten Nikko. If I made these toys, perhaps one would find its way into his life. Moreover, none understood the pain in these children's lives as I. My heart longed to bring them joy and laughter.

"Yes, I have work to do."

"Every child," she reminded me. "I only ask that you leave the mountains their peace. You face too much danger going back, Kris. Unless you find the proper path, the passage up can be treacherous. And I do not trust the memory of your youth to the snow- filled darkness.

"And Kris," she said, hesitating a moment, "you know the traders said plague has returned to some of the villages."

"Yes. I have heard."

"Then leave them to their peace, Kris."

I nodded in response and continued with my drawing.

"Promise?"

"Of course."

I ventured back inside to my workshop and returned to my drafting table, but my mind was distracted by Sarah's discussion and the thoughts of all I had to do.

I unrolled some of the drawings I had made and pinned them to the table in my workshop to study them more closely. They revealed many of the new toys I had recently designed, but I was unsure how I might produce them as quickly as needed and in great numbers.

How would I ever begin to deliver them all in the little time I had?

I began to sketch at my table and focused on an improved sleigh that would carry the many toys I would have to distribute. It would need to hold up under the most severe conditions as I traveled.

As I worked, I began to think back to my youth and the skills Josef had taught me, and I daydreamed about the countless challenges I had faced under his gentle guidance.

As if in response to my thoughts, Gabriella brought me a plate of cookies filled with berries and nuts and placed them beside me at my worktable. I remembered the generous meals she made to keep us healthy and content as we worked to fulfill the duties of our apprenticeships. Gabby touched my shoulder as she left in the comforting silence which always accompanied her on her small, significant acts of kindness.

I paged back through my journal and recalled how Gabriella had first given me this wonderful tool to record my thoughts and imaginings and the designs that would become my toys.

How many pages I had filled throughout the years! They stood as a record of my hollow youth and the ways my life had been filled up again by my developing passions and the people who surrounded me and guided me. I could see myself as a young boy, so lost and angry without a notion as to how I might overcome my burdens, when Josef and Gabriella took me in and treated me as a son.

I remembered the maps I had drawn on the inside covers, which identified the places where I deposited my brothers and sisters, and thought about how those simple directions linked me to them in my heart. I thought of when I had lost Nikko.

I kept those directions with me, always; I had determined I might one day need to rush to their assistance or return and bring them all together again. I labeled every little turn and bend in the trails that connected me to my brothers and sisters, with notes about their gentle qualities and the discoveries I might chance upon as I looked in on them, year after year, and as they grew in closeness to their new families.

In looking back upon all these things, all the good intentions and support, all the love shared by Josef and Gabriella and by my Love, my devoted Sarah, and even those painful memories and recollections that had suffocated me in my youth, I realized now these experiences were in fact gifts to me that fueled the devotion I now possessed to share the gifts of joy and laughter with the children at Christmas.

I once was a young man hungry for purpose and knowledge. The skills I developed filled me up like the glorious meals my Gabriella and Sarah fed me. Soon I would have a son who would be the culmination of this journey of love and the object of our devotion. I don't know when I decided it was a boy, but this was how I thought of him.

I had grown from a thick and troubled youth to the fullness of manhood in the prime of my life, and now it was my turn to share with my child the many gifts given to me by others. It had become my turn to be the teacher and share the truths that life and experience had taught me. I would teach him the act of selfless giving as a gift we give ourselves, that pride and purpose and goodness and worth could be received from the eyes of a child, when a gift of no inherent value other than the smiles it evoked was given on Christmas morning. If I didn't teach him anything else, I would teach him that.

I turned to see Gabriella and Sarah watching me as I daydreamed and worked, and was captivated by the smell of the cloudberry cookies they brought with them. They were as delightful and comforting as the cookies had been in my youth.

Dragging the heavy logs, from which I cut boards and beams and panels and parts for the new sleigh and cradle and this year's deliveries, was a massive undertaking. I made a sledge out of thick tarp and put it to good use in moving logs across the snowy fields and to the doors of my workshop. By the end of the first long day's work, my tunic was soaked with sweat, and my hands were raw and chapped from the friction and the cold.

"Six months!" I shouted to the treetops. I had wasted too much time. Truly I wasn't even sure if I could accomplish the task with a full year's preparation. I looked about the forest, scouring for the best trees and branches and burl with interesting natural shapes and rich grains or coloration. It was all there, but how would I gather it all without breaking my back? And how could I wrap the twine and paint and clothe and finish each necessary piece? Josef had not trained me to be weak-willed, but there was a reality I had to acknowledge. This ambition stretched beyond my abilities.

Then I heard gentle drumming in the distance and the sound of Enok's glorious bark, and I ran from the trees to greet our welcome visitors.

"Pel!" I shouted when I saw his hat bobbing through the trees. By the time I got to him, he was sitting on a stool, casually smoking his long bone pipe. He had placed his wooden drum beside his feet and blew rings of smoke into the wind, which carried it off in dancing swirls.

Enok lay beside him and jumped to greet me as I emerged from the hut. I wrestled with him for a moment as he licked me furiously.

Pel tapped out the pipe on the bottom of his boot, and tucked it into a pocket. "Is it possible you grow wider?" Pel asked.

"Is it possible you grow shorter?" I replied.

We laughed and thumped each other on the back as the old friends we were.

"Welcome. You have returned early,"

"It was time," he said. From around him stepped my beloved Sami, each of them holding a roll of twine or a fold of cloth or bowls of various colored lacquers and paints. They were splitting wood of varying lengths and sizes and gathering the twigs they used for their children's dolls.

"How did you know?" I asked, in awe of their insight.

"The Spirit spoke to us," he stated in his straightforward way. "And Sarah told us you need help."

Pel smiled and strolled over to my old horse, Gerda, who was tethered outside, and rubbed her soft nose.

"Gerda, good friend. You grow old," he said.

"She's not useless. Even if she can't handle this year's delivery," I said to him protectively.

"Reindeer fly fast!" Pel said, moving his arms through the air with the swoosh of a flying reindeer.

"So you tell me. When you have time enough to strap eight reindeer together, you do that," I chided him, laughing at his antics. "For it'll take no less than that to carry my new sleigh. This needs something bigger."

Pel shook his head and chuckled again. "You need a big, big, big, BIG something," he said as he pointed at my belly laughingly, and wandered off chuckling with Enok into the village where others were beginning to appear.

My efforts to create this year's toys went faster now as my preparation and the assistance of the Sami paid off. Their skills allowed me to work with more speed and increase the output of high-quality toys of many types.

Once I had my designs prepared, I would assemble a sufficient number of the necessary pieces of wood and make multiple markings, which allowed me to cut out numerous versions of each toy. When I had the templates formed, I was able to cut finished pieces with staggering speed and skill and pile them near my workbench, where some of the Sami youth would put them together.

Shavings grew on the floor as we labored, and Gabriella or Sarah would sometimes come to watch us work and assist in sweeping wood chips and sawdust shavings out of the way. Gabriella liked using the chips in the stove, and was certain to insist we save every combustible scrap.

Pel offered his assistance but more often would sit in awe as he observed my progress. He had many gifts, but quite frankly toy making was not one of them; he struggled with the carvings I assigned to him. He was preoccupied with the magical movement of the toys and spent hours each day pulling on strings and twisting levers to send the toys into action. The sight of the animals running, dancing, and flying filled him with joy, and he would smile and laugh throughout his time working beside me. Whenever I observed his errors or struggles and frustrations in shaving the wood to its desired dimensions, I remembered the patience and good grace he demonstrated in teaching me the ways of the reindeer. No matter what his level of achievement, his company and unyielding humor were welcomed and important to me, and our friendship increased each day through working together.

One day Pel led me on a journey to the distant stables of a horseman well known to him and the Sami people. He packed his pipe and blew smoke into the breeze and watched me barter with the horseman over four powerful Friesian draft horses that I wanted to serve as the team for the new larger sleigh I had designed. I offered to create tables and strong chairs for the horseman's cottage and to help him fashion newer and stronger stable doors and hinged shutters and barriers to provide his animals with better protection from the elements and keep them safe.

We approached the stables so I could see the horses and inspect the work to be done, the stable doors flew open as if from a horse's kick, and a monstrous horse with a white mark on his forehead lurched from the stables and into the snow. The horseman gave chase, yelling, "Sebastian," and cracking his whip at the now crazed horse.

I ran forward and grabbed the horseman's whip as Pel approached the horse and calmed him by stroking his nose. The horseman was angry with us for interfering, but handed me the parchment to sign and conclude our deal. He was tired of this horse's stubborn behavior and wanted to relieve himself of the burden while he had the chance.

I could see the fire in Sebastian's eyes and sensed he had an intellect as strong as his muscular frame. He was truly an incredible specimen, and I knew we would become fast friends and that he would serve as the leader of the horses that would speed me along my way when it came time for the great delivery of toys.

I scrutinized the agreement handed to me by the horseman and added my signature, hoping impossibly I had found a horse that would be as true to me and dedicated as Gerda had been over so many years.

Once back home we went to work creating new templates and new techniques to mass-produce toys for the many families and children on my list. There is something I have learned of children: give them a polished stone from the river and tell them it has magical qualities, and they will keep it in their pockets until they become old men. Give them the most extravagant, ingenious toy ever created, and they will play with it for half a day. Give them one toy, and it becomes their best friend; give them twelve and they play with none. I began to simplify most of my toys. What I found most important in the exchange of a toy was heart. Did the toy convey and capture the heart of the child? The right gift takes thought and time. And it comes with heart.

I counted the members of every family, and named the children in scribbles off to the side of my journal entries for each town and village. Names of those who I thought would enjoy something special as well as those who needed extra care and consideration in the delivery of their gifts were circled on my list. My journal was filled with information I needed to identify their houses and make my secret deliveries.

On the tables across from me, the piles of toys grew. As I whittled new pieces that required assembly, Pel collected them and blew the shavings away with a magical blessing to thank the raw wood for surrendering such beautiful toys.

Pel continued to have difficulty disguising his clumsiness with the carving knife. On occasion he would yelp and squeal in response to a nicked hand or cut finger, which he tried to hide by jamming his bloody fingers into his mouth.

We spent many hours searching the forest to find the right trees, of good form and quality, from which to make our toys. Locating them was only the beginning of our tasks, for then they must also be cut and trimmed and hauled to the workshop where they were stacked awaiting further sizing, routing, carving, and fitting into final form.

Much of the time I had help from the Sami, but on a day when they were caring for the reindeer, I chose in my hubris a massive log to tow from the forest alone. As my fists clenched the thick rope, I pulled with all my strength but was only able to inch my way forward. I lurched again with another mighty tug and fell flat upon the ground, face first into the snow. I lay exhausted and laughed for thinking myself up to the task.

To my surprise, the towline became taut once more, and I looked up to see Sebastian with the rope between his teeth. He had freed himself from his tethering to help me transport the log. I pulled myself up by Sebastian's bridle and together we hauled the massive tree from the forest.

In considering the ways I could increase the speed of toy production, I first sketched and later bartered with a village blacksmith to build a sturdy lathe that would allow me to turn large sections of logs and cut spiral rings formed to a consistent thickness. I devised a router blade that aided me in gouging out portions of the rings to make crude shapes that I could cut into uniform blocks and carve into a series of toys of the same design. This device assisted me in maintaining the quality of the toys and the accuracy of the design and speeded our assembly process.

Pel directed his men to assist us in cutting the blocks and rough chunks of wood that we would carve in greater detail.

Baldur and Roald worked on a series of blocks destined to become toy horses and reindeer pull toys, and they pursued their assignments in the same dedicated manner they employed as they tended to their herds.

Vidar and Flem cut the blocks we would later shape into wooden nutcrackers. Haakon and Eilif cut blocks of wood that would soon become throwing tops and yo-yos. I began working on a series of stackable dolls carved in the shape and likeness of Pel. Each new doll was slightly smaller than the one before, and each smaller doll fit into the next larger size, in several successive steps of growth. Pel had a mighty laugh when he saw these dolls being fitted together. He said they showed he had the strength and spirit of many good men.

Sarah suggested we add curved beams to the larger wooden horses so they might rock in place. She had seen similar toys and knew how much children enjoyed riding on the rocking animals.

We also built magnificently simple steeds meant to take the older child on glorious quests by combining our beautifully carved horses' heads with rods shaped like broomsticks that children could mount and run with as they wished and to the fullness of their pleasure.

Each day we advanced our efforts and added to the variety of toys we produced.

There were many types of dolls and puppets suspended from strings, which were moved by wooden control arms to which the strings were attached. There were games of chess and checkers whose pieces were placed upon colorful boards made up of wood tiles cut from many different trees, revealing their interesting grains and diverse colors.

Much to the delight of the men, I also designed a wooden puzzle that depicted a scene in which reindeer were grazing in a meadow. I affixed my drawing to a thin board and cut it into a variety of shapes that could be scattered and reassembled. Pel and his men laughed and exchanged notes as they moved the reindeer pieces about and decided where they should stand and how they would fit together.

Enok guarded us with dedication as we worked, and so I carved him a wooden bone that he could carry about and gnaw on as he sat with us in his role as protector. Gabriella's abundant meals and flavorful cakes were the fuel that kept us all going as we kept pace with our demanding schedule.

Our work was directed by our desire to create well-made toys that represented the pride of our craftsmanship while at the same time bringing joy and wonder to their recipients. And the types of toys were as varied as the children that would play with them.

We toiled together, and our collection of toys grew to an impressive size. The workshop became overloaded beyond our capacity to work around what we had already made. But Pel had a ready solution and offered another of his huts as a safe haven for our gifts. He and his men worked to safely transfer groups of toys to our temporary storage area.

Pel also became our primary toy tester as he pulled on strings, tweaked levers, rode rocking horses and hobbyhorses, and danced with puppets to our amusement and delight in the workshop.

One day as I began assembling the pieces of the great sleigh I had designed, Sarah watched me through the window. She was quite heavy with child and I could see the added difficulty she sometimes had while moving about our home.

When I had hammered in the last of the pegs securing the coach to the body of the sleigh, I cracked the reins and sent Sebastian bolting forward. His massive strength ripped the front half of the sleigh right off, pulling the runners and the floor out from under me. Still holding onto the front of the sleigh, I slid for half a dozen paces, then lost my grip and tumbled in the snow. In his enthusiasm he continued to run, and I had to chase him down to get him to return.

I could see Sarah laughing heartily as she watched us through the window despite the fact she tried to hide her amusement.

In the coming days I completed the sleigh and tried another test run with Sebastian. Our efforts were a glorious success and I knew I would soon be ready to begin my incredible journey.

After a long day's work, sleep seemed a welcomed relief. But I remained restless and agitated in my dreams as I considered the great delivery I was about to make and all there was remaining to do.

I hadn't noticed when Sarah left our bed, but I awoke when she returned as the light of the lantern shone briefly in my eyes. She curled into the bed beside me and wrapped herself in the sheets as she drifted off to sleep. I watched her lying there for a moment and reflected on all the love I felt for her, then raised my groggy head and decided to return to the workshop to see if I could finish still more of my toys.

Though my sleep was short, I felt a new sense of energy as I entered the workshop to stoke the fire and set about my duties. Then what to my eyes did appear but little bundles of toys, wrapped in bright red knitted material.

The bundles were scattered throughout the workshop, organized by village. Each bundle had a name to identify its intended recipient, written on a tiny wood plate salvaged from the shavings that Gabriela and Sarah had collected. Some lay on table tops, some in bags, some in great piles on the floor. And there was Pel wandering amid the toys, tapping each present as if counting.

"You have big, big, big herd of toys," Pel stated proudly.

"You wrapped them?" I said with astonishment.

"Sarah," Pel beamed.

I began tapping the presents as Pel had done, and he looked at me as if to question my motives.

"Just checking twice,"

Pel began digging in his pocket and pulled out a wooden doll he had constructed. He proudly set the simple doll, with its large, roughly carved wooden head and a body made from straw and sticks bound by cloth, next to the rows and piles of wrapped toys.

Dejected, he compared his present to the other beautifully wrapped gifts set about the room.

"What's the matter?" I asked him gently. "What's troubling you, Pel?"

"Doll have no blanket like other toys," he said.

I thought for a moment, then walked over to the stove and lifted one of the socks left on the belly to dry. Pel watched me with curiosity. I retrieved his toy, opened the sock and dropped the doll inside. I then tied a clever knot in the top of the sock and set it down upon a pile of toys.

Pel smacked the table with delight, pulled another doll out of his pocket, and grinned at me.

With the help of Pel and his men, all was ready and loaded. When my massive team was harnessed four-in-hand with Sebastian at the left lead, I climbed into the sleigh and took a deep breath of cold night air. I could feel the excitement coursing through my veins and my heart pounding with anticipation. Pel looked up as if remembering something almost forgotten, took off his steeple hat, quickly stuffed it with hay from the floor of the barn, and pulled it down over my head.

I was sure I looked the fool, but he was right. Without a head covering, I would lose much of my warmth to the long winter's night and endanger my well-being. Despite the aversion to my outward appearance, I left the hat on and gave a polite smile. Pel laughed so hard, he fell to the ground kicking and holding his tummy. I wondered how long he had waited and planned for this moment. I knew he loved the hat, and he knew I hated it. But I vowed in that jovial moment that he would never get it back.

Pel pushed the door of the barn wide open. I waved good-bye and threw kisses across the breeze to Sarah and Gabriella who were watching from the windows. I stood chariot-style on a stand behind the sleigh and commanded my team of magnificent horses as they launched their weighty cargo out into the wondrous night and down the tree-covered path. Their thick, long manes and tails and the white feather anklets dancing above their massive hooves, shone in the glimmering light of a moon that cut through the trees as we raced forward.

The horses ran with strength, pride, and determination. The sleigh's lantern that hung above and in front of them from a long pole swayed in response to their speed as the first snow flurries of Christmas Eve began to fall.

I gripped the reins tightly in my hands as we dashed ahead across the countryside, standing behind the sleigh urging my beauties forward, my cape buffeted by the wind.

Ahead I could see a small village nestled among the foothills, and from the windows of cabins spread across the land the twinkling light of lanterns spilled into the night. Above the village, a star-peppered sky cast a majestic dome that brought the heavens and the earth together in a glorious scene.

As I arrived at the edge of the village, I steered Sebastian to a secluded spot and pulled the sleigh to a halt.

I leapt to the ground, shouldered a heavy bag of toys, and set off into the snow.

Sarah and Gabriella had prepared a number of small, fresh cakes to sustain me on my journey, and in my excitement I pulled one from my pocket and savored its rich flavor.

I selected a red bundle from my bag of toys and placed it proudly on the windowsill of the first cottage I encountered then rewarded myself with another bite of cake as I danced away to other cottages along the path.

I quietly moved to each new dwelling and placed my presents on windowsill after windowsill until each was endowed with a special gift intended especially for the occupants of that home, whose names I reviewed in my journal.

When I completed my deliveries in this village, my bag of toys was lightened, and I returned to the sleigh to begin my journey to the next small hamlet on my list. I stopped momentarily to sample more cakes, as I knew I must maintain my strength for the long night ahead.

Along the way, I spied a single stone house nearly hidden by a thick growth of trees. It was immersed in dark shadows and looked anything but inviting.

I stopped my team and reached into the bag of toys resting behind me, where I located a brightly colored nutcracker painted in reds, yellows, and greens.

"What do you think, Sebastian, is this the one?" I asked him, seeking an honest answer that was promptly delivered.

Sebastian snorted at the gift.

I decided he was merely envious of my cake. And so as I walked past him, I turned briefly and whispered in his ear, "Don't tell the others." And I reached into my bag of treats as he nuzzled me only to find in my zeal that I had eaten them all. So I took my hat off to feed him some of the hay Pel had packed within, and he shoved his entire muzzle completely inside, nearly eating the fabric with it.

"That's supposed to keep my head warm." I cheerfully admonished. And when I put my hat back on my head, it flopped to the side, resting on my shoulder like some old stocking. At least I no longer pointed to the sky.

Facing the large house, I could see a pair of snarling stone bears that flanked its entryway as if to scare away intruders.

"Looks like somebody here could use a toy," I said over my shoulder to Sebastian.

The house had a shingled roof and high windows without sills which left me absent a place to leave the toy where it was at least somewhat protected. I walked partway around its perimeter, flipping the nutcracker in my hand as I studied how I might attempt my delivery. Then I got an idea. The size and location of the chimney indicated it housed one of the large central fireplaces that heated the entire home, normally open to a great room that surrounded it. The hearth itself should span 6 to 8 feet on either side, more than enough room to drop a toy down without landing in the fire. The owners probably used the warm stone hearth to dry clothing and such.

I returned to the sleigh and grabbed a coil of rope that I slung over my shoulder. Sebastian watched me with interest. He tossed his head with a loud whinny, releasing giant clouds of his steamy breath, and then grunted as if in disapproval.

"Yes, that's why you're the horse and I'm the driver," I answered in response to his comment.

I found a large crack along one corner of the house and places I could work my boots in between the stones in a long, hard climb to the roof.

With the greatest of effort, I finally made it to the top. I rolled over onto my back and lay on the roof, gasping for air after my strenuous climb. The length of the walls made the roof abnormally high, and I lay there asking myself what I was thinking. When I had rested sufficiently to regain my nerve, I took the rope coil from around my shoulder and scrambled over the ice-covered roof to the chimney.

I looked inside the flue of the chimney to locate the position of the fire below, and I tied a slip knot around the toy soldier's ankles and lowered him slowly into the chimney until he was dangling a safe distance away from the embers of the low-burning fire in the hearth. When I could see he was well positioned, I gave a little tug of the rope, and the toy soldier dropped and rolled just beyond the fireplace and onto the stone floor. I was thrilled with the success of my maneuver and congratulated myself as I began to work my way down the roof. "Ho, ho, ho," I laughed until my foot hit a patch of ice and slid out from under me. I fell, sliding down the sloped roof, struggling to grab onto anything only to fill my hands with powdered snow. Unable to stop my descent, I shot out over the edge of the roof with my legs kicking through the air wildly. "Wh-whoah!" I shouted uncontrollably as I plummeted to the ground and landed flat on my back in a giant mound of snow with a loud WHOMP. Moments later, my bag of toys hit the snow beside me.

Sebastian and the other horses looked over to see what had caused the commotion, and he snorted and blew steam from his nostrils as if anxious that I might be caught.

I could hear the barking of a large dog inside the house, and additional candlelight began to glow though the windows of the upper story. I gathered my wits about me, collected my toys, and quickly limped back to the sleigh with an Ooooo, Aggghhh, Owwww.

Sebastian whinnied in response as he pulled the sleigh forward.

"Quiet," I said to him flatly. "Or next time, you go up on the roof with me."

On we went to village after village and town after town as we covered vast distances to deliver our gifts. Once again I experienced the strange stretching of time that came with every delivery, where I couldn't tell if I had been traveling for days or hours.

Sebastian and the team moved with great speed, despite our long journey, and soon I directed them to the old church where I had long ago left my darling sister.

I pulled them to a halt beyond the sanctuary and jumped down from the sleigh to venture inside. The table where I had set Kendra to rest was still in place. And on it was the same wicker mat and stone nativity display from my very first visit, the one wise man still chipped from my momentary burst of anguish and bitterness.

From my pocket I pulled a figurine that I had delicately carved from stone. It was what I imagined the Sami Noiadi wise man who traveled across the world to welcome a small child might have looked like. When I placed him in the manger scene, I realized that if my hat still pointed to the sky, he might look a little like me.

I knelt down at eye level with the table and explored the tableau of figurines, from the beasts that lay in and around the manger to the bent and tired couple surrounded by shepherds and the wise men who knelt or stood before the child, offering their gifts of precious metal, oil, and incense.

"Merry Christmas, little one," I said, to the small child whose birth was to be a beacon of hope to the world.

Then an old remembered voice rang out behind me in rich, warm resonant tones.

"How are the miracles?"

"I've decided to believe," I confided to the holy man.

"Oh, why is that?" he asked, laying a gentle hand on my shoulder.

"Because it is a much better world with them in it," was my simple reply.

"Yes. Yes, it is," the holy man said. Then he placed a steaming cup of tea and plate of cookies on the table beside me as if he still had them from our first meeting and had simply waited for my return.

Standing with effort, I realized that Pel was right. I was getting wider. And I had already eaten the whole batch of cakes made by Sarah.

"Oh, no. No, I really shouldn't," I said softly as I rubbed my ample belly.

The holy man looked at me with his cataract eyes and patted me on the cheek with a laugh.

"Never turn down a cookie," he said with a smile as he turned to leave.

I selected one of the fattest cookies and took a generous bite. When I looked to say good-bye, he was already gone, though the room seemed filled with his presence.

Sebastian and his companions had waited for me patiently, and when I returned to the sleigh, I rubbed their necks as I walked by and thanked them for the incredible job they had done.

With the light of our oil lantern hanging in front of the sleigh like a guiding star, we set off for the last of the night's deliveries near the mountain spine that divided our Norwegian lands from the lands beyond.

Silent snowflakes drifted down around us as we finished our monumental task, leaving us feeling triumphant and invincible. We surged along a snowy trail surrounded by imposing mountains that beckoned to us and stopped at the fork in the road that lead up to the mountain home of my early youth.

I had toys still remaining in my bag.

"These gifts would make some children very happy," I said to Sebastian and the team. I looked up at my familiar mountains silhouetted against the starry sky, and one of the horses snorted.

"What do you say, fellas?" I asked.

Another horse shook its backside and sent out a spray of snow from its haunches.

I fumbled absentmindedly in my pockets, now replenished by the cookies from the church. I stuffed a small one into my mouth as I examined the fork in the trail that would take us higher into the mountains.

"YAH!" I shouted with my mouth still half full. With a slap of the reins we shot up the mountain path.

I had forgotten the abrupt weather changes of the passes up into the mountains, and our passage became more challenging as we proceeded. Waves of wind-driven sleet pummeled the sleigh with loud THWACKS as our pace began to slow.

The horses' hooves slipped from time to time due to the ice that appeared in growing patches, and it became increasingly difficult to keep the horses on the narrow trail along the side of the mountain.

I stood in the coach to chance a better look as we moved forward, and saw the trail cut away with a sharp edge and a steep drop-off to the boulders littering the valley below.

Pulling on the reins, I steered the horses to the left so Sebastian and the others would hug the mountain wall. The wind whipped down the trail and tore at us relentlessly, making it even more difficult to proceed. As our movement and positioning became harder, I knew we could not turn around on this narrow sliver of trail. There was no choice but to continue our forward momentum however we might, in hope of finding a wider segment of trail ahead, or a place to pull aside in shelter.

The wind would not relent in the punishment it gave us, blowing in gusts so great they almost threw me from the sleigh. I thought of the promise I had made to Sarah, the promise I had made and broken.

What I thought to be the howling of the wind became the howling and snapping of wolves as a snarl drew my attention to a giant gray wolf that ran along the ridge of the mountain above and beside my head, snapping his feral teeth. Behind me in the distance I heard the pack following us, waiting for the moment to leap upon the sleigh and tear at us in our helplessness.

We must continue to move.

"Sebastian! Lead on!"

The wolves began to close in around us, as they were easily able to match our pace running across the looming boulders above us and the icy trail.

You have come for me at last. You are relentless, unforgiving, unyielding in your mission—just as I am! "On, Sebastian! On!" I shouted.

The howls grew in intensity. I snapped the reins again, and the horses picked up speed. Their hoof beats cracked and ricocheted against the mountain wall.

Wolves snarled closer now, first from one direction then another. They were racing across the mountainside and approaching from behind.

Moving in now. Ready to make their attack. Running at us with teeth bared. Growling. Snarling. Chasing us with savage fury. Anticipating a kill.

One of the vicious creatures dropped from the ridge above into the sleigh and launched itself, rabid and biting, at my face. Frantically I swept the beast aside, and he flew past me only to land on the trail behind us, skidding to a stop and bursting into a run, joining the pack at our heels. My movement had cost us, and the sleigh lurched to the side nearly tipping over the edge. Incredibly, I pulled us back to the wall as we sped on.

Up ahead in the distance, beyond the radiance of the lantern hanging in front of the horses, the moonlight revealed a chasm in the trail where a bridge had once been, now gone, leaving a wide fault that separated us from the trail which picked up on the opposite mountain.

The wolves continued their chase, leaping at us now, almost within reach, desperate in their desire to tear at us and feast.

As the sleigh approached the chasm, the wolves were running along the rocks above my shoulders. One leapt through the air, landing on my chest. I dropped the reins, instinctively shoving it away with all my strength. The cabin of the sleigh rocked and swayed from side to side as we struggled. The wolf tore at my arm as I caught it by the throat and wrestled with it until I was able to throw it from the sleigh and beyond the edge of the cliff, where it fell into the nothingness.

Still, I encouraged Sebastian to lead the horses forward. Their hooves gained speed, blurring as they ran.

The other wolves would not relent. Their yellow fangs remained bared as they sprinted after us, so close I could almost feel their hot breath.

The heads of the horses rocked back and forth in a rhythm as they ran, and for a moment I saw a soft light in the sky or perhaps snow drifting in the wind or a cloud illuminated in the ebbing moonlight, and I imagined Pel surrounded by the huge puffs of the tobacco smoke he loved to send adrift. Eerily, I could hear the pounding of drums in the distance. I remembered the song Pel sang of me. I remembered Josef's acts of helplessness.

"It is a choice when there are no choices." And I chose to act!

"Yah!" I shouted, driving the team forward. "If this be our last moment Sebastian, let us fly."

Sebastian and his team leapt from the trail and into the air.

The black velvet night surrounded us, and the stars took on a greater brilliance, silhouetting us as we flew across the sky and the moon hanging in the night, lead by the lantern sparkling towards distant eyes.

With a tremendous crash we landed on the other side of the chasm. The horses were terrified and out of control as the sleigh slid forward, with its momentum carrying it up a steep path. I struggled desperately to rein in the team, but the sleigh swung erratically along the trail, side to side, from one runner to the next.

My lantern broke free as the sleigh twisted and rocked. The oil from its tank sprayed across my arms, inside the coach, and up onto the mountainside as the lamp exploded against the boulders. Fire spread rapidly across the hillside and within the sleigh. I tried to smother it with my coat, but the flames reached for my arms, licking at the oil on my clothing as I fought to extinguish them and control the team.

One of the runners beneath the sleigh snapped with a mighty crack, and the joint securing the team to the coach split in half. The straps holding the horses in place ripped free from the sleigh as the horses fought to escape, continuing their wild flight up the inclining trail.

The cabin of the sleigh shook intensely on its remaining rail and slid backward toward the chasm with increasing speed.

Fire now raged on the hillside, and flames leapt across the trees, as the sleigh passed directly through them.

I tossed my bag of toys from the coach and hung my legs over the front of the cabin, lowering them to the ground, where I attempted to dig my heels into the snow to slow the sleigh's momentum.

With a mighty effort I brought the sleigh to a stop. Then I slipped on a solid icy patch and slammed to the ground, driving the breath from my lungs as I landed, sending myself and the sleigh once again sliding down the icy trail. I rolled onto my belly as I slid and clawed at the frozen ground, the sleigh and I plunging toward the cliff's edge and the dark chasm beneath.

In one final desperate grasp I seized the heavy roots of a tree that emerged from the side of the cliff below the trail's edge just as the sleigh plummeted into the dark abyss, tumbling end over flaming end and crashing onto the boulders below.

My legs grew weary as I hugged the steep wall of the chasm and tried unsuccessfully to pull myself up onto the trail. My arms soon began to tire as well, and I feared my strength would give out before I could climb to safety.

Above me, one of the horses neighed, and a set of reins dropped and dangled within reach. I snatched at them and held on tightly, pushing with my legs as the force behind the reins continued to lift me.

When my eyes reached the level of the trail, I could see Sebastian slowly muscling backward, pulling me up and over the ledge.

Once beyond the edge of the chasm, I flopped over onto my back and whispered, "Thank you, Sebastian."

Across the great chasm two wolves sat silently, their golden eyes shining as a reminder that they would always be watching.

Sebastian nuzzled my hair as I grabbed his bridle and he lifted me to my feet.

"If it had been just you and me, Sebastian, we would have made it," I said as I ran my fingers behind his ears.

I followed Sebastian up the slope toward the other horses. When they finally calmed down, I grabbed my bag of toys and wrapped it around Sebastian's pommel, cinching it tightly.

I turned away from the terrible devastation and disappointment we had faced, leaning on Sebastian for support. "Let's see if we can pick our way down," I said to him gently.

Our return journey was a somber one. I rode upon Sebastian's back as we covered the countryside; my weariness was debilitating, and I frequently slumped across his neck holding tightly to keep from falling.

When we finally arrived at Pel's village and our home, I could see the light of a lantern dancing back and forth by the entryway to my hut. We came closer and I could see Pel holding the lantern as he paced.

He ran to me and called for some of his men to secure the team, and he assisted me as I slid off Sebastian's back and to the ground.

"You walk like old bear. Must hurry!" Pel said.

"What is happening?" I asked him with concern.

"Life!" Pel said to make himself clear.

Just then I could hear Sarah's voice pierce through the open shutter. "Kris!"

I pushed past Pel and ran into the hut. The fire pit was stoked with wood, and the flames brightly illuminated the living area and spilled into the adjoining room where Sarah lay in the throes of labor.

Gabriella passed a bowl of steaming water to Lohcca, a Sami woman who assisted her.

When Gabby saw me, she hurried to the doorway and grabbed me by the coat, whispering, "She's not well, Kris."

I went quickly to Sarah's side.

"Hello love," I said gently.

"Something's wrong, Kris."

"Maybe you should wait outside," Gabriella suggested.

"What?" I said with surprise. "No!"

Lohcca began a rhythmic chant, repeating it over and over.

"What are you saying?" I demanded of the Lohcca.

"Kris, make her save him," Sarah said weakly.

"Why is she saying that?" I asked of Gabriella.

Sarah screamed in pain, and I turned back to her.

"Hold her, Kris," Gabriella said softly.

I wrapped my arms around her, cradling her head. "Don't you leave me! Don't you leave," I insisted.

I held Sarah and watched her give birth in great agony. And then her face relaxed.

"How is he?" Sarah asked.

Gabriella placed the blanket over the baby, then looked at me and shook her head no while the Sami woman spirited away the bundle holding my stillborn child.

But I could not tell this to Sarah.

"He is beautiful. He looks like his mother," I said, smoothing the hair from her forehead.

"We were never very good liars, Kris." The water held in her eyes sparkled from the firelight.

I sighed softly and stroked Sarah's hair.

"I went to the mountains," I confessed, convinced that my broken promise had brought this tragedy upon my family.

"I knew you would," she said in her gentle forgiving tone.

"I failed."

"Never."

I held her and kissed her briefly, but I could feel her body begin to go limp and I set her back onto the bed.

"Don't go, Sarah," I said with tears streaming from my eyes.

Her arm slipped off my shoulder and fell to her side. Her face looked empty and lifeless.

I rested on the crib for a moment of support. Then I screamed, lifting it and smashing it to the ground, shattering and scattering across the floor.

I ran from the room still carrying a piece of the crib's railing.

Gabriella yelled, "Stay!" as I hurried past her and out the door. "Kris!"

Pel was outside holding Sebastian's reins. Pel had separated Sebastian from the team and was preparing to walk him to the stable, my bag of toys still tied to his pommel.

Unaware of Sarah's continued grasp on life and filled with my own egotistical belief that this tragedy was somehow my fault, I vaulted onto Sebastian's back and stormed off into the night, alone.

Chapter

7

Returning

O n I rode, through the bitter darkness, a crest of icy powder from Sebastian's churning hooves spraying the veil of night. The land twisted and stretched past me, blurred by my frozen tears.

If I could just ride until the moon rose to its highest tide I might someday find myself lost beyond its radiance. My sorrows would evaporate as I would enter another land, another life, another time. The radiant northern lights spoke to me in their dance through the sky, as I imagined Pel's reindeer in full flight.

Sebastian and I rode to the edge where the land meets the sea near a wharf by the ocean and a town just awakening from its sleep, and I found myself where a tormented man might, in a tavern.

The snow continued to fall as the wind drove it in waves that splashed against the earth, and I could not stop the fury fueled by my thoughts. In the darkness of the winter morning, I threw open the tavern door and stood silhouetted in the doorway, backed by the silvery reflection off the falling snow. I could hear the loud voices of the seamen who ate and drank and sang in this seaport sanctuary, which was a home for these salty comrades and their local counterparts.

Squinting at the light, I could see weather-beaten and sea-swept faces, both dark and light, from lands far and near. I was a stranger among these strangers, and for a moment they stopped to look at me and the rail of my child's crib that I still gripped tightly in my hand.

The fire in the hearth swelled as the proprietor fed it thick dry logs that crackled like flames of the netherworld. I walked to it and threw the crib rail into the fire. The light and shadows washed over my cheeks and every other face in the room.

Across the bar three sailors, no doubt rugged men from distant lands, were already deep in their cups. They watched me to see what dust I might kick up.

In a moment one muttered to the others, and they all broke into heavy laughter, as if I were the butt of their joke. I threw my coat down on a bench next to a vacant round table and walked directly to the men. A large knife rested on a counter nearby, and I snatched it up and stabbed it into the table between them to challenge their derision.

Eye to eye, I looked for what I wanted, a focal point of my pain and anguish. Then I remembered the carpentry and the rage of my broken childhood. I remembered Josef's words, "None of us gets to own pain." And I knew I was not ready to give mine up today. But none would challenge me.

When I finally turned to retrieve my coat, a sailor grabbed for the knife, but his friend caught his wrist and placed a warm, steaming mug into his hand to calm him, telling him not to stand.

I slapped the bar to attract the attention of the proprietor, whom I soon came to know as James from the orders shouted at him from across the room. He was built strong and, from the looks of him, had dealt with many unruly and dangerous men in his day.

James wiped his hands and called for his young bar boy to assist me. "Cai!" he barked loudly. A tuft of dirty blonde hair followed by two tiny ice-blue eyes rose up just beyond the counter's edge.

Cai extended his small arm to place a tall, wooden cup before me. I took a long and deep draft then set my mug down with a thump on the empty counter where I sat.

Again the tavern door burst open. Two laughing men, no more than twenty years of age, stood arm in arm, framed by the light reflecting off the snow behind them.

"James! Pour us a mug. We broke away from the women!" said one.

James gave them a nod and shouted, "Cai! Grab me two mugs. And make sure they're dirty. We want these men to feel at home."

Cai seemed somewhat confused by this command and looked around the room as the men broke into laughter.

"Grab me two mugs, son," James said in a more restrained voice.

The taller of the two men in the doorway responded next, "Better get ready, James. Service is out, and we're the first."

"Hardly the first," a fat sailor said.

"We're placing bets on who it was made so many unusual toys for the children," the tall man's friend chimed in.

A man from a nearby table lifted his face out of his soup and muttered, "You know about this?" Then his head fell back into the bowl.

A short, round man drying his socks near the hearth yelled, "It's not one of our men. They can't even make their beds."

All the men laughed.

A stout old man, with the necktie of a pastor, stepped into the doorway from the penetrating cold outside and slammed the door behind him, drawing our attention to his entry.

He shook off his jacket and sprinkled the floor with powdery snow and ice crystals. He walked to the bar and put his hands on the shoulders of his friends and spoke: "Man from down south said the last two villages he passed through had the same story. Toys everywhere. Nobody knows where they came from or how they got there."

"It's true, Pastor!" one of the sailors shouted. "I'm from Kirby, and we was trying to figure that out too!"

The door burst open again, and a little runt of a man tripped over the threshold and fell into the sawdust. The sailors laughed, and one of them shouted, "Shorty still gots his sea legs."

Another sailor yelled, "What'a you mean? I can't see his legs. Hey, Shorty, you got legs?"

Shorty was fully bundled and struggled to get off the floor while the sailors laughed and sprayed ale across the table.

A gentle giant of man in his late teens came in behind Shorty a moment later. One of the men near the bar shouted out to him, "Ian, come join us for a cup once you're done helping Shorty up."

Shorty worked his way to his feet and began to unwrap himself, casting a challenging eye to the others.

"Careful who ye' mock," Shorty said, "or I may be adding a little boot to your ballast."

"What do you know, Shorty?" another odd-looking fellow shouted.

"What I know is someone's gone up and down the countryside delivering presents to every house with a child," Shorty announced with authority.

"Shorty, if you aren't late for everything," said the man still drying his socks.

"One of the towns is calling him the Santa," Shorty said smugly, as he revealed news he seemed to feel the others would not know.

"Santa?" James asked.

"It means Saint," the pastor said.

"Sent to look after the children," added Ian reverently.

"It's magic!" one of the sailors mocked.

"Shut up!" the grizzly sailor sitting next to him cautioned.

"It's a blessing," the pastor said gently.

"Right you are!" hollered another of the sailors to the affirming grunts of the men surrounding him.

"He is a saint!" Shorty proclaimed.

"That's a lie!" I found myself bellowing. "He's a lie! Your Santa does not exist!"

I shouted above them all. I stood and lifted the huge round wood table before me, smashing it to the ground, sending a cloud of dust into the air.

There was a stunned silence from the stillness of the men in the room as the dust settled.

Ian stepped up from behind me and set his hand upon my shoulder. "It's Christmas," he said in an effort to calm.

I had forgotten.

No one moved; their eyes fixed upon me.

"Forgive me," I said, averting my eyes from theirs in shame.

As I turned to leave these people to their peace, a small hand reached up and tugged at my shirt. Cai, the blue-eyed son of the tavern owner, stood innocently if bravely before me.

"You're wrong, Mister," he said with as much firmness as he could muster. "Santa is real," Cai affirmed, "and he gave me this."

Then he thrust his arm into the sky and brandished a wooden toy reindeer as proof of the Santa's existence.

There are moments of life when we are humbled to ourselves, and for sure no one humbles us quite like a child. I had forgotten my delivery of the long night, and in one moment this child had robbed me of my right to wallow. I had been given a greater purpose in this life, and everyone around me had seen it but me. I had not been willing to look at my contribution to the world, and in that refusal had insulted the God-given gifts and experience with which I was blessed. I wished Sarah could be with me to see what our efforts had wrought.

"You can have it, if it would make you feel better," he said to me with the innocence of a lovely boy.

I gently placed my hand upon Cai's head. "Thank you. But I am sure Santa would want you to keep it," I said to him and walked through the tavern door back into the morning light.

I made my way slowly to the stable, drifting like the snow swirling in the breeze and all the while considering what I would do next in what remained of my wind-tossed life. Sebastian waited for me there with a forgiving and welcome look in his eyes and a gentle nuzzle as I approached. My bag of toys remained where I had tied it and drew me forward once more to look inside and determine what my destiny might be.

"These are the last of our toys," I said to Sebastian, who snorted his acknowledgement and his insistence I put them to good use.

"I don't know, dear fellow," I said to him. "Could we have really made it on our own?"

Sebastian whinnied and stomped his hooves, emphatic in his desire to see the toys delivered.

"It will be challenging," I said to him. "We would have to go back up that mountain."

Sebastian reared up into the air and cut at the breeze with his massive hooves, lurching and snorting in anticipation of departure.

"You're right," I said. "I cannot forget that you will be with me."

And, with that, I secured the bag of toys on his pommel, leapt onto his back, and shouted, "Let's go, good friend. Go!"

Sebastian burst from the stable at a mighty pace and raced into the snowy confusion outside. Ahead, I could just make out the misty image of that great and threatening mountain awaiting our return in the distance.

The deep blue twilight of the northern winter day surrounded us as Sebastian drove forward up the mountain, buffeted by the wind and ever-changing snow.

Up the trail we surged without a second thought, hugging the mountain wall to stay as far from the perilous drop-off as we ought.

In my mind I could see a vision of my home and the Sami people. They had befriended me and adopted my challenges as their own. They brought clever solutions and backbreaking efforts to meet the looming demands of my great journey of giving. They had struggled so hard and with so much love to help me answer the needs that drove me. They worked together in a fury of activity that far exceeded the one day's challenges this mountain trail would now present.

I could see Pel in his vast wisdom and cunning laying out a path for me within my thoughts. I could hear his powerful drumming and recall the Yoik he once sang in my name. That song now pounded in my veins and echoed against the walls of the mountains surrounding me. I could feel the strength of his people, my people, and the belief of the children inspire my strength and spur me forward on this day's last delivery.

Time seemed to open its arms to me and pull us forward in its mystical embrace as without a second thought Sebastian reached the great chasm in the mountain trail and leapt into the air, sailing, soaring, flying, he and I, as we became one with the sky. All around the wolves howled in awe at the force we had become as they watched us float right by.

Time, place, and the fear once etched upon my face were distant now from all that lay ahead as Sebastian finally brought us back to earth to land on the other side in the cresting and billowing snow.

Knee-deep in powder, Sebastian remained relentless in his venture up the mountainside. I heard the distant sound of bells that reinvigorated both Sebastian and me. We took the last thirty feet up the hill one lurching, powerful leap at a time.

There at our pinnacle we saw the remains of an old and burnt-out village that once had been my home and the flickering amber candle-light of a newly built cabin that had made this place its own.

Illuminated by the gentle starlight on the mountain's other side, white smoke curled from the cabin's chimney, and on the railings of its porch hung a leather strip of sleigh bells that fluttered in the wind.

With exhilarated and determined hearts, Sebastian and I made our way down to the cabin and to the depths of my distant memories.

Here, where everything once had been destroyed, new life had begun. I vowed that I would embrace this new image given me, built upon the love, effort, and sacrifice of so many. I pledged I would work to be worthy of this title, this mantle of the "Santa."

I pulled Sebastian to a stop in the trees near the hill and cautioned him to wait for me in silence. He stroked the ground in gentle accep-tance as I made my way quietly toward the cabin with a magnificent toy dancing bear that I hoped would thrill any child, whether girl or boy.

I placed it on the windowsill with caution and backed away slowly to watch the moon illuminate its rightness.

And just as quickly, I was gone.

Sebastian and I returned to the mountaintop and gazed out over the starlit night and the countryside below.

I looked back on all the memories I had made here, all the glories and joys of those lost days, and the crucible of experiences that had forged and formed my life and character. My coat billowed in the wind as the remembrances of things past fluttered in my mind.

Sebastian and I rode along the trail to the twisted, gnarled tree. "This is where I left my childhood," I said to Sebastian. "This is where I set about to shape my destiny and the destiny of my brothers and sisters. This is where my life began."

I had made this passage back to a place where all seemed lost. Where love was both salvation and the sum of all its cost. Now I could say with certainty that even the pain of all things past had significance and value to me here at last, in the way it laid the pathway to tomorrow. The triumph I experienced would forever be in the joys and laughter of children on Christmas morning.

Our journey back to the Sami village blessed me with memories of all the love that I had known, and thoughts of how that love had shaped my life and the ways that I had grown.

Life would be different now, to be sure, but I owed it to dear Sarah to continue with our dreams. I tried not to focus on the impending loneliness of the coming years. It was inevitable, and I decided I would wait for those days and strive not to fuel the fires of what was to come. From the ashes of my past and the flaws of my experience she had built with me a family beyond our imagination.

All the children were ours. Ours to bring joy. Ours to care for. All the children of the earth are our family, and I was dumbfounded that the world did not carry this inherent awareness. Why were not all brought up to understand this simple truth from early childhood? This profound understanding consumed my thoughts for most of my passage home.

As we came at last upon the Sami village, I paused and prepared to enter my home, now absent my wife.

The snow here was piled high and wide. I walked Sebastian inside the stable mound so he might rest after our mighty journey and rubbed the weary soreness from his overworked muscles. "Thank you, dear friend."

It was the last year he would ride on the great delivery with me. Now that I had gone back to the mountains, I would return every year, and the horses were just not built for that terrain. The next year I would expand my list of children even farther. A new sleigh was to be built, and I would come to find that Pel's reindeer were to become my reliable companions on my yearly deliveries. But that is a story for a later time. Thankfully my day was not yet complete and my belief in miracles was once again to be fulfilled.

At the entry to my home, I collected broken pieces of the cradle that still lay there like the splinters of what I once imagined would be my life. Then I threw open the door to a glorious vision.

"Sarah!"

Sarah sat bundled in my big rocking chair beside the fire, very much alive. Pel, sleeping in a chair beside the door with Enok snoring at his feet, jolted awake. Gabriella took a steaming cup from Sarah's hand and gently touched her shoulder.

My heart leapt with joy. I ran to Sarah, collapsing at her feet, and wrapped my arms around her knees.

"Gently," Gabriella cautioned me and smiled kindly. My tears began to swell as she signaled Pel and Enok and led them out the door.

I held my dearest Sarah as so many times before. "My love."

A small cry escaped from her lips, and she began to sob. "I can never give you a family Kris," she whispered through her tears. "I can never give you a child."

"No, no, no, my love." I said quietly as I stroked her face and hair. "We have more children than we could ever dream of."

I watched realization ignite in her eyes.

"Yes," Sarah whispered.

"What would I do without you? Who else would dare to believe this dream of ours could really come true?"

"The children, Kris. The children will always believe in you." And we broke into gentle, tearful laughter as we held each other.

"How will we ever take care of them all?" Sara asked most sincerely.

"We simply must live forever."

"And how, my love, do you plan on accomplishing that?" she asked now with a small smile.

Playfully I tweaked her nose and teased, "Don't stop believing in me now."

The world continued to spin, and the snowflakes continued to swirl, and we continued to deliver fine toys each Christmas to our children as our world continued to grow.

Chapter

8

Comfort and Joy

Crackles of orange and red flames licked into the darkness from the stone fireplace of an old, wintered wooden cottage. Wrapping the mantle were sprigs of crisp evergreen and boughs of holly tied together by colorful, bright ribbons. Above the hearth, hung in a row, were the long winter stockings of a boy and a girl.

Snuggly in bed, a rough-and-tumble nine-year-old boy named Olaf lay wrapped in his covers. Surely his head was filled with dreams of Santa and his mighty sleigh that sped through the night filled with toys.

I carefully shouldered my satchel of gifts and moved stealthily through the moonlight, my silhouette cast upon the cabin's broad sides, my boots crunching through crisp icy snow hidden well underneath the powder.

Inside the cabin, Olaf breathed the gentle and comforting rhythms of sleep. At the window, I laid two wrapped toys quietly down on the sill.

Abruptly, a little girl's face popped up in the glass, her eyes wide with exhilaration.

"Santa!" Ona exclaimed with excitement as she threw open the windows and tumbled out into the snow. "I knew you'd come! Daddy said 'Go to sleep,' but I knew you would!"

Ona ran barefoot to the reindeer that stood attached to the sleigh. "What are these?!" she asked joyfully. "Can I touch him?" Then she wrapped her arms around him, patting and scratching his neck and ears.

"He's a reindeer," I replied as the reindeer she petted moved his hooves to the rhythm of her scratching.

"Why is he dancing?" she asked with delight.

"I suppose the joy of Christmas has made him merry, not to mention he likes being scratched behind the ears."

"What's his name?"

"I'm not sure I could pronounce it for you in a word that you would understand."

"Dancer!" she proclaimed. "I will call him, 'Dancer'!" And she giggled as the reindeer nibbled the back of her hair and neck.

"I think he likes the name. Now you'd best go to sleep, little one. We don't want your father mad at us, do we?"

She shook her head emphatically and began to shiver as if realizing she stood barefoot in the cold for the first time. As I bent down to lift her, she asked me a sweet and honest question, profound from her simple nature as a child: "How will I know this isn't a dream?"

Little wooden snowflakes hung from the necks of each reindeer's collar and tackle. I removed the snowflake from Dancer's neck and handed it to her so that she might remember and prove to herself this memory.

"Like a snowflake, there is no one in the world like you," I told her as I lifted her from the snow, carrying her back to the open window. "You are unique."

"I am?" she asked sincerely.

"Yes, little one," I replied, "you are special."

I lifted her and placed her inside the window.

"Santa?" she whispered as she clung to my neck. "I had a dream of Christmas, and you were in it."

"That's funny," I told her, laughing, while trying not to wake her brother, "I had a dream of Christmas, and you were in it."

Letting go, she ran to her bed and dove under the covers.

"Merry Christmas, Santa," she called back to me.

Merry Christmas, What a beautiful sentiment. I chuckled. Merry Christmas. Yes, it was. Merry because we make it and will it to be so.

"Merry Christmas, Ona." I replied in a loud whisper.

Then with a start, she sat up in bed.

"You know my name!" She gasped.

I gave her a wink and pushed the window shut. Christmas is much more special when it carries a little magic, and all that is required to create magic is a little mystery.

I leapt into the sleigh as the reindeer readied to charge forward, and once more we were on our way.

Hooves dug deep and pounded the ground in a heavy, steady beat that served as a driving rhythm that urged the team forward. Snow plowed aside, and sleigh runners sent up plumes of ice crystals that twinkled in the moonlight. Reins taut, we sailed over the pristine snow as their bulging muscles flexed and stretched while the sleigh raced ahead at dazzling speed.

Celestial lights washed over the endless snowy white expanse, and we dashed across the glowing landscape.

I stood boldly in the coach, chariot-style, while commanding the team to make haste through the twilight end of night and felt the icy wind kissing and pinching at my cheeks. The flapping panels of my thick, red coat floated through the endless winter wonder around us, which could only be matched in scale by the bountiful wishes we had carried with us for the dawning Christmas Day.

After our long and challenging journey to towns and villages across the land where we shared our gifts of joy, Dancer and my other lead reindeer, whom I had now decided to call Dasher since my meeting with Ona, led the team and me home again to recover and rest. Each of the reindeer on my team had their Sami names, but Ona's naming of Dancer had captured the heart of my antlered steed perfectly, and I decided to name each one in kind. With a little thought, I discovered that I knew the noble names deserved by each of the others; Dasher, Dancer of course, Prancer, Vixen, Comet, Cupid, Donder, and Blitzen.

Dasher was simply the fastest in the short run. He had troubled me with many a chase when Pel and I first worked to put the reindeer in harness. We had spent weeks just choosing the finest and most suited from the herd. Prancer was the most beautiful with his flowing white mane. And he walked as if he knew it. Vixen was spirited and sprightly, although she could be fierce with her nipping bite, putting any of my team in place if they crossed her. Comet I named because he would explode through the herd, ramming and throwing any challengers with his magnificent antlers. Cupid, because he was so obviously in love with Vixen—and any other female reindeer that he happened across, for that matter. And of course Donder and Blitzen, which mean, "Thunder," and, "Lightning," because they were inseparable and also because they were the power that pulled the sleigh. I called to them by name, and they flew across the land as if delighting in their newly acknowledged identities.

I was thankful we had made such progress in providing presents to so many deserving children, but I knew there was more we could do in future years: more presents, faster progress in making them, and more children we could reach with our mission to spread happiness and celebrate the wonders of Christmas.

Each year our great journey was both tiring and punishing, with the severity of the cold and the complications brought by winter's unflinching grip and the vast distances we had covered. My health was challenged in the weariness I faced once we had returned safely home.

I had left behind my well-intentioned gifts of Christmas toys, but I had also stirred up a sea of question and concern that soon would grow from the excitement Ona and Olaf expressed on Christmas morning.

Unknown to me, a controversy was about to build in a powerful storm that would draw me into its center and envelop my past, present, and future.

In the weak morning light that filtered through the windows of Ona's cabin, young Olaf awoke ready for Christmas day and all the discoveries it would bring. He quickly opened the window to see what secrets he might uncover, plucking two wrapped gifts from the sill, then ran back to rouse Ona from her sleep to share his exhilaration.

"Ona! Ona! Look, see," he exclaimed as he jumped onto her bed and shook her awake.

Ona rubbed the sleep from her eyes as she crawled out of bed and ran into the main room after Olaf. They danced with glee at the joy they felt this Christmas morning.

"They're gonna be even better than last year," Olaf shouted as he heard a loud STOMP outside, near the cabin's front door.

The door swung open, and their father, Jacob, a sturdy, work-hardened family man of some thirty years, stood in the doorway. He stomped again to loosen the snow from his boots and watched the children celebrating their unknown presents.

"That's enough, Olaf," Jacob said firmly. "You know the rules. The Christmas gathering first, and then you can open and play with the stranger's gifts."

Jacob's wife, Johanna, admonished him sweetly. "Jacob," she said. "Let them play."

Johanna's softer, gentler, demeanor was often used to temper Jacob's tendency toward abrupt communication with the children.

He approached her slowly while she continued stirring a bowl of pudding batter with a wooden spoon.

"It is my house and my family." And then he sniffed at the air. "Do I smell pudding?"

Jacob quickly grabbed at Johanna and tickled her. Giggling, she escaped from the room to finish her preparation of the food they would bring to the great Christmas feast that was to be held in the assembly room of the village church.

Jacob took the packaged gifts from a pouting Olaf and placed them high on the mantle over the fireplace. "That's no face for Christmas Day," he said sincerely. Then he held out two closed hands, giving Olaf first choice at the surprise he was hiding inside them.

Olaf tapped one hand and waited.

Jacob slowly opened his fingers to reveal a mighty chunk of rock candy.

Olaf scooped it up and popped the sweet into his mouth, while he looked longingly at the mysterious toys that had been taken from him.

"That's something you won't find on a windowsill," Jacob said earnestly. "Now don't tell your mother." Then he called to Ona, "Come on, Winklet." Jacob picked Ona up, gave her a tender hug, and rubbed noses with her.

"Daddy! Merry Christmas," Ona said softly to her father.

Lifting her high in the air and tossing her, he questioned her playfully with a chuckle. "Merry Christmas? Merry Christmas? What is this Merry Christmas, Winklet?"

"Where is it?" Ona asked breathlessly, giggling heartily, pulling at her father's coat.

"What?" Jacob teased her in return.

"Stop it, Daddy," Ona laughingly insisted.

"All right," Jacob said. He set his wriggling daughter down and explored the depths of his pockets. "Well, now. Let's see here. Nothing in that pocket."

Ona watched him carefully in an effort to discover where the candy was hidden.

"Maybe there's something over here," Jacob said. "Oh! What's this? What's this?"

Jacob held out a clenched hand and opened it slowly to reveal three pieces of candy.

Distracted, Ona ignored the candy and pointed to the undiscovered toys on the mantle that had once more caught her attention. "Let's see what Santa brought me, Daddy," she cried out with delight, running for the presents.

Forgotten, Jacob closed his hand and returned the sweets to his pocket. A sense of jealousy overtook him as he watched his children roughhouse near the toys.

"Who's ready for pudding?" Johanna called from the doorway.

"Ona, Olaf. Your mother has finished the pudding. Come along now."

But Ona and Olaf continued to wrestle on the floor.

"What did I get? What did I get?" Ona said.

"Santa didn't bring you anything!" Olaf answered unmercifully.

"He did too! I saw him leave the toys."

"No, you didn't."

"Yes I did. I even went outside to meet his reindeer," Ona shouted at him. And she waited to see his reaction.

"Ona, what did you say?" her father asked with concern from across the room.

"I saw him," Ona said timidly.

"Did not," Olaf mocked.

"Did too. I talked to him."

Jacob looked to his wife with an expression of anger. "Ona,, come closer," he said to her solemnly.

Jacob grabbed Ona by the wrist and covered the side of her face with the palm of his hand. He then pulled down each of her lower eyelids with his thumb and forefinger, searching for signs of plague. His steely eyes examined her intensely.

"Open your mouth, Ona," Jacob instructed.

"Did I do something wrong?" Ona asked with a mystified look.

"Ona! Listen to me!" Jacob said sternly.

"Jacob! You are scaring her," Johanna said. Then she called to the children. "Come on Ona, it's time to go. Olaf?"

The children retreated to their mother's side, and Ona clung to Johanna's hip as she led them away.

Jacob was left standing alone in the main room looking at the colorful toys that had been brought by the visiting stranger called Santa.

At the Christmas feast, a gathering of jovial townspeople sat ready to eat, filling rows of wooden benches that framed decorated tables covered with platters of warm breads, big bowls of nuts and berries, fresh cheeses and roasted meats, chunks of cod, thick, fragrant puddings, pies, and mounds of cookies and candies, along with Christmas cakes that rested beside large pitchers of fresh milk.

The villagers talked and laughed together in a genuine spirit of holiday joy as they celebrated Christmas Day.

The children sat impatiently while their parents exchanged greetings and gossip and dashed off in reckless abandon when they finally were excused from the table to play.

A group of men gathered away from the women and children, who remained working clearing the tables. The men were engaged in a serious discussion that increased in its intensity as it progressed.

Gill, a cantankerous man in his forties, who was as soft as a Christmas cake, grumbled to the men. "It's the imaginings of a child, I tell you."

"And I'm telling you she spoke with him," Jacob said.

A man named Thatcher, a tall and strapping, well-reasoned ranger in his mid-thirties, gave their comments his consideration and said flatly, "Nothing like this has ever happened in the past."

"Jacob, would you wish to take this little bit of joy from our children?" asked Rolf. The weather-beaten old tracker seemed perplexed that such a commotion was being raised over the visit of the Santa.

"If it protects us, yes," Jacob said, looking him in the eye.

"What do we do if we find him?" challenged Gill.

"Shake his hand and buy him a pint!" a willowy boy-faced man named Darren mused, and the men erupted with laughter.

Jacob was intent on making his point. "This strange man, bringing God knows what sort of disease with those toys–"

"So you're worried the toys are sick?" Darren jabbed.

The men laughed again.

"Jacob, it is Christmas," Thatcher said with a tone of forgiveness. "Let's say we give it a couple of days, and look at this with clear heads."

"By then it will be too late!" Jacob said sternly. "We'll miss any chance of catching his tracks!"

"We don't even know if she is telling the truth," Gill said as Ona quietly snuck up behind her father.

"I am telling the truth," Ona said, much to the embarrassment of all.

"Ona, you are too old to make up stories," Gill said.

"I promise! His sleigh is pulled by reindeer."

"You see!" Jacob shouted. His voice was loud enough that the women clearing the tables turned to see what had happened. Not seeing the immediate response he desired, Jacob stormed off to collect his gear and weapons.

"Now I've heard it all. Who would harness a deer?" Darren mocked, sending the men once again into riotous laughter.

"Have you seen the tracks?" Thatcher asked, bringing the men up short. A few of them nodded and grunted in affirmation.

"Rolf, do you think you can find him for us?" inquired Thatcher.

"Deer I can follow," was Rolf's sound reply.

"Saddle the horses!" Thatcher said.

"You are not serious?" Darren asked.

"I'll get the dogs," Rolf said.

"It's Christmas!" Darren complained to no one.

"Go inform the women," Thatcher said to a lean, awkward teen named Percy who seemed determined to join the men.

"I will; then I'll get the muskets," Percy said enthusiastically.

"You're staying here!" Thatcher said to him curtly. "Now, go tell the women!"

"Yes sir." Percy replied dejectedly, nearly tripping over his own feet as he ran off.

"I'll round up food and supplies," Gill announced.

"And if he has the sickness?" Darren asked with a bit of fear in his voice.

Thatcher grimaced at him and shooed Ona away so she would not hear his response. "Bring torches," he whispered harshly.

"I'll grab Jacob and tell the other men. Meet back here. We'll stay together and spread out as a group so we are sure not to lose the track," Thatcher said as the men hurried off to prepare.

The sound of determined rummaging filled a small, cluttered shed near Jacob's cabin. Inside the hut, a rambunctious husky dog, a tiny horse though little more than a puppy, sniffed around at the rubble.

Like a gust of winter wind, Ona ran through the front door of the shed, calling for her dog. "Wolfie!" she cried out. "Wolfie, come here."

Olaf stepped from behind the clutter, holding an ice axe in one hand as he struggled to adjust the heavy, overfilled satchel slung over his back. Trying to hold the sack in place with the same hand holding the ice axe, he reached down to pick up a disk sled attached to a rope the children used to pull each other around with.

"Where are you going, Olaf?" Ona asked him with surprise and worry.

"Why should I tell you?" Olaf said to her in a rude, ugly tone.

Ona's eyes began to tear as she weighed Olaf's response.

"Where are you going?" she asked.

Olaf continued his preparations, determined to ignore her.

"Why won't you tell me where you're going?" Ona cried.

"I'm going to find Santa," Olaf said sharply.

"I want to go with you," Ona said, pleading with him.

"Don't even talk to me," Olaf barked at her.

"I can help you," Ona told him, seeking his acceptance.

"I said, don't talk to me!"

"What did I do?"

"You are so stupid. Papa has the whole village out looking for Santa. Because of you!"

"I didn't mean to."

"Dad told you to go to sleep, didn't he? Didn't he? Now Santa is in trouble because of you!"

"I didn't mean to," Ona cried again, now completely in tears.

"Just go home, Ona. You are such a child," he said to her. And he pushed past her, heading out the door. "Come on, Wolfie," he called, throwing the sled down and plopping on top, sack and all. He attached the rope to the husky's collar, and together they embarked, loyal steed and wayward adventurer. "Let's find Santa before the others can hunt him down."

I hunched over steaming bowls of water in an effort to loosen the tightness in my chest and to relieve the persistent cough that so frequently interrupted my breathing, choking the life from me. My body was punishing me for ignoring its call for needed rest and sustenance over the last few days.

Gabriella and Sarah brought me tea to soothe the harshness in my throat and were ceaseless in their efforts to tempt me with fruited cakes and cookies and other treats to lift my spirits, which I could only turn away, much to their concern and dismay.

I sat in my chair near the hearth in an effort to keep warm, watching the fire dance and lurch into the air and listening to its crackle. I paged back through my journal and gave thought to the distance I had crossed in time and space, and emotion, to get to this day, and of all the powerful lessons I had learned within the memories that washed over me.

I rocked in my old chair to the music of the fire and drifted into the spirit land, as I had so many times listening to Pel's drumming and the songs he and other visiting noiadi would sing or through the tales they would tell of heroic deeds done in a discordant world. I thought of the reindeer herds and the migrations they tolerated majestically as part of the natural cycle of life, and I realized with clarity that the challenges and migrations I had endured were no less than theirs, and still, no greater.

Sarah continued to watch me from a distance. I was not well, and Sarah and Gabriella knew this and fretted over my health and the ragged breaths I took. I struggled to sleep as best as I could, but the punishing force of my cough interrupted me each time I drifted off, and roused me from my slumber. When Sarah could no longer restrain herself in response to my restlessness and discomfort she said to me, "Kris, you can't keep this up. I love them too. But you are venturing beyond your capability. The people may call you the Santa, my love, but you are just one man."

A loud knock at the door interrupted her, and before Sarah could complete her thought, I lifted myself from the chair and crossed to see who might be calling at our door.

My dear friend Pel stood in the snow, and I motioned him inside. He eyed me with apprehension as I launched into a round of deep coughs that shook me as I stood before him.

"You look bit thin," Pel said with a worried grin.

"You look a bit taller," I said, smiling in return.

"I miss you, friend," Pel said, watching me as I fought to restrain another cough. "You no well. I sing to spirits in the sky. Give you breath of reindeer."

"Thank you, Pel," I said to him with some difficulty.

"Baldur say many men look for you, and Flem say one boy is lost," Pel nodded his head and held up one finger to underscore his concern. "Baldur see men with weapon and fire in the night, watch everywhere. They ask question of you, with anger in eyes. Baldur say men hunt for big man with sleigh pulled by deer."

I nodded, confused. Obviously they were looking for me, but why?

"Baldur tell them, big man, he go other way."

I laughed at Pel's comment, and he smiled, but I returned quickly to the issue at hand.

"You say a boy is lost."

"Flem like Christmas feast and sometime send little girl to trade for food. She say boy lost but no men home to find him. They look for you. She say boy's name is Olost."

"Olaf," I said in response and realization as I began to see the connection that might have been drawn to me. Had Ona come after me?

"How long has the boy been lost? Was he alone?" I asked to see what Pel had learned from his men. "Was it only the boy? Was there also a young girl?"

Pel shrugged his shoulders.

"Are the men searching for the boy or for me?"

"Men look for you. No one look for boy."

I threw off the blanket keeping me warm and reached for my coat.

Sarah quickly stepped before me to block my exit. She had fire in her eyes. "Don't you dare," she said with powerful emotion in her voice. "You are not going out there. No!"

She struggled with me as I continued to put on my coat.

"Stop, Sarah. Please. Let me do this!"

"You're already ill," she said, almost crying.

"It's one of the children, Sarah. I must help him. There is only us. And I fear somehow this is my doing."

Sarah leaned into me and released my coat. But she looked into my eyes and with a heavy heart said, "You find him. And then you come home to me."

I nodded in acceptance of her wishes.

I looked to Pel, who waited patiently for me to see how he might assist my efforts. "The boy may have followed the coastal trails where passage seems easier," I said. "This time of year, with the westerly winds, the fjords won't be fully frozen, so I doubt he could have gotten far. I will go there. You take the trail leading to the forest and circle back to find me if you are able." Pel gave a nod.

"If he's further in, the men will probably stumble into him. But I will look for him along the river trails and the pathways just north of his village."

I gave Sarah a strong hug and quickly released her to make haste in finding Olaf.

Pel loaded a small sleigh with blankets and furs and shot off along the trail to the forest.

Sebastian saw me approaching with another stack of blankets and a satchel filled with supplies. He neighed and stomped in greeting.

"Hello, old friend," I said to him as I prepared him for the ride and loaded the gear. "It's been some time since we have journeyed together, but I need your help now to find young Olaf."

Sebastian sputtered and whinnied, signaling his allegiance to the cause.

"He's in danger, I fear. We must find him before the wolves and winter can claim him for their own," I told him.

I climbed into the saddle and made sure all was secure. With that, Sebastian lurched from the stable mound and made haste through the powdery snow, driving ahead with fervor toward the trail where we would begin our search, onward to the river.

I thought back about young Ona and Olaf as Sebastian raced on. They were children of good heart and as devoted to their parents as they were to their adventures and dreams. Ona was a brave young girl with the radiant light of excited youth in her eyes, and Olaf was a bold adventurer, who no doubt felt above all risk.

Olaf had come looking for me. It was clear the boy's message was one of intended warning. I guessed that the torches of plague, spurred by fear, searched for me once again.

Chapter

Searching

ebastian and I poured our strength out on the land in our search to find our errant champion. As we rode ahead on our way to the river, searching along the trail and through the trees, a new snow began to flutter and tumble from above. Then, as if a hole had been torn open in the sky, the frozen tears of heaven fell upon us: heavy, slushy ice rained down and grew in intensity, making passage difficult and increasing the risks we all might face in our efforts to track down Olaf.

Now, once more, the wolves began to howl as I expected, for I had come to know their devious ways and the endless plaintive melodies that announced their intentions and desires. I knew they would follow us without pause and challenge us for young Olaf when at last we discovered him.

Sebastian and I pushed on as I surveyed the land, watching for movement in the shadows between the trees which might indicate Olaf's presence or other signs that he had passed this way.

It was difficult to estimate how far he might have traveled in the time that had elapsed since his journey began. I did not know precisely how he had set off, when, or whether he had come by horse or sleigh or on foot. I only prayed that he would be found before the wolves and winter could hurt him.

Near a dense stand of trees, I directed Sebastian off the trail to examine the area for signs of human crossing or shelter that might have been constructed. Slowly we marched on through the faint pillars of light and shadow that painted the forest floor. The woods were newly frozen from the downpour, and all life seemed suspended in time as if it had cocooned itself in some protective enclave until the strong grip of winter loosened its hold and dissolved.

We pressed forward, and I sought to reach higher ground in an effort to gain a wider view of the land. Sebastian was my brave companion, and he carefully picked his way across the open, rocky expanses that we covered over stone and ice as I surveyed all that was before us.

Higher we climbed, but no matter what our vantage point, we were unable to detect any speck of movement on the white sea of snow that flowed before us to the horizon.

Is this a futile search? I feared that the wet and icy fingers of winter already had caught Olaf. I begged God that Ona and her parents would not feel the pangs of loss with which I was so familiar. I had such grief in my heart to know that somehow I had contributed to Olaf's peril, and I wanted desperately to make amends.

Quick movement in the trees jostled me and pulled me from my drifting and fearful thoughts. A large group of reindeer burst from a clump of trees and sprinted across the snow pack. They were farther south than they should have been. I watched them glide forward, flexing powerful muscles to master the thick crusts of ice and snow that had formed on the hard earth floor where they ran. And as I watched them, I thought about the first time I had seen them glide across the snow in this manner as if they were flying above the land amid the broad plumes that sprayed up behind them as they dashed ahead in pursuit of safety and isolation from any man or beast that might wish them harm.

We paused in tribute to this spectacle of freedom and unbounded elegance. The world spoke to us about our place in its magnificence and in this vast spectrum of life and wild majesty to which we served as constant witness.

Wolves howled in the distance, and I encouraged Sebastian to increase his speed.

Olaf rode his sled, pulled by his dog, slowly over the rough terrain. Both were tired now and challenged by the cold.

Olaf knew that they would have to rest soon and grew worried about the night's gale.

Wolfie slowed to a halt and yelped at Olaf.

"What is it, boy?" Olaf asked. "You think we should find some place to stop now?"

Wolfie barked at him and howled, encouraged by the boy's voice.

"We can go there by the rocks for protection from the wind," Olaf said. And he dragged the sled toward a collection of boulders and a ledge in the distance.

Olaf stopped briefly to gather a sizeable collection of broken branches and fallen wood in a rich section of forest and piled them on the sled. He stopped near the rocks and unloaded the wood so he could build a fire to keep them warm throughout the night.

The flames heated the bitter air and reflected off the rocks surrounding them to bring some relief for now.

As time passed, Olaf grew more worried and soon realized that he was desperately lost. He had seen no sign of Santa or of anyone since they had left his village home. The food he had brought was enough for a day but no more. Olaf lamented his shortsightedness.

He broke off pieces of dried meat for him and Wolfie. Olaf remained determined to find Santa. If he could just warn Santa, he thought, maybe he could help Santa avoid the wrath of his father.

Olaf held Wolfie close to him as he laid down to rest near the blazing fire. He covered himself and his dog in mounds of blankets and felt the heat from the fire sharing its warming breath as he drifted off to sleep.

In his dreams Olaf searched for Santa endlessly through the snowy wilderness. In the distance he could hear the call of his mother, but he could never find her. So much time had passed that he was certain his family would be frightened, and he wished there were some way to show them he was still safe. In his confused and troubled dreams, he could not discover a solution to the difficulty he was now facing.

Olaf awoke with Wolfie licking his cheeks.

Ahead, suddenly, I could make out evidence of movement on the horizon. What seemed to be a small group of men and sleds passed slowly across the ice and snow toward a large patch of forest. I directed our course toward them and hoped to catch them to learn what they had seen while traveling this region. The men halted as they came to the wooded area and appeared to be unloading their sleds to make a camp for the night. They continued working while Sebastian and I rode on, making haste to confer with them.

As we approached, one of the men warned the others that a stranger had arrived. The men stopped working and gathered tools that were near them. A tall and solid man who could have been their leader raised his hand and signaled to me in the distance.

"What ho there?" he yelled as he raised one large hand to signal that I should slow or stop.

I reined in Sebastian and prepared to announce myself in a way that would not alarm them. From this distance I could see the men were hunters "My name is Kris," I said. "I seek your help."

"And how do you think we could help you?" the tall, solid man said simply.

"I am searching for a lost boy" I told them.

The men were unresponsive to my statement.

"What is your name, my friend?" I asked of the stranger in an effort to encourage more communication.

"Canute," the stranger said flatly.

"I see your men are hunters," I said to Canute. "You must know the land well."

"Well enough," Canute said.

"Canute knows this land better than he knows his wife!" one of the men shouted.

"The ice out here is nothing compared to the ice he finds at home," laughed another.

"Jorgen and Vegar are simple men," Canute said, tilting his head back toward them with a wink. "But I told their mums I'd look after them. You see, they was lost boys, too."

He looked me over for a good while as he thought. "We will set up a small camp here to rest our teams and prepare for tomorrow."

"I have ridden long through the wet snow," I said. "May I join your camp for a few moments of rest?"

"Can you gather wood?" Canute asked.

"Yes," I responded even as I coughed.

"Then gather wood for the fire, and you can join us," Canute said.

I tied Sebastian's reins to a tree and followed Jorgen and Vegar into the nearby forest to gather firewood.

We dragged large sections of wind-broken branches and fallen sticks toward the camp and returned several times for more until we had an impressive pile of firewood ready for the night. We then created a perimeter for the fire pit with thick branches that we cut and positioned in a circle around the shallow hole Vegar dug with a short, blunt shovel.

Canute was busy near the fire pit lacing together long poles which would support the canvas sheets that would serve as barriers to the wind and moisture and reflect the heat from the fire upon us as we prepared a meal. When the wood was piled in sufficient quantities to last them through the night, we joined Canute in securing the canvas to the poles. Jorgen and Vegar moved their sleds closer to our sanctuary, and I brought Sebastian beside my shelter near the fire so he could stay warm and safe.

At last we had a raging fire underway and shared the blessings of its heat and the smell of roasting meat sizzling over the flames. I had cakes that I gave to Sebastian and the men. We all ripped off big chunks of roasted bear that Canute had presented for the meal.

"This brown bear came upon our camp last week," Canute said to me as the others ate. "We invited him to stay with us, too."

"Then we'll both enjoy your hospitality," I said in a friendly tone.

"It's not usual to see a man travel this harsh land alone," Canute said.

"I'm not alone. I have Sebastian," I offered in response.

Sebastian stomped his hooves in approval.

"Well, your companion is a mighty war horse," Canute said.

"He delivers joy, not war," I corrected Canute.

"I see," Canute said, wiping his greasy hands on his pant legs. "Then, you'd be delivering joy to the boy you be looking for?" Canute asked wryly.

"Only if I can find him," I said. "Bringing him home will be a great joy for all."

"We seen some men was looking for someone," said Jorgen.

"Where?" I asked with interest.

"Where we came from," said Vegar. "Over there." And he pointed off to the vast wilderness behind us.

"How many men?" I asked.

"More than one," Jorgen said with a laugh.

"We didn't count 'em," Canute said. "But there was a group of men, maybe ten, maybe more. They was spread out." He looked at me closely to see my reaction. "They was looking for a big man, too."

"Oh," I said. "And what was their luck?"

"Can't say," Canute muttered.

"The boy came looking for me," I said at last.

"Did he?" Canute said.

"Yes. I think he came to bring a message, or warn me."

"And, how do you know this, if the boy is lost?"

"Herders in my village spoke with people from his."

"I see," Canute said.

"It would be a miracle to find him alive," I said.

"Do you believe in miracles?" Canute asked. And the other men watched me closely, awaiting my response.

"Yes. Yes I do. I was once lost too," I said. "And by a miracle I was saved." The men looked at each other and exchanged subtle glances and indications of trust in my assertions by a nod or tilt of the head.

"Well, we didn't see no one," Canute said. "That's what we told the other men too." And he looked me over again. "But they was angry men. Full of hate, it seemed." Canute picked scraps of meat from his teeth as he talked. "And we did not believe they would not harm the man they was seeking."

"Some men make the world dangerous when fear and anger fill their hearts," I said.

"I like you," Canute said after a moment. "There is no hate in your heart. So we will help you."

"How will you do that?" I asked, coughing harder now.

"We didn't see the boy you want. But we did see some sign of tracks awhile back from here. Looked to be a dog pulling some kind of sledge. Could have been your child."

"Where?" I asked with amazement, standing and coughing.

"Sit. You need the food, and a few minutes of rest won't hurt you," Canute said. "In the forest near the fjord we found the strange tracks; we can tell you where to search. Or, we can take you."

Then Canute added an air of apology to his words. "We didn't know it was a lost boy, or we would have helped him."

"Thank you," I told Canute and his men. "I must set out for the fjord immediately to search for him."

"Eat first. You need the strength."

The wolves moved relentlessly through the forest searching for small animals they could feast upon. But the cold forest floor offered little promise they would find what they were seeking on this night. They wove in and out of shadows like phantoms that appeared and disappeared at will. Any creature that should try to avoid them would have little suspicion of their numbers or their stealthy approach.

The pack leader changed his course and climbed up onto the slope that led to the rocky shelf jutting out beyond the forest's edge. The other wolves followed his path through the white mist, and soon the ridge was dotted with moving shadows that passed between and disappeared among the greyback boulders and glided along the open spaces between them.

At the crest of the ridge, the pack leader surveyed the land below. The full silver moonlight cast across the vast expanse of rock and forest leading to the fjord. And then as the others joined him near the highest point, the wolf caught a trace of movement in the distance. It was too far away for him to know precisely what it might be, but he could see something move slowly across the snow, signaling that it was alive and easy prey.

The wolf watched the creature continue in its journey and howled in his anticipation of the kill, and the other wolves joined in chorus as their songs of hunger changed into a statement of intent.

I startled awake, immediately guilty for having fallen asleep.

The men were packing the camp. "You needed the moment of rest." Canute handed me a cup of warm broth.

I quickly drank, feeling better for the warmth, and went to check on Sebastian.

Canute looked at the satchel on Sebastian's pommel as I handed him his cup. "We heard stories from the strangers. They said the man they looked for was the one who brought toys to children in the villages."

I looked into his eyes to assess his meaning and intent and listened as he continued.

"They was fearful of the plague," he said.

"Plague drives fear through the hearts of many men, especially those easily consumed by fear."

"Well, we ain't the fearful type," Canute said. "And I can see as you are not fearful either."

"No. Not fearful. But concerned for the boy. For his safety."

"You may not have the plague, but you are not well. Your illness should be your concern too," Canute said.

"It is just the wet weather leaving its mark," I said, suppressing a cough.

"Out here the cold and wet weather will kill you surer than the wolves."

"Well, I will continue on as my strength allows. It is important the boy is found."

"Yes, it is." Canute said.

"And what of you?" I asked. "What brings you to this distant place? And why do you persist?"

"We are hunters," Canute said. "So, we are here to hunt. And, now we hunt for a child, with you."

"We heard many stories of you," Jorgen blurted out.

"Stories?"

"Yes," Vegar said. "Of the man they call the Santa."

"And, do you think I am the Santa?" I asked.

"Yes." Jorgen said. "Some say he wears a great red coat." Then he paused to look me over. "And you wear such a coat."

"You leave behind a long trail of stories," Canute said.

"In my village, children wait for you each year," Jorgen added. "Their parents tell them to be good or the Santa will not come."

"And I tell Jorgen to be good or the Santa will pass him by too," Vegar said. "But, it don't matter much, 'cause Jorgen is still a bad boy." He laughed as Jorgen pointed a thick finger to caution him.

"I am just a toy maker," I said. "I am no saint."

"But children dream because of you," Vegar said.

"They dream because there is much to dream about," I said "and many miracles to behold."

"These men who wish to harm you do not understand miracles," Canute said.

"Maybe not," I agreed "but perhaps one day they will experience one."

"Yes," Canute said, "and they will learn that miracles exist even in things they fear. Like gifts and toys and joy brought to them by the Santa."

"Canute, Jorgen, Vegar," I said to them directly. "Let's be on our way."

"There are places to shelter near the fjord," Canute announced as he leapt into his sleigh. "The weather is warmer there, as the wind comes from the west off the currents in the water. If the boy lives, I think he will have gone to shelter."

"Then we shall go there," I said. "And we will find him."

"How do you know we will find him?" Vegar asked.

"Because I believe in miracles."

Jacob and Thatcher roused the men from their cold sleep on the frozen earth.

"We haven't had much luck, Jacob. We've lost the first few days of Christmas," Thatcher said. "How about we let the men go home and spend the rest of the holiday with their families?"

"What if he carries the plague?" Jacob demanded.

"Then I'll be a horse's keister, because I don't think this man would put our children in danger for anything," Rolf spat from behind them.

"You don't know that," Jacob retorted.

The sounds of breaking branches and the gallop of a fast-approaching horse broke the silence of the morning. Percy rode at full speed from the trees, leaping from the horse's back and landing at the feet of the men.

He had aged from the day before and looked as if he'd ridden through the night.

"It's Olaf," Percy shouted.

Pel guided his sled along the forest's edge. Haakon, Baldur, and Eilif drove their sleds behind him and fanned out across the open ground as their reindeer surged ahead. They had searched the major forest trails, but Pel began to doubt he would discover Olaf in this manner. He issued a shrill cry to the others, who slowed in response. At his signal, they moved closer together once more and stopped to examine the options before them.

Pel told the other men he worried about Kris and felt they would do better by reconnecting with him. He decided they would circle back toward the fjord in an effort to find Kris and the boy. "If the boy is alive," Pel said to his men, "the wolves already have discovered him."

As Pel positioned himself in the sled, he signaled to Baldur, Eilif, and Haakon, and they charged off once more in an effort to find Kris and Olaf.

Olaf marched through the slushy snow, dragging the sled with his satchel on his back. Wolfie lagged behind. Olaf was unsure what to do except to walk ahead and look for shelter or someone to help him.

"You stay right beside me, Wolfie!" And Wolfie wagged his tail and marched along with Olaf as they continued through the slush.

Olaf was unaware that the wolves were following them now and watching every move, waiting patiently for a time to sweep in and attack.

As he trudged forward, Olaf shared his thoughts with Wolfie, who was an eager listener, tail and ears at attention. "We have to find Santa," he said. "If we can tell him what happened at the Christmas gathering and warn him, maybe it will keep him from getting into trouble with Papa and the men from the village."

Wolfie seemed to agree with that idea, and so Olaf convinced himself once more that he was doing the right thing.

But after walking for a considerable distance, Olaf began to tire, his hunger grew, and his pace began to slow. Wolfie barked at him to encourage him forward. This triggered a response in the wolves as the pack leader began to howl and other wolves joined his song to announce they were not far behind.

Olaf heard the wolves and began to run, with Wolfie keeping pace beside him. He was breathless with fear as he could tell the wolves were coming closer with every chorus of howls.

The wolves became excited now too and raced ahead, spreading out across the snowy plain to circle around Olaf so they could begin to close in on him.

Olaf pulled the ice axe from his pack as he stopped briefly to take several deep breaths and look for someplace where he might be safe. He was terrified as he listened to the wolves calling to one another in the dim light. As he looked ahead, Olaf could see the land slope down to a lower elevation where it met with a wide river. He could hear the wolves howling and yelping from almost every direction now, and he was not sure which way to go for safety.

Pel and his men drove their sleds with fury toward the river, where they hoped to find Kris and the boy. They could hear the wolves now and knew this was a bad sign, for it meant the wolves were working to unnerve their prey as they stalked and hunted it.

In cry after cry, the wolves announced they were the masters of this land.

On the crest of a high plateau, Pel pulled his sled to a stop, and the other men did the same. Haakon and Baldur yelled that they could see movement below and pointed in that direction so Pel could move closer and observe the party of men they had come upon.

Eilif asked Pel if he thought it might be the men who hunted Kris and the boy.

Pel signaled for them to be quiet and watch.

And as the three men on sleds and one on horseback moved through the muted light in the distance, Pel was able to make out Kris's red coat and Sebastian's powerful form. He announced to the men that it was Kris, but that he did not know the others.

The wolves continued their echoing cries, and Pel ordered his men to hurry onward so they might join Kris and his companions.

As I listened to the cries of the wolves, I knew they would attack their prey soon. I was convinced beyond question that their prey was Olaf. I rode faster and pushed Canute and the other men to follow me with increased speed. We split at a small bridge that spanned the river on the chance that Olaf was on the other side.

Halfway across the bridge, I could see both sides of the river into the distance, but the wolves and the prey they hunted were not visible in the dim light.

Canute and his men hugged their side of the river. He felt that was where the wolves would go and where any creature trying to flee from them would likely run, for there was no other route of escape.

Jorgen and Vegar pulled the muskets from their packs and secured them within reach across their sleds. Canute signaled to me to go ahead.

As I made it to the other side of the river I could hear the sound of men calling. I turned to see Pel and his companions racing down the slope not far from Canute.

Olaf was exhausted from the energy spent running through the wet snow. He stumbled as he ran, falling to his face in the slushy mess. Wolfie jumped on him and licked his ears, but Olaf chased him off and cautioned him to stop playing now that they were in danger. Wolfie took the admonition well and looked about, listening to the wolf calls as Olaf regained his footing and got up. His clothing was wet, and he knew he must find shelter from the wolves. The ice already was beginning to form a heavy crust on his pants, and the stinging cold of its abrasive surface rubbed his legs raw and made it harder to walk.

Before he could fully consider the predicament he now found himself facing, he heard the growling of a wolf that snarled at him as it charged.

Olaf gripped his ice axe and swung it at the wolf as it lunged at him, clipping it squarely in the head and wounding it severely as the wolf knocked him to the ground. For a moment, Olaf lay stunned while

Wolfie barked and growled at the whimpering wolf. Olaf got to his feet and ran calling for Wolfie to follow him.

The fear in his heart removed the sting of the cold and the pain he had felt when he fell. He threw his pack off and continued running toward the river with his ice axe held firmly in his hand.

There were many wolves now moving across the snow, in and out of shadows. The wolves had caught their scent and now searched aggressively stalking the boy.

Olaf continued running with Wolfie close behind. As he got close enough to hear the rushing river, he decided that he would plunge into it with Wolfie in hopes that it would carry them far enough away to escape the wolves. But a pair of wolves began to charge at him from the shadows, and he screamed in fear, knowing he could not evade them. He ran a few more steps and heard the crack of a musket shot that felled one of the attacking wolves. Olaf turned to see who had fired the rifle, but the second wolf continued its attack and charged directly at him. Olaf ran for the river.

I rode at high speed toward Olaf behind the wolves that chased him. Across the river, Canute and his men fired weapons at them.

But the wolves did not relent so easily.

Three more wolves made a sudden charge at Olaf as he approached the river and scrambled over rocks at the water's edge. I called out to warn him, and Olaf turned to see who had shouted his name, but a wolf leapt at him and knocked him back into the river, where he fell and was swept off by the current.

I jumped from Sebastian's back and ran to the water in an effort to save Olaf. Canute and the hunters fired shots at the remaining wolves, hoping to score a hit or discourage any more attacks.

The wolves scattered and ran in defeat as the shadows amid the rocks and forest reclaimed them.

Wolfie danced in worry on the large boulders beside the river where Olaf had fallen. He barked and barked, trying to arouse Olaf, who floated without movement in the water. Then Wolfie sprang, leaping into the air and landing in the raging water beside Olaf, struggling to stay afloat. Somehow he wedged himself under one of Olaf's arms, propping him up and lifting the boy's face from the water.

I rushed onto the rocks and ran beside the river where Olaf floated and threw off my coat. I flopped onto my stomach near the edge of the water, reaching for the boy and the dog. Stretching and crawling as far as I could, I was finally able to grab Olaf by his collar and drag him up onto a large flat stone. Then I snagged the dog by the scruff of his neck to pull him to safety, too.

Wolfie shook himself off and sprinkled us with icy cold water once he was standing on the stones. I was soaked by the river's frothy wash that sprayed up over us as I held Olaf to determine whether he was alive.

Carrying the boy to where I had deposited my coat, I wrapped the freezing child inside my red jacket, still hot from the warmth of my body. Sebastian loped up behind me and nudged me with his nose. The boy moaned, and his eyes opened lazily.

"Just rest now," I said soothingly. "I have you."

At Sebastian's top speed, I could have the boy home in little more than an hour, which I determined was the best place for him. He and his dog had covered a lot of ground for their tiny legs. And his mother was sure to be sick with worry. Besides, he needed warm shelter, fresh clothing, and food.

I draped the boy over Sebastian's back then stepped up to sit behind him to hold him in place.

Pel and the other men waved from the other side of the river. I waved back, letting them know all seemed well, then launched Sebastian into a run. Wolfie ran persistently alongside.

Chapter

Silent Night

Olaf slept through the ride home.

I watched him sleep under this great canopy of sky. He looked so much like my young brothers whose faded images I had carried with me in my heart and mind throughout my life.

We had been so blessed to come upon Olaf before the wolves had taken him. As I had said to Canute, it was indeed a miracle—a miracle due in great part to the good hearts of Canute and his men, who came to our aid.

Despite my own weakness and the chills that had overtaken me, I was determined to return Olaf safely to his parents and his sister and his village this day. I could only suspect that they had lived in endless fear since his disappearance. And I knew Christmas had gone quite sour for Olaf's family and those who worried about him.

I was still unsure of the precise reason for his journey, though I suspected he was warning me about the men tracking me. Regardless, I was sure his parents would be pleased to have him in their arms, safe once more. What I did not know was how they would treat me when they realized who I was.

Olaf's breathing was ragged, and my own breathing was even more difficult. Exposure to the icy cold water and winter's unflinching grip had brought us past the limit of our endurance. I too needed rest now. But my health was less important than getting Olaf safely back home.

Thatcher led Jacob and the other men over the long trail back to their village. Jacob remained agitated and uncomfortable that they had accomplished so little.

"I want to try one more pass, this time near the fjord," Jacob said finally.

The other men were worn out from the search and wanted nothing more than to be warm at home with their own families, but it was Jacob's son who was missing, and they realized the agony he must have felt.

"We'll take one last pass," Thatcher said after looking at the other men, who reluctantly nodded their heads. "If we don't learn something more of value, or find Olaf, we will head home and re-provision."

"Agreed," Jacob said. He was pleased the men would not give up so easily.

And so they turned in the direction of the fjord, seeking the lost boy.

The cold air bit at my lungs, and I relied on Sebastian's strength to carry me forward. Olaf was alert from time to time, and I told him to rest as quietly as he could and not to worry because we were returning to his home.

He didn't question me or seek to know why we had rescued him, but the relief showed in his eyes each time I spoke to reassure him.

As we neared his village, Olaf finally said to me, and to the dimming light around us, "I was looking for the Santa. I wanted to warn him about my father and the men."

"And what did you want to tell the Santa?" I asked.

"I wanted to tell him the men were angry he brought toys into our house." And then he thought for a moment. "I wanted Santa to show them, so that they would understand."

"Understand what?"

"That he is good."

"You are a good boy," I said to Olaf.

"Will you see him?" Olaf asked. "Will you see the Santa?"

"I believe I will. The world is full of miracles."

"Will you tell him that my sister and I love him?" Olaf asked. "We don't want to see him punished. He makes the greatest toys."

And with a tear in my eye I said to the boy, "He loves you too, Olaf, and your sister Ona. As he loves all of the children he visits at Christmas time."

"Do you know my sister Ona?" Olaf asked in a bewildered state.

"Yes. Yes I do, Olaf. I know your sister and your family. And they are a very good and loving family who will be happy to see you home."

As we approached Olaf's house, he was sleeping once more. Wolfie lagged beside us, tongue hanging from his mouth.

I had taken the path that bypassed the main village road, as I did not want to bring too much notice to our arrival. I was not sure what I would say to them, except to let them know Olaf was safe, and that he had a good heart. And no matter how he might have frightened them with his departure in search of me, they should forgive him and comfort him.

As Sebastian walked to a stop, Wolfie stood up, his forelegs on the side of Sebastian, and licked Olaf's nose and his cheek. Olaf twitched awake and started to giggle as Wolfie's tongue tickled him and brushed across his face.

They were quite a pair of adventurers, these two.

I swept the bundled boy up into my arms and carried him to the cabin. Wolfie jumped in the snow, running to the house barking.

When I reached the cabin door, I knocked with the back of one hand while I continued to hold Olaf.

The sky was darkening now, and I could see the reflections of candlelight bouncing off the windowsill as someone moved through the cabin in answer to my knock, and I heard the sound of feet rushing to the door.

Olaf's mother, Johanna, threw open the door and looked at me with her jaw agape and her eyes puffy from tears.

Olaf was awake now, and despite the fact he was snugly wrapped in my coat he began to shiver.

Olaf's mother reached out for him, crying as she held Olaf in her arms. "Thank God and this good man you are safe," she said, her voice filled with emotion. "Oh, Olaf, we were so worried we had lost you."

And then she looked at me and invited me inside the cabin to sit near the fire and warm myself.

"Thank you! Thank you so!" she said to me. "Please come inside. Please."

"Thank you for the offer of your kind hospitality," I said. "But I need to leave. There are others waiting for my return, just as you have waited for Olaf to come home."

"Please stay. If only for a few moments. You look terrible."

I looked at her, sincere in her concern for me as she embraced Olaf, and nodded.

"Let me fetch you a blanket and get him out of these clothes," she said. "The men will be back, and my husband will want to thank you."

Olaf's mother carried him off to a nearby room to get him warm clothes, and I decided it might be better and easier for all if I departed.

I walked quietly to the door and reached for the handle, but just as I did, Ona scampered into the room and began to hug my legs.

"I'm sorry, Santa! I'll never stay up late again. I promise."

"Slow down little one, all is well." I patted her on the head while she continued to squeeze my legs.

"No. It's my fault Papa's mad at you. He told me to go to sleep, and I didn't listen. I'm sorry. I'll never do it again. I'll go to bed early next year. I promise."

"None of this is your fault, Ona. Your father loves you and wanted to protect you and Olaf, that is all."

"Will you come and eat your cookies?" Ona asked so sweetly.

"You are a very kind girl, Ona, but now that everyone is safe I must go."

"Are we strangers now?"

"No little one, we will never be strangers. I remember the day you were born and when you lost your first tooth."

"This one?" Ona asked, pulling her mouth open to show me where the tooth had come out.

"Yes, that one," I laughed.

"Why are you laughing at me?"

"Oh. I'm not laughing at you, Ona."

"Then why are you laughing?"

"Why does anyone laugh? I don't know. Happiness. Hope."

"Hope?" she asked, confused, squinching up her nose.

I thought for a moment and then tried to answer her innocent question. "There will be times in your life when you may disappoint yourself, Ona, or when you feel all is lost."

She looked at me with her eyes still questioning.

"I laugh because it brings me joy to see the goodness in the world, the goodness in you, even as life reminds me how stupid I can be."

"You shouldn't say stupid. Mommy says that is a bad word."

Again I could not help but chuckle at the simple truth of a child. "She is right, of course. I am sorry."

"It hurts my brother's feelings," Ona explained.

This caused me to laugh even harder as it revealed a deeper truth to her experience. If we could only teach children not to be cruel to each other, we might learn as adults how to create true peace on earth.

"Always be sensitive to the feelings of others. And never forget how to laugh, even during the hardest times of life. Even when you are old, like me."

"My brother is mean to me and calls me a child."

"It is good to be a child, Ona. You should be happy to be a child in a loving home such as this. To a child, all things are possible."

Ona hugged my leg again, and Wolfie began to run around the room barking.

"Were you ever a child?" Ona asked me sweetly.

"Oh, yes, my little one. And in many ways, I still am."

I lifted her into the air and kissed her on the forehead.

"Now really, I must go." Then I set her down near Wolfie and he began to lick her feet and wag his tail wildly.

I turned to reach for the door handle, but Johanna rushed into the room and gripped me by the arm. As she handed me my red coat, she leaned forward and kissed me on the cheek.

"Thank you, Santa," she said warmly. "In bringing my son back to us safely, you have given our family the greatest Christmas gift we could ask for."

"I know the pain of losing a child. And the pain of losing a brother," I said to her and Ona. "And I have learned that even in the midst of that terrible pain, miracles can occur. Never stop believing."

And then I wished them a Merry Christmas and went out into the night.

Sebastian carried me homeward in his ever-faithful way, though I was a heavy load upon his back, coughing and struggling to breathe in the cold winter air.

Our journey seemed so much more long and difficult as my illness advanced. Sebastian realized I was not fully in command of my senses as I grew delirious and weak. I could feel him trying to get his haunches under my weight, trying to keep me balanced on his back. Try as I might, I could not keep my head from lolling in exhaustion. Each time it dropped and I jerked awake, I felt sicker and more nauseated.

Eventually, despite Sebastian's efforts, I fell backwards off my loyal horse, who stayed standing vigil beside me. The powder from the soft snowfall that gently filled the air softened my impact, and I stared up into the blurry night sky, remembering the end of my first delivery a lifetime ago.

"Don't worry, Nikko. It won't be long now. Merry Christmas."

At Jacob's home that evening, Ona sat near the hearth playing with Olaf's Christmas present, while Olaf was off resting in his bed.

"Ona, it's important that you not mention anything to your father," her mother said to her in a serious voice. "Do you understand me?"

"Yes," Ona said.

Her mother took Olaf's toy away from her. "Listen to me. This is very important. Your father just . . . You just can't say a word. Do you understand?"

"Santa doesn't want anyone else to know who he is," Ona replied.

"Yes. Yes, sweetheart. Santa likes to be a secret. Can you keep his secret?" Her mother looked Ona in the eye and whispered, "Shhh."

"Shhh," Ona whispered back at her. And they both laughed at their shared secret.

"What secret?" Olaf said from the bedroom door. "Where did the man go who brought me back?"

"Olaf doesn't know the secret," Ona laughed.

"Shhh," her mother said.

"Shhh," Ona repeated again, giggling.

"What secret? Tell me the secret!" Olaf insisted.

"The man who brought you back is named Santa," Ona blurted out.

"He's not Santa," Olaf scoffed.

"Yes he is, Isn't he, Mama?"

"What! Is he still here?" Olaf yelled.

"No. Olaf, he has gone. Your sister and you must promise . . ."

Olaf ignored his mother and ran to the door yelling, "Santa! Santa! Wait! Come back!"

As Olaf burst onto the porch, he collided with a strong pair of legs. "Santa?" he began to ask. But when he looked up, he saw the weary face of his father staring down at him.

"Why all this shouting about Santa?" Jacob said harshly as he hauled Olaf into the cabin by the scruff of his neck.

Thatcher, Darren, and Rolf followed him onto the porch and inside.

"Where have you been, boy? Is this some kind of joke?" Jacob said sternly, grabbing the boy by both arms. "We were searching the countryside for you, son. Where have you been? When did you come home?" Jacob looked at Olaf with fire in his eyes, and Olaf was too frightened to speak.

"He's home safe," Thatcher said, trying to sooth the anger Jacob expressed. "That's all that matters now."

"What is going on here? Someone answer me," Jacob continued.

"Olaf got excited and went out," Johanna said in a protective voice. "But now he's back. He's safe. Everything is fine now. Thank you, gentlemen, for your kind help. I'm sorry for your trouble."

"We thought we had lost you, son," Jacob said in a deeply serious manner. Then he wrapped his arms around the boy, hugging him as he buried his head in the boy's soft and messy hair. He shook his head, still holding the boy, then without looking up asked Johanna to get the men refreshments. "Is there something warm for the men to drink, Johanna? It's bitter cold out there."

"None for me," Darren said. "We need to be heading home."

"Someone needs to go inform the others that your boy is safe," Rolf said.

"I'll take care of that," Thatcher replied.

"Yes. Thank you," responded Jacob.

"Well, we are all home now. Safe and sound," Johanna said, handing Thatcher and Rolf warm steaming mugs.

"Thanks to Santa," Olaf said with admiration. "Santa brought me home."

The room froze.

"What is this?" Jacob asked loudly.

"Olaf, it was supposed to be a secret," Ona whispered loudly to her brother.

"Jacob," Johanna said, "he only meant to help us and bring Olaf home. He was sick. He endangered himself to help our son. He saved our son, Jacob."

"Let's get a good night's sleep and look at this fresh in the morning," added Thatcher cautiously.

"I went to warn Santa, because I didn't want you to hurt him. Then it got so cold and I didn't know how to get home. I only wanted to be home. But Daddy, I knew that you would find me. And then the wolves chased me, so I jumped into the river, and Santa jumped in after me."

Jacob simply stood looking down on Olaf.

"He saved me, Dad, just like you would have."

Silence rung throughout the room as all eyes rested on Jacob. Then Jacob collapsed to his knees and wrapped his arms about the boy, burying his head in the child's neck. Jacob's breathing came in stuttering gasps as he held onto the child.

"Olaf, I was afraid that you would like Santa more than me. In my jealousy I almost truly lost you. Forgive me for what I have put you through."

Jacob stood and looked about the room.

"What I have put you all through."

"How could you think that, Dad?" Olaf asked, looking up at Jacob with innocent concern.

"I don't know," Jacob said, bending down to look Olaf in the eyes. "I have been stupid, son."

"You're not stupid, Daddy, you're special," Ona said sweetly. "You have a snowflake like Santa gave to me."

Sure enough, the old weather-beaten snowflake left with the infant Nikko hung from Jacob's neck as he bent over, looking down at his son, Olaf. Ona held out her hand, displaying her tiny replica that had once dangled from Dancer's collar. The room was silent.

Jacob stared at the only connection he had ever found to his past. He lifted the tiny snowflake from Ona's hand, inspecting the cuts and curves that unmistakably imitated the form of the snowflake that he had worn from his earliest memories.

Stunned, Jacob pulled on his jacket as if in a dream and prepared to venture out into the night once again in search of Santa. Only this time he sought a connection to his past and the connection to a family he had never known.

Thatcher caught his arm. "Johanna said he was unwell. He may indeed have the sickness."

Jacob looked Thatcher in the eye, gently pulled his arm free from Thatcher's grasp, and walked out the door into the cold night.

"I'm going with him," Darrin announced, then shouted, "Jacob!" as he followed out the door.

"I don't know about you, Thatcher, or the rest of the men, but I am not letting them go alone," Rolf added.

"I don't know where they are going. We need fresh horses and some food, preferably warm, before anyone is leaving," said Thatcher, holding the door for Rolf.

Jacob rode long and hard in pursuit of the Santa, accompanied by all the men from the village except for Percy, who said it was his job to stay and watch over the women and children should there be a problem. The hunting party followed the trail left by the Santa. Finding the tracks had been relatively easy due to how recently they had been created. Following was a different matter. The snow continued to fall, making the hunt increasingly more difficult. No one knew for certain where the man they called the Santa lived or how far north they might be traveling.

Jacob and the other men on horseback fanned out though the trees. The snow was falling faster, creating an impenetrable sheet, impossible to see through at twenty paces. Echoing calls passed through the trees from man to man in a steady, monotonous rhythm. Then, a frantic hollering broke the repetition, sending the men converging.

My father stood above me, surrounded by men of our home village.

"Does he have the sickness?" I heard one of the men ask.

Father bent down and cradled my head, wiping the sweat from my forehead and smoothing my hair. "No. But I am not sure it matters."

"I waited a long time for you," he said to me. "There is so much I would like to tell you and learn about you."

I could almost hear sleigh bells in the distance. My father looked so young, younger that I remember him ever looking. He was strong and confident.

"I did everything I could," I told my father.

"I am sure you did."

"I am sorry. I lost Nikko."

"Nikko?"

"Nicholas, Dad, I lost Nicholas."

Then I broke into coughing.

He's delirious, but he is alive," Jacob said hopefully to the group.

"If we are going to do something, we'd best do it," Rolf announced. "I don't believe he'll last the ride back," he added, putting his hand on Jacob's shoulder.

Jacob stood looking around frantically for any solution that might present itself, as if out of the snow would appear some undiscovered village or roadhouse. And again the jingle of bells rang in the distance.

Pel spotted the red coat and smelled the horses long before he saw the men. Without his hands on the reins, Pel sat inside the sleigh as if he were merely a passenger on the ride. Absent of any goading or guidance, the magnificent reindeer pulled the sleigh alongside the men, who stood looking at the team and sleigh as if they had just flown out of the land of fairies.

Rolf broke the spell and cut to the chase. "Gentlemen, this big fella is gonna take the lot of us."

One by one, men from my home village stepped up to stand beside my father. I felt guilty for having forgotten the faces of these once dear friends and neighbors.

"Don't worry," my father said to me. "We have you." As one they reached down and lifted me up, placing me gently in my sleigh. Then my father stepped in the sleigh with me. "I need to go with him," he said to our neighbors. "Don't worry about me; I will find my way home."

Chapter

11

Redemption

J acob was *fascinated when the Sami in their colorful clothing* appeared as if from another world around the low hills that the sleigh passed by. The people matched the unique appearance of the old, short, gruff man who rode in the sleigh grumbling as he ministered to the Santa. As of yet he had not spoken a word to Jacob, barely even giving him a look.

Jacob was completely stunned when a door opened up from one of the hills, and a beautiful woman in her late forties ran to the sleigh, desperately worried about the Santa's well-being. She called him Kris, and though all her attention was dedicated to assisting the Santa, she gave Jacob a warm if brief greeting and had some of the Sami lead him and the extraordinarily bizarre deer into the back of the hill, which astonishingly encompassed both a stable and workshop. The strange men unhitched each of the deer and stabled them, then wordlessly left Jacob to explore the unusually large and peculiar room.

Wooden snowflakes hung all about the workshop. They were cut in the arches that supported the latticed dome of the earthen structure. They were repeated in the elaborate scrollwork that covered the cabinets and counters. The workshop itself was a mystical combination of two worlds, colliding in a beautiful fusion of purpose and meaning.

Everywhere Jacob looked there were replicate designs of his snow-flake. He was overwhelmed by the evident connection that he held to something that seemed so much greater than him. From beneath his shirt he pulled his snowflake pendant to compare the exact designs.

Unknown to him, Sarah entered from the door in the back of the carpentry and watched from the shadows. "He spent a lifetime looking for you," she said, slightly startling Jacob.

Sarah stepped from the darkness and walked directly to his side, then touched the dangling snowflake with her fingertips.

"How is he?" Jacob asked softly.

Sarah struggled to hold off her overwhelming emotion, placing the back of her hand over her mouth until she regained her composure. Looking up at Jacob, she inspected the familiar lines of a face so like the one she had fallen in love with a lifetime ago. Reaching up, she placed the palm of her hand on the side of his chin.

"Who can deny that miracles exist?" she whispered. "Come. I think your brother would like to meet you."

"Brother." Jacob stood there, testing the thought and tasting the word.

"I believe," she affirmed for him. "Were you found as an infant one early Christmas morning?"

Water gleamed in Jacob's eyes as he nodded.

"Then it is so."

"Does he know I am here?"

"He knows you are here. He does not know the significance of who you are." A tiny cuckoo clock struck the half hour.

Jacob approached the clock. It looked like a tiny cabin with a porch, and instead of a bird, two figures, a man and a woman, poked out the front door as if calling for someone. Along the porch were the carved statuettes of eight children, four boys and three girls, with the tallest boy holding an infant. Around the neck of the woman figurine set the pendant Jacob now held in his hand.

"There was love?" Jacob asked, identifying instinctively the truth of the scene before him.

"Yes, and there was tragedy," Sara said.

Jacob saw an open bag of toys lying before him at his feet. He carefully rummaged through the toys and selected one to examine more closely. It seemed similar to the ones his children had received on Christmas.

"I was so angry with him. Finally I had my own family, and someone was trying to take my place. I was so afraid he would steal their hearts from me." Jacob paused. "He's sick because he jumped in a frozen river to save my son. This is my fault."

"Now I know you are related, taking responsibility for that which is outside the powers of any man." Sarah smiled, shaking her head.

"I never meant any harm," Jacob said mostly to himself, unsure what to say or do next.

Sarah came to his aid. "Let that rest, child. You have a lifetime of questions that you may now fear to have answered. Nonetheless, the time is here."

The cabin was still except for the sound of the crackling fire that illuminated the main living area. I sat propped up under a thick pile of blankets covering the massive bed as Gabriella fussed over me, wiping my brow and forcing warm broth down my throat despite my protestations. She finally relented when my lovely Sarah sat down, rescuing me from Gabby's care.

What was to be was to be. I knew how badly I must have looked because I felt it. No matter how much hot liquid they put inside my body, I was where I was.

My loving Sarah kissed me on the lips and stroked my forehead.

"I have someone who would like to meet you," she said coyly. "This is Jacob."

And there he stood, the image of my father. What I had thought to be a dream was some uncanny reality.

"You're the one," I said, beckoning him over.

"I am?" he asked, standing there comically, almost like a timid child.

"The one who saved me," I said, clarifying my meaning. "You look so much like my father, long gone now. In my delirious state, I thought you were he, coming to rescue me."

"Maybe it was," Jacob said.

"That is a nice sentiment," I replied as I ruminated for a moment. "How did you find me?"

"You gave my daughter this." And Jacob held up the little snowflake I had given his daughter.

"Ona . . . I am sorry for any fear or trouble I have caused your village."

But he waved off my comment. "The illness was the fear inside me," he stated; then he handed me the tiny snowflake. "You have them everywhere."

"They remind me . . ."

"Of what?"

"Many things. That all the children on the earth are our family."

"Where did you get it?"

"That is a story almost forgotten."

I lost my battle to suppress my cough and began hacking against the fluid that filled my chest. Sarah ran to my side once again with the warm broth, which actually made me feel a little better.

"Sometimes I can still smell the smoke."

"Hush, my love." Sarah touched my hand, standing up from the bedside and crossing to the fire in order to refill the cup once again with steaming liquid from the small cauldron that hung there.

"Tell me," Jacob said earnestly, taking the cup from Sarah and sitting beside me. He truly was the image of my father.

"I think my life began on that day," I said to him. "My village died of the plague when I was but a boy."

I could clearly recall the vivid images of the flames bursting into the sky and the searing heat of the burning houses.

"Stealing her last hours of life, my mother bade me find homes for my seven brothers and sisters before she passed."

Visions of my confused and frightened siblings danced before my eyes.

"And so on that Christmas Eve we set off to find places of shelter for each of them. And I left them to their fates, with families and people unknown."

As I told him the details of every delivery, my animated movement on the bed caused the mattress to nudge the bedside table, and a carved miniature horse began to rock back and forth as I spoke.

Jacob watched the rocking horse as it continued on its timeless journey to nowhere.

"When all the children, save my infant brother Nikko, had been dispersed, and my mother had finally lost her struggle against death, we found ourselves alone."

I remembered how Nikko and I had trudged through the snow and surrendered to the night. And I told Jacob how I had lain in the snow beside the infant, sure that death had caught us at last. Then I told him of the star flash and the embers from the chimney. How I had fooled the older couple by knocking on the door, and how I had reached in through the window while they were distracted, leaving my tiny brother in their care.

Jacob listened with sincere attention, asking probing questions at times, but remained silent for most of the telling.

I told him how I was rescued by a man and his wife who were to become my family and my salvation. How I finally came to understand, after so much pain and loss, that there was goodness and happiness in the world. And, I learned that I had a gift for woodwork and for the invention of toys.

I could see back into the distant corners of my mind to my work-bench and knife as I carved the rough ends of a wood block in an effort to shape it into a beautiful duck. I could see and feel the shavings as they fell in my imagination until I held up the roughly formed pieces of wood that would fit together to form the moving, flying toy.

"I would go each year in search of my brothers and sisters and secretly observe them in their new homes. I would not disturb them for fear of spoiling their new lives. And so each Christmas I would leave them toys and gifts I had made as a way of telling them I still cared for them and still remembered their beauty and their love."

I looked at Jacob as he stared at me, transfixed by my story.

"And the infant?" he asked.

"The very next Christmas after the separation of my family, I went back to reunite us. All the others had new families, but I had lost Nikko. I found the cabin of the old cottager with whom I had left him abandoned."

I stopped to take a deep and painful breath.

"The deliveries grew as I dedicated myself to bringing joy to others at Christmas. I have learned our tragedies are the ashes from which we are intended to rise again, reborn." I reached over to the rocking horse and stopped its motion.

"Who adopts eight abandoned children from a plague-ridden coun-tryside?" Jacob asked almost comically.

And we laughed.

"I don't know," I said thoughtfully. "God, I guess."

Jacob stood near the wall examining a shelf laden with colorful toys. The fire gave a pop from a burst of resin it had discovered. Sarah set down another steaming mug for me and went to the fireplace to stir the concoction brewing in the pot.

"And you crafted these for the children?" Jacob asked as he lifted one of the toys off the shelf.

"No. Those toys are Nikko's. One for each year."

I began to cough violently again, and Jacob rushed to my side, lifting the mug Sarah left me to my lips.

"I don't know if it would have made a difference, but I would have liked a gift on Christmas," Jacob said quietly.

The snowflake hanging from Jacob's neck swayed as he moved beside me and emerged from the opening in his coat. It was a vision I never thought I would live to see.

"Nikko?" I said to him in my shock and sudden recognition of who this man might be.

"Nikko," Jacob said softly to himself. "I never knew my true name. My new family called me Jacob."

"It was Nicholas," I told him. "As a baby we called you Nikko."

"I used to dream my true father was a great hero, searching for his stolen child." Jacob removed the snowflake from around his neck and ran his fingers across it. "That my mother was a beautiful princess longing for my return."

We laughed.

"It's all true," I said, and our shared laugh slowed to a knowing silence.

"I was always out of place there. I never allowed myself to be a real member of the family. I never let them love me, the couple you left me with. I didn't feel I deserved to be loved. If my own parents didn't want me . . ."

"I wanted you," I said to him. "For years I thought if I could just find you, all would be forgiven, all our pain would be forgotten."

Jacob placed the snowflake and its cord necklace over my head. I grabbed his arm and held onto it for a moment as I struggled against my violent and painful cough.

"Come brother, we have to get you better," Jacob said with deep sincerity and concern. "There are only eleven months to prepare. What would Christmas be without Santa?"

Epilogue

A sea of plush red cloth moved through the winter snow toward the cabin as Santa made his way to Olaf and Ona's window with a large bag of toys slung over his shoulder. He gently placed two gifts on the windowsill and turned to make his way back to the sleigh. Looking over his shoulder, Jacob beamed with delight at the feelings that swelled inside after he had left the gifts for his children. He climbed into the sleigh and set off to spread more holiday joy as he traveled through his village where he planned to share presents with neighbors and friends still asleep in anticipation of Christmas morning.

Now it is the late 1700s, and a Russian merchant just back from his travels carefully places a colorfully wrapped package on the satin cloth covering a table in his store. He smiles with pride and happiness at the gifts he is about to share. His thick, black hair and mustache are expertly groomed and ready for the party that will soon begin in his establishment.

He steps back with two more packages in his arms and eyes the setting to judge how best to arrange and display them. After a brief consideration, the merchant gently slides the second package into place, and sets the final gift lovingly on top of the other two. He lays sprigs of holly carefully around them all to give an added accent of color.

Now it is 1812 in an energetic London suburb. Inside the Georgian home, pine needles and the ornaments of a Christmas tree rise above the gifts. Three partygoers enter the room and sweep up the presents from underneath the tree. The three quickly move to an archway and cross into another room where their Christmas celebration is in progress. Friends are singing and laughing there, but when the three enter the room and begin to hand out gifts, everyone pauses to cheer in excitement.

Now it is 1871, and a weathered wooden passenger ship prepares to depart from a port in Venice, Italy. A simple young woman carries a small gift in one hand and a suitcase in the other. She walks behind a line of plainly dressed people boarding in the steerage class of the ship. As she makes her way onboard, she sees a man of her acquaintance and greets him with a gentle smile. He wishes her a happy holiday, and she hands him the gift. He hugs her warmly, and tears fill their eyes.

Now it is America in 1910, and a woman's extravagant hat flops about as she walks along the pier. She halts in front of a large cruise ship anchored there. A line of people exit the first-class decks, making their way slowly down that ship's long, heavy ramp. A wealthy man suddenly appears behind them and waves to the woman from the top of the ramp while holding a beautifully wrapped gift in his hands. As he approaches her, the sunlight glistens off the brightly wrapped package. She runs to welcome him home.

Now it is World War I; along the western front explosions of mortars fade to silence. The land is covered by a sea of bitterness and blackness beneath a dome of sparkling stars. Interrupting the silence of the night are the low rumbles of shells fired in the distance and bursts of bright red light that punctuate their explosions in the sky. A British soldier sits in a muddy trench as he opens a Christmas package from home. He laughs when he pulls out a cookie shaped and decorated like a Christmas tree, which brings loving memories of home.

Across no-man's-land, the thick stretches of mud-trenched earth that separate the armies, a German soldier bites into a gingerbread man that he withdrew from the opened package beside him.

Now it is Brazil in 1956, and a poor old man sucks the last drops of soup from a dirty bowl, settling back against the wall of a dilapidated building where he hopes to sleep. A care worker covers him with a blanket so he might have a bit of warmth throughout the Christmas night.

Now it is 1984, and a sleepy young Indian child is held warmly in the arms of her father, who tucks her into bed, giving her a gentle kiss upon the cheek. Beside him, on the girl's nightstand, a small gift sits beautifully dressed with a red velvet bow.

Now it is 2003, and all across China, children dream of the gifts that will be left by Santa this Christmas Eve.

Now in a vast department store, children wait anxiously to greet Santa. Tabby, next in line, runs past the elf helper and plops onto the big Santa chair, scooting and pushing to make room.

"I'm Tabby," she says. "I know you're not really Santa, but that's OK. I'm getting too old for that."

"I never liked that excuse."

Her little hand tests the softness of the white fur lining the thick red Santa coat.

"I've seen Santa before in other malls," she says as proof of her perception.

"You know, even Santa needs a little help now and again."

"Santa needs help?" she asks, having never quite considered it that way.

"Oh, yes, there are many children . . ."

"I want to help Santa, too."

"That's easy, Tabby, be the Santa in you. Santa wants you to know that if you are good, you will have a surprise under your tree at Christmas."

"Really?"

"Really."

Tabby wraps her little arms around my belly and gives me a hug. Hopping from my lap, she runs to her mother and tugs on her blouse. "Mommy, Mommy, Santa says if I'm good I'll get the Barbie Dream House for Christmas!"

"What's this?" her father asks, excited to hear what Santa said to her.

"Santa says if she's good he'll get her a Barbie Dream House for Christmas," Tabby's mother tells him resolutely.

Her father lifts Tabby high above his head and lowers her for an Eskimo kiss.

"Well, then we had best be good for Santa, hadn't we?" he commands with a smile.

Her father looks at me as he sets his daughter on the ground, and gives me a smirk and a nod.

I wink back at him and smile. He's a good boy, John. Always has been.

Without warning, Matthew, a fiery five-year-old boy, hops up onto my lap.

"Santa?" he asks, to make sure I am the jolly guy that he has come to see.

"Yes, Matthew," I assure him.

He gives me a quizzical look as if to ask how I already know his name.

"I remember you from last year," I say with a grin.

Matthew reaches toward the white fringe of my coat.

"Why is your workshop in the North Pole?" he asks.

"Oh, because they say people live forever up there."

"Forever?" he asks in awe.

"Forever!" I respond in equal enthusiasm.

Matthew lifts the wooden snowflake pendant hanging from my neck and runs his fingers across it, feeling its engraved designs and pointy edges. "And how do reindeer fly?" he asks.

I look him directly in his eyes and whisper, "One secret at a time, little one. One secret at a time."

The End

Acknowledgments

I truly hope you have enjoyed the story. Like a piece of theatre on opening night, this book represents a collaboration of friends and colleagues whose love and toil have coaxed from the fires of its creation a greater complexity than can come from one individual's inception of an idea.

The simple story was born in 1995 when I first stepped in for Santa and wore the Santa suit for a group of kids in New Jersey. They were singing "Here Comes Santa Claus," and I threw open the doors to be greeted by a four-year-old girl whose eyes grew to the size of silver dollars. Lifting her arms to the sky, she beckoned to be picked up. That day I lived as the man that would never do a child wrong. I was more than friend—I was confidant. I was more than character—I was a living legend in their minds. At the end of the day, three fathers, probably in their mid-thirties, asked if they could take a picture with me. Without thinking I said, "Have we been good this year?"

"Yes," each one replied most earnestly.

I realized then that there is a child inside every adult who still yearns for Santa. I decided that day to start searching for the story that would give teenagers and adults back the hero of early childhood and to create the story that would resolve the question for all time—*Is Santa Real?*

The story I found was a story that reveals a man who, like all men, faces trials, failures and self-doubt. A man who teaches us the obvious truth that Santa lives in each of us and whose very existence is a call to action: "Be the Santa in You!"

I can only say that God placed the core story inside my head because I woke up one day, and it was there. Then years of research and the contributions of many expanded its scope and detail. The first person I told the story to was a dear friend of mine, Dan Mackler, whose intense response launched me into a committed pursuit to see this story made into a movie. He, along with Bill Hill, John Higgins, Dominick Salfi , Bob Di Cerbo and others, spent the next six years of their lives in the dedication of that cause. The original short story was taken in dictation by my amazing and supportive wife, Joanne, who on that day kept me from making a tragic mistake in its writing. She then gave me two beautiful children, Caius and Jinnai, who taught me what a challenging and rewarding task Santa has taking care of all the children on the earth.

Over the next eight years, the story took multiple forms—from the screenplay to the pseudo-historical documents of the first *Santa is Real* book published in 2006. Each form has influenced the subtleties and depth of what is in this novel. I would like to thank my incredibly talented collaborator Joseph Kenny who served as a contributor and writer on this novel. His work helped me transition the story from its many forms into the book you read today. Without him there would be a beauty missing from its reading. I must also thank my primary writing partner on the screenplay and many other aspects of this project, Donte Bonner. His thoughts flow throughout the entire story. Early on in the screenplay process, Ben and Stephanie Lowell were very helpful. Sandy Thrift lent me her years of experience. Stella Sung gave him music. Connie Chattaway gave him poetry, Huaixiang Tan gave him art, Eric Craft and Alvin DeLeon designed his first home, and Bill Brewer gave him clothing. Chris Sprysenski gave us legal counsel, Frank DiPietro made us accountable, Tim Baker and Doni Keen gave us the "Santa Talks," and Per Heistad pulled no punches on his analysis of our entire project. Shannon O'Donnell helped me keep it together, Peter Weed gave me heart, and Jayson Stringfellow gave me motivation to jump. My dear friend Jason Diller brought his incredible writing talents to this project and even lived with my family for more than a year as we refined the total work. The song about snowflakes was written by my friend and business partner John Higgins, and the song about the lumberjacks is an American folk song from the mid 1800's.

Without doubt my stalwart business partner Dominick Salfi has been mentor, friend and champion from the beginning of this project in 2001 and has given over his law firm, Salfi Law, to the dedication of this endeavor. Gayle Hair has been my faithful cheerleader from the very beginning. My partner and CEO of KRS Media Group, Bill Findley, brought personal resources and then jumped into the trenches with us—his effort has been monumental. Marcia Findley's faith and tremendous assistance made this book a reality. Pam Findley, outside of her constant support, has personally project managed the distribution of this book.

Without her, this venture would have had little hope for success. My great love and thanks to them all. As well, I would like to thank Kennan Burch and all of my Dream Builder friends for stoking the fires of my dreams and for always showing up, including Mark Carbone for his social media expertise, Roy Reid for his public relations guidance, and Derric Johnson for his counsel.

I must thank my publisher, Dave Welday, owner of Higher Life Publishing, for his immediate dedication to the creation of this novel, my production manager, Marsha McCoy, for keeping us organized, my supervising editor, Alice Bass, for her love and expertise, and my copy editor, Kathryn DiBernardo, for her brilliant if sometimes brutal comments. Their truth and artistry can never be paid for. (The extraneous preposition is just for them.) My great appreciation goes to Doug Berger and Simon Jacobson for the "Kris" titling and Santa is Real website, my friend and colleague director of photography Elie Alakji for taking pictures in the Arctic cold, Kaye Hanna for her masterful calligraphy, and Dave Murray for the cover illustration. I should probably thank Doug twice for all the different versions of the story I made him listen to and for graphic designing most aspects of the project over the last eight years.

It is important that I not forget to thank my Norwegian friends, whom I miss dearly. Kjetil and his wife, Gunn, opened their home up to me and made me feel like family. To their friends Mikal and Marianne, who introduced me to the living folk musical art form thriving in Norway today. Much thanks to Svein Anderson, who introduced me to his Sami relations. And maybe most of all to the Sami leader, Ole Mathis, who somehow got me up into the mountains of Lapland three hundred miles above the Arctic Circle and then brought me back out alive. He transformed the story completely by teaching me that elves and reindeer are real. He is Pel.

The goal of this project is to add a piece to the global legend of Santa, and it is hard to express the sheer hours and collaborative thought that it has taken—though the above list looks long, it is by far complete. To all who have walked this journey with me, I thank you for your belief and contribution to the cause.

Christmas is a time of joy, a time of hope, a time when we are just a little better and the world is a little brighter. As I write this, I realize there are two very important people whom I have forgotten to thank.

Santa, thank you for the gifts. Thank you for never really caring if I was naughty or nice, for inspiring my dreams and imagination, and for sharing your story with me. I will look for you in the eyes of children this Christmas season.

And to the Child whose birth has inspired the season, thank You for hope. God bless.

Here are more ways to keep the magic of Christmas alive...

❋ Tell friends about this book on Facebook, Twitter, your blog, and other social networks.

❋ Download the **eBook edition of *KRIS—The Legend Begins***. It's available through Kindle, Nook, iBookstore and other popular eBook download sites.

❋ Order a deluxe hardbound edition of ***KRIS—The Legend Begins*** to share with friends and family.

❋ We are working now on a fully illustrated children's edition of the story, illustrated by Huaixiang Tan. To request a special premier edition, visit our website at www.santaisreal.com

❋ ***KRIS—The Movie***. We are seeking investors to produce KRIS as a major motion picture. To find out more about this exciting adventure, visit www.santaisreal.com

❋ **Enjoy our advent calendar** filled with short inspiring videos that embrace the meaning of the Christmas season. You'll find it on the homepage of our website at www.santaisreal.com.

Coming Soon...

❄ The fully illustrated children's edition of the story titled *Santa Is Real*. To request a special premier edition, visit our Web site at **www.santaisreal.com**.

❄ *KRIS—The Movie*. We are seeking investors to produce KRIS as a major motion picture. To find out more about this exciting adventure, visit **www.santaisreal.com**.

Note: The nationwide release of this book will be mid-2011, so prior to that, copies are only available through the Author's Web site, **www.santaisreal.com**.

Connect With Me...

To learn more about *Kris—The Legend Begins,* please contact me at:

www.santaisreal.com

A Christmas Wish

May the spirit of Christmas fill your world with joy and wonder all year through.

Be the Santa in you!

J. J. Ruscella